SECRETS PAST:

INFINITY'S END BOOK 5

ERIC WARREN

Part of the Sovereign Coalition Universe

Cover Design by Dan Van Oss www.covermint.design

Content Editor Tiffany Shand www.eclipseediting.com

ISBN 978-1-0867-4646-4

For Ossie Marie Cox, who instilled in me a love of story

ERIC WARREN

<u>The Sovereign Coalition Series</u>

Short Stories

CASPIAN'S GAMBIT: An Infinity's End Story

SOON'S FOLLY: An Infinity's End Story

Novels

INFINITY'S END SAGA

CASPIAN'S FORTUNE (BOOK 1)

TEMPEST RISING (BOOK 2)

DARKEST REACH (BOOK 3)

JOURNEY'S EDGE (BOOK 4)

SECRETS PAST (BOOK 5)

PLANETFALL (BOOK 6)

BROKEN SEEDS (BOOK 7)

<u>The Quantum Gate Series</u>

Short Stories

PROGENY (BOOK 0)

Novels

SINGULAR (BOOK 1)

DUALITY (BOOK 2)

TRIALITY (BOOK 3)

DISPARITY (BOOK 4)

CAUSALITY (BOOK 5)

Special Offer

Sign up on my website and receive the first short story in the INFINITY'S END SAGA absolutely free!

Go to www.ericwarrenauthor.com to download CASPIAN'S GAMBIT!

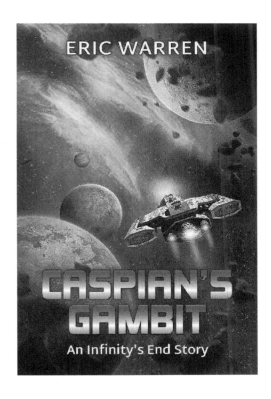

ERIC WARREN

The ship resembled a gem in space.

It wasn't more than a few thousand morbs away, but from the way Opaous glinted off the surface and scattered the light rays Vrij could have sworn it was a jewel. Until he flew the ship closer that's how it had appeared. It wasn't like the Bulaq ships—no. This was shiny, new, *gleaming*. It had damage but that wasn't a problem for Vrij, not when he had all his tools. And they wouldn't mind a borrow. He'd borrowed many things. Everything came around again in the end. They were all connected, like the Great Ones used to say.

The Great Ones had been back on Laq. Now Laq was lost. Vrij patted his eyes. *Think on them later.* Now it was time for work. Hard, quick work. He drove his small ship close to the jewel's surface, scanning for the parts he needed. It wouldn't take long. Then he'd be back on his way, gone in a flash. No traces. The scans looked very good, many power conduits. They wouldn't miss them. He couldn't borrow them if they noticed. He couldn't leave them helpless. But this ship was powerful, strong. *Redundant.* Vrij would borrow, then good fortune would come to them, they would see. They wouldn't even notice. Vrij's shuttle was much too small. Much too camouflaged.

"Ahhh." Vrij smiled. The perfect spot for borrowing. It wouldn't take long at all. He stopped the shuttle, less than two morbs from the side of the jewel. He removed one of the twelve identical canisters from his belt. Activating it sent shivers up his back, it was always the same. He grinned. Good sensations. Vrij grabbed his case of tools and the openway yawned before him. He stepped through into the space. No gravity. No heat. Only cold and empty, like him. No, Vrij wasn't all cold. He was warm, sometimes.

He got to work, cutting through the hard metal of the jewel. It was thicker than he'd thought, took longer to cut. He checked the field holding in his heat; holding in his air. Less than a quarter gone so far. He still had time.

The panel came away and Vrij aimed it for the opening in his shuttle, pushing it until it went inside. No waste. Everything can be reused, that's what they said back home. Couldn't afford waste, no matter what. That was okay with Vrij, waste was bad anyway.

"This is it." Vrij liked talking to himself. Kept himself company all the time. Today was no different. Behind the thick metal were two power converters and a distribution node. Perfect. His was almost d-ceased. The borrowed pieces would work great, with some modification. He removed the first canister, humming a tune Mother had taught him. Vrij didn't know the words, but that didn't matter. Humming was good enough today even if all he could feel were the vibrations in his own ears.

The first converter came out easy. No alarms. See? Easy to borrow, no one would notice. He clipped the first converter to his belt. Too fragile to throw back into the shuttle. He'd take them both at the same time. He just had to be careful. No one else was careful. Everyone else tried to shoot the jewel.

Stupid. Nothing but a waste of energy. Energy they didn't have. But this would guarantee Vrij didn't run out of power for a while. It had been a long time since a borrow this good. He couldn't wait to get back home.

Something sharp poked him between the shoulders. Vrij furrowed his brow. What—?

When he turned, he saw their great transparent, bulbed heads and he screamed, flailing his arms back which only made him rotate. Stupid. He should have tethered on. What were these things? Their bodies were made of wrinkly material that was thick and fully opaque. Except the heads. Inside the great bulbs were smaller heads. Vrij screamed again, the sound lost to space. He motioned himself away but without anything to grab onto he couldn't move. Wait. The jewel. Yes, he'd just—

One of them grabbed him with its swollen hand. Vrij tried to fight back until another one hooked onto him as well. How were they moving? They had jets on their backs? Impossible. But wait, no, these were not their true forms. These were suits. The smaller animals must be inside, that's what he saw inside the bulb. That was the true animal. But still, the animal held a weapon pointed right at him. And canister or not, he didn't want to test their weapons. If they had a ship of this size, they could probably defend it well. Stupid. He should have been better. More careful.

The lead animal motioned for him and the others to follow, to a shuttle like Vrij's a few morbs away. How had he missed it? They'd snuck up on him and he hadn't even seen them. Too impressed with himself. Too happy about the jewel. The converter still hung from his belt, bouncing back and forth as they pulled him along. He could detonate it, get them off him, but it would probably kill them all. And Vrij wasn't about to be killed. Not when there was more borrowing to do.

They pulled him in the back of their craft, leading him in with their jets until the gravity took over. He was glad they had gravity. Some animals had nothing, just let themselves float in the emptiness. Vrij only liked floating sometimes. He checked his protection unit. He was only about halfway through its use, but he deactivated it anyway. No sense in wasting it.

The first thing that hit him was the smell and Vrij almost lost his last meal all over the alien ship's floor. It was a tangy, pungent smell and Vrij didn't like it. Like the sickness of death or very bad food. Was this the animals' smell? He gagged as the animals removed the bulbs from their heads. Underneath were nothing but small heads, with something on the top. Like a mane, but it was longer on some of them than on others. And different colors. Vrij felt along his own smooth head. Manes were annoying.

The lead animal said something, but it was gibberish. Vrij crossed his hands in front of his chest: the universal symbol for "I don't understand". The animal looked to the others and mimicked the movement. *It* didn't understand either? Or was it just copying?

"Ugh, animals." Vrij reached for something on his belt. All the animals shouted at once, pointing their weapons at him and Vrij froze. He could understand *that* at least. He was only going for the translator. How were they supposed to understand Vrij if all they did was shout at him? No movement for Vrij. Not until the animals calmed down.

The lead one shouted something again. Didn't they understand? Vrij pointed to the small device on his belt then his mouth. The lead animal's eyes flicked from the translator to Vrij and back again, all behind the raised weapon. Vrij sighed. Maybe the jewel wasn't so pretty after all. The shuttle bumped as it entered the ship. They were taking him. Not good but not surprising. Vrij had seen ships. Many jails. Fewer lately. But always jail.

With its weapon still on him, one of the animals reached over and unclipped the power converter from Vrij's belt, stowing it away. Vrij only hoped they had no torture. Torture was the worst. He pointed to the translator again, then again to his mouth where he opened and closed it, making sounds. The animal's eyes got bigger. They were all so soft-looking. Like he could puncture them if he tried hard enough. Beneath the suits they had no kind of protection. No scales, shells, plates, nothing. Just soft and squishy. Did they always wear the suits? He had questions.

Vrij made a motion for the translator again, slow this time. The animals liked slow. Not fast, not jerky. The lead animal moved its head up and down. Was that good? Or was it a warning? Only one way to tell. Vrij took the translator off his belt, slow. Very slow. Then pressed it to his neck where it stuck. He motioned for the animals to begin speech, but they only stood silent.

Vrij stared at the ceiling of the shuttle. They'd landed in the jewel but hadn't moved yet. No one would leave until they could talk. "Long day," Vrij said, his bones tired under his muscles. Supposed to be an easy borrow. Not all this mess.

The lead animal cocked its head. Did they have translators too? Did all he need to do was talk? "Can you u-understand Vrij? I am him. I came h-here on my ship. You took it. I need to b-borrow your converters. My s-ship is falling apart."

"Wait, hold on," the lead animal said.

Yes! They did have translators! They worked! He understood what the animal had said.

"You understood! You s-should have said s-something. S-said you had translators. You made this very hard."

"We made this hard? You were outside trying to take our ship apart," the lead one accused. But they weren't using the weapon. Good.

"Not t-take. Never," Vrij replied. "Borrowed. Only borrowing. T-the universe will provide." He twisted his fingers into the salute of the Great Ones. Even though many had forsaken them, Vrij had not. Even after...everything.

"I think he's insulting you, Chief," the animal behind Vrij said.

"No. No insult. T-this means blessings on you," Vrij replied, his sharp teeth clicking as he spoke.

"What do we do with him?" The animal with the long mane asked. A female animal. They had males and females too. Like Bulaq, not so different. But strange. Never seen them before.

"We'll take him to the brig then the captain or Robeaux can figure out what to do with him," the leader said, lowering the weapon. She was a female too. "If he's a threat, he's a poor one."

"W-what's row-bow?" Vrij asked.

One of the animals took him by the arm. Vrij had the idea of using his apparatus but no. Bad idea. They'd shoot him quick. Better to comply. "The man who decides your fate," the animal said. "C'mon, we need to process you through custody."

"What's custody?" Vrij asked. Easy concept. But no need to reveal more than needed. Maybe if animals thought him dumb, they might let their guard down.

The animal pressed a lot of air through his mouth. It was much smaller than Vrij's. And without sharp teeth. Straight teeth. Very strange. "We're going to hold you until we know what to do with you." Jail. Always jail.

"I-I know what you can do. Let Vrij go. No threat." The animal made a strange movement with his mouth and looked back at the leader.

"Got a funny one, Chief."

The "chief" stepped out of the suit. Much smaller than expected. Only two arms. No other appendages. Very strange. Vrij felt the need to flex his mandibles but kept them tight under his jacket. Never know. Maybe the animals didn't even know they existed. Good surprise if necessary. Good for getting out of jail. "Funny or not, he goes in the lockup. Don't let your guard down."

"Aye, aye." *Strange. I. I. Yes, Vrij owns two eyes. So do animals. Maybe the translator is on the fritz.*

The animals still in the suits escorted Vrij through the ship. Very clean. *Many* resources. No wonder so many had targeted. But Vrij was the only one who got close. And now inside. Good for research. Maybe to borrow more later. Always a way around. So many more animals. Though not all. One insect Vrij saw. One...not sure what. More than one species. Different kind of animals, all. So many. All stared at Vrij with interest.

Doors opened automatically in front. So much power. Lots of backups. Vrij needed to see schematics. So much on the jewel worth borrowing.

"Search him?" the female asked.

"Why? It's a force barrier. I doubt he's carrying anything that can break it. You saw the ship he came here in."

"Vrij's shuttle. *Makumba.* G-good ship. R-reliable." Vrij wiggled his fingers. Sign of respect.

"Yeah, whatever," the male said. He placed his squishy hand on Vrij's back, Vrij's heartbeat jumped. But the animal didn't feel mandibles. Instead guiding Vrij forward. Vrij complied. Better than a fight. Wait it out. "Someone will be with you when they get a chance. You've probably noticed we're busy."

A blue barrier appeared behind Vrij as he turned around, separating him and the animals. He was alone in a small room. A shelf built into the wall was behind him. And a bowl. He'd investigate later. "Repairs. F-from all the damage," Vrij said.

"Yeah, well…" The male exchanged looks with the female. "Sit tight." They turned and left.

That's what Vrij would do. He sat. It would be as tight as he could manage.

2

"You found him doing what?" Caspian Robeaux asked, maintaining a brisk pace down the corridor with Chief Rafnkell beside him, having no trouble keeping up.

"Pulling out the fucking power conduits, like they were pieces of a puzzle. I don't know how the hell he didn't kill himself or blow a hole in the side of the ship. Somehow he managed to get one off with no trouble. Those aren't supposed to be removable from the outside. If we hadn't cornered him when we did, I'm sure he would have made off with a couple." She didn't look at Cas, instead kept her gaze in front of them as they made their way down the hall. Whoever this alien was, he'd set off a proximity alert on the side of the ship and the chief had taken it upon herself to investigate without checking with the bridge first. Though it was probably a good thing she did, otherwise their "visitor" might have gotten away. Cas and the chief had never gotten along, especially not after the loss of Grippen during Cas's operation to save the ship. But ever since the ship had been disabled by the minefield at Omicron Terminus, she'd been more professional than before and this was one of those instances he was happy she took the initiative.

"Did he say anything else? Anything useful?" Cas asked.

The woman shook her head, her short, blonde hair swishing as she did. "He's one weird little fucker. Never seen anything like him. Tried to sweet-talk us into letting him go. *After* we almost shot him." Cas glared at her. "He wasn't making any sense. It took the auto-vox a minute to read the syntax."

At least he didn't have to deal with a dead body today. They were having enough issues on the ship without an incident with an unknown alien culture. Engineering had just reopened and he needed to be down there helping Zenfor and Sesster get things back up and running rather than figuring out who this guy was and what he wanted. But it was either him or Lieutenant Uuma, who was elbow deep in the disassembled weapons control systems.

Cas sighed. Ever since Evie had forced him into being *Tempest's* first officer after Captain Greene had been critically injured at their encounter at Omicron Terminus, he'd felt a growing pit in his stomach. He'd tried this before and it hadn't worked out for him. And while the past two weeks they'd all been too busy to even think about something like a former criminal filling the second highest posting on the ship, it had been in the back of his mind, brewing. This time though, he'd made a personal commitment he hoped would facilitate his new role: he'd given up drinking for the duration of his time as first officer. Last time he'd become too dependent on it and if he was honest with himself, he was *always* too dependent on it. Perhaps this could be a better situation for him.

The ship had taken a lot of damage by those mines the species they called *Andromeda* set for them, and in the end it had nearly cost them everything. Had it not been for Zenfor stabilizing the undercurrent drive and Evie's intuition in getting them out of that system they never would have made it. But now they were adrift again, after the engines had failed for the third time in less than two weeks. Thanks to Lieutenant Tyler and his team, Engineering had once again been repressurized. Sesster had taken his post again; they could only hope he'd be able to get them up and running.

If everyone would stop attacking them for five minutes.

Cas was determined to find out this guy's agenda. He suspected he belonged to the same race of beings who had been strafing *Tempest* with their tiny craft for the past ten days. They would come in quick and take a few shots, getting close to the ship before taking off again, in their own undercurrents. At first it had been more annoying than anything, but now the ship was starting to take substantial damage and they couldn't ignore the advantage of interrogating one of their would-be assailants.

Cas entered the brig with Rafnkell by his side and took stock of the creature before him. His skin was a mottled gray, but it resembled scales more than skin, with small plates overlapping each other all over his body. His eyes were large and dark, and he had small holes for ears on either side of his head. Only four fingers protruded on each hand with sharp claws at the ends and his heels were locked high, like his legs were built for running. He resembled one of the dominant species on Sissk, though he had no tail and his mouth was larger and full of sharp teeth.

The being regarded Cas with what he assumed was a genuine curiosity, but he was hunched on the bench inside the brig, unmoving. His clothes were old and patchwork, much like the ship they'd pulled into Bay Two, which was Cas's next stop. But first, answers.

"What do they call you?" he asked, facing the creature.

"Vrij. Always Vrij," he responded, his face animated as he spoke. "Y-you?"

Cas's eyes narrowed. "Robeaux. What is your business with us?"

"No business. Only b-borrowing. I borrow to s-survive." He shifted on the bench like he wanted to stand but couldn't.

"It's not borrowing. It's stealing. You're stealing vital components of our ship. Why?"

"No, only borrow. It will come back. Always c-comes back. I-in the end. I needed—my ship—running on low power. Jewel in s-space." Vrij seemed more agitated, he was almost shaking on the bench.

Cas leaned over to Rafnkell. "Is the translator working properly?"

She took out a diagnostic device. "As far as I can tell."

"Look, Vrij," Cas said. "Stand up, you're making me nervous jumping around like that." Vrij shot up and approached the barrier separating them. He studied Cas, his movements jerky and uncontrolled before moving on to Rafnkell and performing a similar examination. Cas turned back to Rafnkell. "Was he in a suit out there?"

She shook her head. "Just what he's got on now. I wish we were that tough."

"No s-suit." Vrij reached down to his belt. He removed a small orange canister not more than a few centimeters in diameter. "*Skin curtain.*"

"Skin curtain?" Cas bared his teeth. "What—?"

"H-hugs skin tight," Vrij said. "Air supply. K-keeps the cold out, warm. Good for space."

Now he understood. "We have something similar," he replied, thinking of their repelfields. "But it's only to keep out disease and protect against low-energy attacks. If we want to leave the ship we need full suits to protect us from the cold and vacuum."

"Bulaq spend a lot of time in space," Vrij said, replacing the canister. "Needed a b-better solution."

Was Bulaq the name of his race? "You attacked us to get parts for your ship, yes?" Cas needed to get this back on track. He couldn't be sidetracked by what was clearly advanced technology.

"Yes. Many thanks for your g-generosity. Repair *Makumba*. Keeps me alive."

"No, you don't understand. You can't keep the parts. We need them for *our* ship." Vrij's face fell. "Your friends out there have been damaging our ship for ten days now. Why?"

Vrij growled a low frustration. "Other Bulaq are stupid. I a-am the only one s-smart enough to g-get close. Others waste energy. They are not Vrij's friends."

"Are you saying others of your kind want our supplies?" Cas asked. It was what he'd suspected. The attacks hadn't been critical enough to do any real damage, more like test runs to see what they could get away with and see how much they could damage in a strafe. He'd surmised their plan was to wear *Tempest* down to the point where she couldn't fend for herself anymore. Then they'd take her. And it wouldn't be too far from the truth. What reserves they did have were dwindling.

"All Bulaq need supplies. But the others—stupid. Vrij clever. Get in close."

"Not clever enough, you little bastard," Rafnkell said. "Caught your ass, didn't we?"

Vrij only eyed her. Cas couldn't tell if it was with contempt or interest. But the alien brought his hands up so the ends of the claws on his fingers clicked together. "Did he have anything else other than those canisters on him?"

"Not that we saw."

Vrij grinned in response. Cas decided he didn't like that grin. "I'm going to look at his ship. See if we can figure out how to detect these guys before they appear out of nowhere. Then maybe we can get a weapons lock on them."

"Good. Good for m-me. Takes care of c-competition," the alien replied. "Let me go. No harm done."

"No harm? Do you realize we have to go back out there and repair the damage you did from removing those power conduits?" Rafnkell accused, stepping closer to the barrier. Vrij took a step back, cowering.

"Easy fix. No problems. I can go. Won't t-try to b-borrow again."

Cas sighed.

Rafnkell turned to him, her eyes boring into him. "You can't be thinking about doing it."

He shook his head. "I'll have to talk to the captain. See what she thinks. We can't hold him forever."

"Ugh." Rafnkell turned and stormed off in a huff. Just as well. She needed to cool off and had other responsibilities. Like how they were supposed to execute such a delicate repair on the outside of the ship. Not to mention the sections where the mines had struck were still open to space.

"You n-need parts, yes? I can help," Vrij said. "In exchange for f-freedom." He made a strange motion with his hands, as if he were shooing away a small creature. "All the p-parts you could need. Good p-prices."

"If they're so good why don't you just *borrow* from them instead of us?" This guy wasn't going to be much help. He'd have better luck searching through the shuttle. Maybe if Tyler could spare someone they could get through it quicker.

"Vrij has no m-money. N-nothing to trade. Parts are good, but expensive. High security."

Cas almost laughed. He was more than familiar with the problem. He'd talk to Evie, see how she wanted to handle their newest passenger. More than likely they'd let him go under the threat of disintegration if he ever came back. That was, if Uuma could get the weapons back up and working again. "Anything I should know about your ship before I go searching?"

That grin was back, the one that told Cas he wouldn't like the answer. "N-no. G-go ahead. S-shuttle clear."

Yeah, right. He should grab his old boomcannon before boarding shuttle. Maybe these Bulaq had no concept of subterfuge as it had to be the poorest lie he'd ever heard. Cas would need to do a few sweeps before boarding that ship. "I'll be back later," he said. "Don't go anywhere."

"No," Vrij replied. "I'll s-stay right here."

3

Exhausted from scanning the unending report, Evelyn Diazal ran her hands down her face, massaging the deep sockets that had become the receptacles for what was left of her eyes. Ever since their escape at Omicron Terminus it had been one thing after another in what could only amount to a slow cascade failure of every system on the ship. If it wasn't the life support systems it was the propulsion. If it wasn't propulsion it was the weapons. On and on. Those mines had done some major damage and she wasn't sure *Tempest* could recover. At least not without a couple weeks or even a season in spacedock. They didn't have the supplies out here to complete all the repairs on their own. The engineering section alone was a mess, with the adjacent sections on deck eleven still open to space from where one of the mines had nearly crippled them. They'd only managed to get Commander Sesster—their resident Claxian—back inside yesterday and the news hadn't been good. They'd had to stop *again* because some of the raw fuel was leaking into an adjacent system. Which was both a curse and a blessing. A curse because they had to find a way to re-coagulate the material for use again and a blessing that it hadn't just vented into space and been lost forever.

And then there were the attacks. They'd began just after they'd left what she and Cas had dubbed "Option C", a possible planetoid that might have provided raw materials for the ship to use. But on the first trip down it had been clear the planet was too volatile to mine and they'd given up, returning to open space in hopes of finding a new source of materials. That's when the first of the tiny ships appeared.

At first, they were nothing more than small points of light in the distance, studying perhaps. But after repeated communication attempts had gone unanswered (not that the comm towers were in the best of shape anyway) Evie had chosen to ignore them, in hopes they were nothing more than curious. Which, in hindsight hadn't been the best decision. Every twelve hours since they'd send another one of their tiny ships to make runs against *Tempest*. And despite Lieutenant Uuma's best efforts, the things were damn hard to hit. They had a scattering field which confused the sensors and made manual targeting the only option. When she finally would get a lock, they were back on their way out of the system, out of range. So far there had been fourteen attacks, not counting whatever Rafnkell found this morning. She checked the comm, Cas should have been back with the report by now.

Just as she moved to get up, the door to the command room chimed. "Enter," she said, readjusting herself in the seat.

"Sorry," Cas replied, walking in, data bar in his hand. His face was covered in sweat and his brown hair—which had grown shaggy since the attacks—was plastered against his skull. "That shuttle of his is damn hot. Took longer than I would have liked."

"You talked to him?" Evie asked. Cas handed her the data bar which she tapped, bringing up a short report. It was brief but gave the basic information. So far Cas was turning out to be a competent first officer when he wasn't worried about the chain of command. It had turned out to be a better situation than when he'd temporarily taken his commission back without a role. Then again no one'd had much rest in almost two weeks, and she didn't expect anyone to care too much about decorum.

Cas brushed his shoulder, checking behind him. "You okay?" she prompted.

"Yeah. Fine. Just…really big spiders in that ship." He shuddered.

She had to work to keep a smile off her face. "Arachnophobic are we?"

"No, I just… look, the shuttle's got a level six barrier around it now. So they can't get out. It could be a health issue. You never know what kind of diseases a creature like that might be carrying."

"You mean in its fuzzy little abdomen?" She stifled a laugh. It was the best she'd felt all week.

"It's *not* funny." He checked his back again and took the seat across from her. It was so strange being on this side of the table. Usually *she'd* be on the other side, giving her reports to Greene.

"*Anyway*. He says he needed parts for his ship and considering the shape it's in I'm not surprised," Cas said. "I've seen better Sargan garbage scows. If it had made it another five light years I'd be surprised."

"Does he know anything about any of the other attacks?" She turned the data bar off and setting it to the side.

"Claims not to. Called them a waste of energy. He might just be a scavenger, looking for a way to survive."

"By poaching off us." Evie shook her head. The worst part about this was being so cut off from the Coalition. The closest Coalition ship was at best almost two-hundred days away across an unexplored expanse of space. And that was if they could even call for help which, because of the damage to their long-range communication grid, they couldn't. They barely had internal comms. So that meant they were all alone out here—something Evie wasn't keen to advertise. Not to mention there was still the possibility the entire reason they'd come out here—the *Andromeda* aliens as the Coalition had called them—could still be close. Or they could be on their way to Earth already. It was impossible to know because they had some method of disguising themselves inside pockets of time. That's how Cas had encountered them when he and some of the others had gone looking. And even though they had some limited information, Evie wasn't sure it was enough to report back. They hadn't discovered any weaknesses, only more strengths.

She sighed and stood, facing the large window behind the desk that looked out onto the obsidian tapestry of space. How had Captain Greene done it? And when would she be able to hand the job back over to him? She'd been happy to take over when he was injured, but this was nothing more than a temporary assignment. Just as Cas's position was. When Greene was better, she'd retake her position as first officer and he could go back to doing whatever it was he did in his off time. She'd always wanted her own command. But not stranded and with the ship falling apart around her. Even further back in her mind were the twenty-two members of the crew they'd lost in the attack. For whom they *still* hadn't managed to have funeral services for.

"Tough day?" Cas asked.

She rolled her eyes. "Smartass. I just don't know how much longer we can keep this up. I've been thinking about emergency preparations. We already have people on rations and have diverted all the energy from non-essential parts of the ship to support our primary functions. But what else can we do?"

He shrugged. "We could cut power to the lower three decks and have people double up on their bunks. Save some energy there. Any maintenance could be done in an enviro-suit."

It wasn't a bad idea. It would conserve some energy at least. But they couldn't limp along forever. At some point they'd need to find some source of raw materials and energy otherwise they'd have no choice but abandon the ship. And that wasn't an option under her watch. She wasn't about to have her first command ending in the loss of her ship. "I also want to lower our general power output as soon as we're ready for another jump. I'm afraid we're lit up like a bunch of fireworks out here and that's how those ships keep finding us. If we can't find a way to defend ourselves they'll eventually wear us down."

"That's a good idea. I tried to find a way to use Vrij's ship—"

"Vrij?" She arched an eyebrow.

"That's what he called himself. I'm not sure the auto-vox is working correctly. But I couldn't find anything on his ship that resembled the scattering field they're using. Whatever it is, he doesn't have one."

"Great," she said, her sarcasm seeping through. "The one ship we could have actually taken out and he's dumb enough to try and peel parts off the ship. Did he give you anything else?"

Cas huffed, like he was holding something back. "I don't know how reliable it is. He *says* he knows where to get the parts we need."

She arched an eyebrow. "But?"

"But they're expensive. If they exist at all. If it's not a trap."

She locked eyes with him. "What's your feeling about it?"

He leaned back, taking longer to formulate his thoughts than she would like. Was this how she had been with Greene?

She always gave him her honest opinion, even if it was hard to hear. She hoped Cas would do the same.

"I know you're not going to want to hear this, but we need an ally out here. This is obviously an inhabited part of space. I think we find someone, bargain some kind of trade and get these assholes off our backs."

He was right. She *didn't* want to hear it. "That's ironic, coming from you." It was his turn to look intrigued. "You want to start your own little Coalition out here," she added.

"I don't have a problem with the Coalition when it's founded on trust," he replied. "Plus, it doesn't need to be permanent."

"And you think we could really trust someone out here? Someone we know little or nothing about? For all we know our guest in the brig could be a spy, sent by whoever has been taking these shots at us."

"I said you wouldn't like it."

She walked around the desk, keeping her eyes on him. "Say we do find someone to ally ourselves with. What do we have to offer? We can barely stay afloat as it is."

He shook his head. "I don't have a clue. And we probably won't know unless we try and find out."

"And what if we end up attracting the wrong kind of attention? Say we seek out one of these species and they see us as nothing but an easy target to be captured. It seems to be the modus operandi out here." She sat back on the edge of the table, crossing her arms. No matter how she looked at it, she didn't like the outcome. There were too many variables and too many unknowns. Searching for an ally close to Coalition space was difficult enough, this far out and there was no telling what they were in for. There was a reason exploration ships didn't come out here anymore: none had ever returned. She wasn't sure how much this alliance idea appealed to Cas or if he was just making the suggestion to give her options.

"I don't see that we have much choice. For now we can afford to remain solitary, but for how much longer?"

She made a grumbling noise in her throat. He was right. If they didn't find a natural source of base materials soon or something they could convert into energy they'd end up adrift before they made it even halfway back to the Coalition. "Have you talked to Zenfor?"

"Not since they got Engineering opened. I was headed there when this genius showed up."

She stood again. "Let's get a status update from her. I want to know what the odds are of getting her engine modifications back online. They're what's stranded us out here." Zenfor had provided them with the technological means to cover a great distance of space in a short amount of time with proprietary technology from the Sil. Except it had been damaged during the attack and hadn't worked since.

He stood as well. "I'll check. But if we can't even keep the undercurrent in place I doubt—"

"Just...let's not make any more assumptions until we know all the facts." She dropped her head, pinching the bridge of her nose.

"How's the big chair working out?" Cas asked.

"Not exactly like I'd hoped," she replied, her voice muffled by her hand. She snapped her head up again and blinked a few times. "I'll be glad when he's back."

"Have you been down there lately?" Cas relaxed his posture. All semblance of formality between them was gone. In an instant they'd passed back into that easy relationship they'd shared from the beginning. She shook her head. "Maybe it will do you some good to get off the bridge for a few minutes. We can talk to Xax, check on his prognosis."

"Yeah," Evie replied, even though she had half a dozen things that needed taking care of on the bridge. Maybe a break was what she needed.

SECRETS PAST

<u>4</u>

"You said our visitor looks Sisskian?" Evie asked as they got out of the hypervator on level fourteen. She seemed to be making conversation to fill the uncomfortable silence between them.

"One of them anyway," Cas replied. He hadn't met a representative from each of the Sisskian's dominant species, but he had seen one that resembled their new prisoner. "Back on my parole board, there was a reptile Sisskian as one of the board members."

"They hate that," Evie replied, a smile in her words.

"I know, but I can't help it. They look…*reptilian*. What other word is there for it?"

"They prefer the term *simmilist*. As do all the species on Sissk. If you go around calling people reptiles, mammals, or anything else you're bound to get the shit beat out of you. But the proper name for the species you're describing is Ashkas."

They turned the corner that headed down to sickbay. "How long did you live there?"

"Fifteen years. It's like a microcosm for the Coalition itself. All those different species, sharing the same planet, the same resources."

Cas laughed to himself. "Now I see where you get it."

"What?"

"Your eternal optimism." Before she could counter with a quip of her own, he continued, "Well, he looks Ashkasian then. Except he doesn't have a tail and his skin, or his plates—whatever they are—are thicker."

"That's fascinating," she replied. "All this way out here and there's another species not too different from one in the Coalition. Maybe they're distant cousins."

He shrugged again. It wasn't impossible. There was plenty of evidence of ancient species migrating all over space, there was no reason a species from this region couldn't have found its way to one of the Coalition's outer planets. Many of his ancient maps were from civilizations long gone who used to chart the stars before humans learned how to farm.

As they reached the doors to sickbay Cas noticed Evie wasn't beside him anymore. He turned and saw she'd stopped a few meters away, staring at the door. "Hey. You okay?" She nodded, but the movement was short and sharp. "Have you been here to see him since it happened?"

She shook her head. "Not since that day we got the news. I've been too busy."

Or this was harder for her than he'd thought. Maybe she hadn't been trying to fill the silence between her and Cas, but her and what she was about to face. She and the captain hadn't served together a long time, but they'd developed a respect for each other. That's how it went when a captain and their XO matched up well; it was something he thought he had with Rutledge. But it had all turned out to be nothing more than lies. For Evie, though, he suspected it was real.

"We don't have—"

"No," she replied. "I want to. I just…needed a second." She stepped past him and the doors slid open for her, revealing the inside of sickbay. It was a wide space, with a lot of stations around this side of the room with tall ceilings. Three of the beds were still occupied by injuries from the attack a few weeks ago. Cas hadn't realized some people still hadn't recovered. He'd need to pay more attention to the personnel reports coming through to him; it was something he shouldn't have missed.

Off to the side stood Box, his companion for five years and newly minted "doctor" for the *USCS Tempest*. Since passing his written tests and earning the title six days ago Cas had heard of little else when the robot decided to drop into whatever he was doing. Box turned upon seeing them and his yellow eyes flashed in excitement.

"You came! I assume you're here to see a top-level medical demonstration from the Coalition's newest and most experienced *doctor*. I'll just take Henderson over here—" he strode over to one of the crewmen lying peacefully on the beds. "And we'll induce some mild cardiac arrhythmia—"

Both Cas and Evie jolted forward before Box stopped mid-stride, his eyes blinking at them. Cas recognized it as his version of laughter.

"He's been pulling that crap all day," Crewman Henderson said from the bed, coughing. "Anyone who comes in—" He coughed again, harder.

Box finished making his way over to him, adjusting one of the sensors on his bed. Henderson's coughing subsided. "I told you, pretend to be asleep. It's much more morbid when they think I'm going to do it to a sleeping man. You're not supposed to be talking anyway." Box glanced back up at them. "He's been my best patient so far."

Evie went over by the crewman's bed. "Thank you for humoring him."

Henderson shook his head. "He's a…delight. Keeps a smile on my face."

"One more word and I'll induce a coma," Box replied. Henderson nodded, smirking. Box turned to them. "He inhaled a lot of actinium and it's taking his lungs a while to heal. But he's doing much better now that we've started the second treatment."

Cas took stock of his friend. Most of the time he'd known Box he'd been barely more than a lazy, self-centered ass, concerned with little else other than watching net dramas. But ever since they'd come aboard *Tempest* he'd seemed to have found his calling as a healer. Though he cringed at the idea of referring to him as "doctor".

Box finished adjusting some of the readouts on the display beside Henderson's bed. "So what can a doctor do for the captain and her first mate?"

"Don't call me that," Cas replied.

"Arrrr," Box said.

"We're here," Evie asserted, glancing between the two of them, "to check on the captain. I wanted to get a status update."

"Oh," Box said, his tone neutral. "Sure. This way." He led them through the large partition separating one side of sickbay from the other. On the far side sat the chief medical officer, Xax, where she sat inside her office, working on her terminal. She glanced up when she saw them come into view.

"Captain. Mr. Robeaux, I wasn't aware—" She stood from her desk. Cas noticed she had not one but two different input terminals. One set on the desk itself and one she held in her second set of hands. He bet she could write reports faster than anyone on the ship. Except maybe Box.

Evie held up her hand. "This is unscheduled. We wanted to see how he was doing."

Xax's face fell slightly. "I'm afraid there hasn't been much change. And since we won't be getting back to a starbase soon I'm taking the situation into my own hands. I'm working on developing a new treatment right now, one that I hope will allow me to get a better look at the kind of damage the captain has suffered." She turned the face of her terminal to them.

"See, the captain suffered a lot of trauma in this area," she pointed to the longitudinal fissure that separated the two halves of the brain.

"The central sulcus," Box whispered to no one in particular.

"There's some deep bruising in there. I'm hoping this new round of calorcium will allow us to figure out how much damage we can heal and how much we can live with. Otherwise, his condition hasn't changed."

"How long until the treatment is ready?" Evie asked, her voice betraying its anxiousness. If Cas noticed, he bet Xax did as well.

"I don't want to say," she replied. "This is experimental, and I can't give a timeframe or even a guarantee it will work. But I'll keep you updated."

Evie nodded. "I guess that's all we can hope for. Thanks, doc."

"Anytime." Xax took her seat again while Evie turned and left. Cas and Box followed, close behind. That hadn't been what either of them had wanted to hear. Captain Greene was the foundation on which the crew was built. Without him in the captain's chair, Evie was left to do it on her own, despite Cas's "promotion". His role here was temporary, which is why he assumed most of the crew followed his orders and did what needed to be done, because they knew they'd be rid of him soon enough and they didn't want Evie coming back to her job and finding out they hadn't been pulling their weight. He was a substitute, temporary and replaceable. But that didn't mean he wasn't going to do a good job. This ship needed all the help it could get, and until things returned to normal, he would do his best to ensure their survival.

Perhaps it would help to take Evie's mind off the subject at hand. As they reached the doors to sickbay he leaned over to Box. "Hey, you remember that time the Erustiaan boarded the *Reasonable Excuse* and tried to steal her from us?"

"Absolutely. The first thing you did was cower in the corner; your arms wrapped around your knees. Classic Caspian," Box replied. Evie turned and eyed him with interest.

"*Obviously* that didn't happen," Cas replied, his face growing red.

"Sure it did. He blew the hatch and you screamed this really high-pitched scream, so loud that I thought I'd lost an audio processor," Box said. "And then you ran into your room like a child." Box lifted his chest. "I, of course, had to fight him off in hand-to-hand combat, in which I managed to overpower him and take his weapons. I then unceremoniously tossed him out the airlock."

Cas crossed his arms. "Oh really? Because if I recall correctly, he shot you three times, blowing your main power source and it took me two weeks to get you back on your feet. Was all that what you dreamed while I was in the middle of taking you apart and putting you back together again?"

"You mean I bravely *allowed* him to shoot me to give us more time to formulate our counter-attack," Box replied.

"What does this have to do with anything?" Evie asked, tapping her foot.

"The point I was trying to get to," Cas said. "Was that I managed to send a distress signal to one of Veena's ships nearby. They made it over to us and together we took care of the Erustiaan while the tin man over here was out cold. I didn't scream. I want to be very clear on that point."

Box huffed. "It wasn't my fault you didn't upgrade my armor. And he had split-point rounds. Those could penetrate unprocessed alchurium ore."

"You're not going to give up on this, are you?" Evie asked, ignoring Box.

"I think it's worth exploring. At least until a better option comes along."

"Give up on what?" Box asked.

Evie stared up at his yellow eyes. "Caspian thinks we need allies out here. That if we continue like this we won't have a chance to make it back home."

"He's not wrong. In our current state there's no way we're making it back to Coalition space. We'll probably be destroyed long before then, or dismantled, or get sucked into a dark fissure, or—"

"Box!" Cas yelled. "You're not helping."

Evie took a deep breath. "Get down to engineering. See what Zenfor and Sesster say about the engines. Then I'll make a decision. In the meantime, I'll have one of the science crews go over our new friend's shuttle, just in case you missed something."

"Just tell them to wear enviro-suits," Cas replied. "In case one of those things had egg sacs or something."

A smile played at her lips. "I'll make sure they know."

Evie took the hypervator up one level to thirteen, alone. It would have been just as easy to comm science lab two, but she had another reason for visiting in person. And since the day had been terrible so far, she felt like she deserved a little indulgence.

She'd hoped the news about Greene would have been better. Though, had there been any significant developments Xax would have commed her instead of waiting for her to visit. It was wishful hoping on her part. The slow realization of the situation fell on her like snow, blanketing the ground. There was a good possibility Greene wouldn't wake up and she would need to take on this mantle permanently. She wasn't even sure how she was supposed to do that. Being captain was a lot different from being first officer. The first officer always had someone else there to help guide them, and while a seasoned XO might not need any guidance, *Tempest* had been Evie's first posting as second-in-command. She'd fully expected to spend four or five years getting used to the job before being offered her own ship. She'd imagined something much more formal, something with more gravitas to mark the occasion. Not that she wanted the pageantry, but she did want it to be significant. More than just an assumption of power. He hadn't even been able to transfer command to her due to his injuries. She'd just *assumed* it. Assumed she was qualified.

She needed more sessions with Sesster. They were helping to calm and focus her mind, even if she couldn't quite remember all the images from when they were close to the alien ship. Evie had managed to get them out of that situation by tapping into something deep within herself, something she couldn't even explain. And in what little downtime she'd found since, she'd worked with Sesster inside his *mind-place* to try and figure out what it all meant. Unfortunately she hadn't made much progress since that very first session. And now that he was back in Engineering it was unlikely he'd be able to find the time for her. All of which fed into the anxiety of what-if. What if the hallucinations came back? What if she couldn't sleep again? What if she just couldn't do the job?

Evie reached the primary science labs and made her way over to science two, tapping on the door. It slid open to reveal the large space in disarray. After one of the mines had exploded it had eventually caused a power conduit to rupture in this section, blowing out half the relays on the deck. Which technically wouldn't have been a problem since the science wings weren't essential to the ship's operation, except that two of *Tempest's* main weapon systems: the dart controls and the blade generators ran behind the same bulkheads and had ruptured along with the power conduits. They'd had to remove half the equipment so they could start tearing the bulkheads away to get to the affected systems.

A maintenance crew had the entire wall exposed while Lieutenant Laura Yamashita directed them as to which systems needed their attention first. All the scientists who worked in this lab had already migrated to other areas to assist in repairs. Laura turned when Evie entered, and a smile flashed across her face before hiding it again. "Yeah, right there," she said, "Between the backup vacuum chamber and the muon prism. Remove those and get the plating off to expose the conduit."

After the weapons systems had gone down, Lieutenant Uuma had assigned Laura down here to oversee the repairs since she was familiar with both the weapons and the science systems, having come from exobiology. Evie couldn't have made a better call herself. "Lieutenant? May I have a word?"

"Of course, Captain," Laura replied. She had to hand it to her, Laura was good at keeping her emotions under wraps. There was barely a hint of anything in her voice other than a standard reply. "Keep working on that and I'll be back in a few minutes." She turned and sauntered her way toward Evie, throwing in a little extra emphasis in her walk, but not enough to be readily noticeable unless someone was really paying attention. Which Evie was. She'd been paying *very close* attention ever since Omicron Terminus when Laura had helped her through her episodes.

"What can I do for you, Captain?" Laura asked, a wide smile on her face. She had specs fluid dotting her face, like one of the hydraulic systems had ruptured too. But it didn't detract from her beauty. Evie had always found her attractive, but ever since she thought Laura might have died in the attack she couldn't suppress the feelings any longer.

Evie glanced up at the maintenance crew. All of them were focused on the power conduits, not paying them any attention. She leaned forward and placed a gentle kiss on Laura's lips before pulling away quickly. Laura barely had any time to react, but her smile grew even wider.

"I just needed a friendly face," Evie said.

Laura's features shifted into understanding. "How bad is it?"

"It's not getting any better. And I just came from sickbay. There's been no change with the captain."

Laura rubbed her arm sympathetically. "You're the captain. And you're doing a great job."

Evie sighed, lowering her voice, "The ship can't keep withstanding these attacks. If we don't do something drastic—"

"Like?"

"Cas thinks we should make an alliance with someone before these little ships cripple us."

Laura grimaced. "What do you think?"

"On one hand I think he's right. An alliance makes sense. We could pool resources, fix ourselves and get home faster. On the other hand, I can't ignore the possibility we'd be opening ourselves up to even further trouble. Who's to say whomever we make an alliance with decides to take what we have by force? Or sabotage us?"

Laura wiped something at Evie's cheek. Her finger came away with a dark smudge. Some of the fluid from Laura's face must have transferred to her own. "It's a gamble, you're right. But do we have a choice?"

"For the time being we still do. But if Zenfor can't get those engines back up and running we'll be out of supplies and energy in less than a season."

Laura's eyes danced. "Are you just venting, or do you want my opinion?"

Evie shrugged. "Both. Neither." She chuckled. "I don't know. I just…wanted to see you. We haven't had much time together since…this." She waved her hand at the back wall.

Laura turned to face the maintenance crew, still working hard on removing all the necessary components. "Yeah, it's great because when the designers built this ship, they put the most essential components of the defense systems *behind* everything else. Which was stellar planning on their part."

Evie almost laughed out loud. "I'm sorry. What's the prognosis?"

"Maybe another day to get it fixed?" She turned back to her. "And before you tell me that's too long because they'll be attacking again soon, I already know. But we can't go any faster, it's delicate work."

"Damn," Evie replied. Laura had read her mind. They needed to get the weapons systems back online for the next attack, which could come anytime in the next six to eight hours if they kept to their "schedule". "Looks like we'll have to send the spacewings out."

"Because I'm awesome I'm going to go ahead and tell you why you came down here in the first place." Laura leaned in.

"What?"

"Not only did you need the opinion of the most qualified member of your crew about our current predicament, but you also wanted to ask me out on a date."

Evie crossed her arms and mirrored her movement, giving her an easy shove. "Is that so?"

"By my count we're a few behind. And you can't blame me for wanting to see you more."

Evie huffed. "I'll just have to rectify that. I have an excellent assortment of ration bars stocked in my quarters for later."

"*Gourmet* ration bars?" Laura asked, her eyebrows wiggling.

"You know it. Only the best for you."

Laura laughed and turned to face Evie. "Sounds wonderful." Her eyes flicked back and forth, and Evie felt more vulnerable than she ever had in her life. But it was a good kind of vulnerable, the kind she wanted but so rarely obtained. She felt as if Laura could see the real her, the her beneath the surface, the one where all the bullshit was stripped away and what remained was Evie's true essence. She'd never felt that with anyone else, and before Laura, hadn't even known it to be possible. But she was sure in her conviction that Laura saw her for who she really was.

"What do you think I should do?" she whispered.

Laura's face softened. "You really want my opinion?" She hesitated a moment. "I agree with our first officer. I think if the principles of the Coalition can work back home, then they can work here too. It's like starting over."

Yeah, except out here we don't have the Claxians to watch over us as we reach out to other species. Was she the only one who thought seeking out other species was a bad idea? All she could think of was how it had led to a Coalition full of subterfuge and secrecy. As best she knew the Claxians still didn't know about what Admiral Rutledge and the crew of the *Achlys* had done when they'd captured a Sil ship and tried to use its technology. And that was something she was complicit in. If they were willing to hide something like that from their closest allies, how many more secrets did the Coalition hold? Were the Claxians or the Untuburu or the Yax-Inax keeping secrets from the humans? And where would it end?

"Evelyn? Sweetie, are you okay?" Laura asked.

Evie gave her head a little shake, fluttering her eyes. "Sorry. I just zoned out there for a minute. You really think we could make an alliance work?"

"Well, I mean don't go after the biggest and baddest species out there. I'd talk to someone who was in a similar position as us. Someone who couldn't necessarily overpower us if they got too desperate. But who also needed help."

"That's a fine line to walk," Evie replied. "Especially when so much of this space isn't charted."

Laura grinned. "You'll figure it out. Now let me get back to work otherwise I'll have to file a formal complaint."

"That sounds like a threat," Evie replied.

"You know it," she said, echoing Evie's earlier words.

She took a deep breath. "My quarters for dinner? Fifteen hundred?"

Laura began strolling back to the maintenance crew. "I wouldn't miss it for the world."

Evie kissed her index and middle fingers and stretched them out to Laura. Laura mimicked the movement then turned her attention back to her job. Evie let her eyes linger a moment longer before leaving the science wing. As she made her way back to the hypervator to return to the bridge, she pondered Laura's advice. Maybe she and Cas were right. But they couldn't go into this thing blind and full of optimism. They needed to be careful. But if the only reason she was hesitating was because of the current state of their own Coalition, then it didn't make sense. She needed to wait to hear back from Cas. In the meantime, it was imperative they defend themselves against the next attack. She tapped the comm in the back of her hand. "Chief Rafnkell?"

"Go ahead, Captain," the chief said.

"I need you to prepare four of your fighters. It seems our primary weapons systems won't be back up in time and we're going to need some defending against the next attack. Be prepared to launch at a moment's notice."

"Finally," Rafnkell said. "A suggestion, Captain?"

"Go ahead."

"Let us sit out there in wait for them. We can use *Tempest* as cover. They won't know we're there until it's too late."

"Will you be okay out there for a few hours on your own?" Evie reached the hypervator, stepping inside.

Rafnkell chuckled. "The space corps can take much worse, trust me. They used to drop us out on Set and make us survive a week on our own. A couple of hours in a spacewing is nothing."

"If you say so, Chief. Proceed at your own discretion. They could be here any time."

"Acknowledged. Rafnkell out."

Evie took another breath. Hopefully they'd have better luck. Now, if only Engineering would cooperate.

<u>6</u>

Cas stepped through the main rollaway door that separated Engineering from the rest of the ship. It was stuck halfway in place and when he pushed on it, it didn't budge a centimeter. There was barely enough room for a human to make it through the opening, he didn't even want to know how the four-meter-tall Sesster made it through.

"Commander!" Cas glanced over to see the newly promoted Lieutenant Tyler jogging toward him. Tyler had been instrumental in keeping Engineering from collapsing entirely during the attack and Evie had rewarded him with a well-deserved promotion. But his already-present anxiety had only seemed to increase in conjunction with his newfound authority.

"You don't have to call me that, Tyler, I've told you before. I don't have an official rank, just a position on the ship," Cas replied.

Tyler took a breath. "I know, it's just easier. Commander, it's a mess down here. My guys did the best they could while it was depressurized but we've got a lot of major systems that will need full overhauls. Those mines really fucked us."

Cas blew out a long breath. "Give me the worst of it."

"Long-range comms are down. Probably for good. We have internal ship communications and we can do short range to shuttles and nearby planets but that's it. Nothing beyond a light year. The transmitters have been destroyed and building a new one will take longer than getting back to Coalition space."

Damn. He was afraid of that. Without the comms they couldn't even reach out to any nearby ships; they'd have to wait until they came in close. "What else?"

"Sesster says the undercurrent system is salvageable, with the right components. For now, any further use is going to put strains on the system and possibly cause a rupture. We've only got three of the four emitters working. I realize we're out in the middle of nowhere and we can't stay here, but for the time being we recommend sparing use of it only." He wiped his brow, sweat was pouring down from under his crop of red hair.

"Have you spoken to Zenfor about her technology?"

Tyler's face turned into a grimace. "I tried. She wasn't in a mood to talk."

Cas nodded. "Don't worry. I'll speak to her. Anything else?"

"I've spoken to Uuma and we think we can get the weapons back without too much of a problem, but we've got multiple parts of the ship where I'm worried about the structural integrity. Volf and I agree we'll need to focus our efforts on containing those sections unless we want the ship to pull itself apart in the undercurrents. If we could find a fresh source of galvanium we could be back up and running with modest repairs. Our other option is to build an energy collector with what we have on-hand and try to synthesize what we need. But that will take a lot longer."

Cas sucked his lips between his teeth, thinking. They needed the collector, even if it would take forever. "If you can spare the people, get started on the collector. There's no guarantee we'll find the materials we need out here. The sooner we get started, the better."

Tyler nodded. "Yes, sir." He turned to some of his staff. "Sophie! Get down to science one and find Doctor Amargosa. We're going to need her help." He turned back to Cas. "She's got a background in thermal dynamics."

Cas wasn't sure if he meant Sophie or Amargosa. Either way it didn't matter. It was clear Tyler had really stepped into his role here and was handling things nicely. Cas glanced over to the massive form of Commander Sesster, who lay in his custom-built cradle at the far end of the room, operating many of the Engineering components from inside. "Where's..." He saw her before he finished his thought. She was over close to Sesster, bent over a console, her stern face like a blade in its intensity. He hadn't been looking forward to this. Cas turned back to Tyler. "Carry on."

Tyler nodded and returned to his duties while Cas made his way across Engineering. There was debris everywhere. Evie had filled him in on how they barely got out after the mine had blown a hole in the deck below. And how Box had been instrumental in helping everyone escape. He'd never tell him to his face, but Cas was proud of how far he'd come in such a short time. And he felt guilty for keeping him on the *Reasonable Excuse* for all those years. Box thrived when he was around more people and when he had something worthwhile to do. Piloting a junky courier ship hadn't been enough for him and Cas couldn't help but think where Box might be had he not been holding him back.

Probably fencing stolen net dramas in the Sargan Commonwealth a voice deep inside him said.

He approached her from the side, making sure to stay where he knew he was in her peripheral vision. From the scowl on her face the last thing he wanted was to startle her and have her rip his head off in retaliation. He'd already endured two punches to the face and wasn't sure he could take another hit without some brain damage. "Consul?" he asked.

"Caspian."

"How are you feeling?"

"What does that matter?" Her eyes hadn't left the screens she'd been staring at. Though it didn't seem like she was changing any of the inputs.

"I just figured since you almost died out there—"

"I told you. Sil lungs are resilient and Xax didn't need to keep me. I'm fine." She tensed and Cas's eyes narrowed. She'd managed to reset the undercurrent system by exposing herself to the vacuum of space, and she'd only needed minimal recovery time in sickbay. But he knew better than to push the issue. It was a bad idea to argue with a Sil. Or, at least, this particular Sil.

"What's the story with your enhancements to our engines?" Cas asked.

"I told you I'd get them fixed and I will." There was an anxiousness in her voice he'd never heard before. Even when she was wrong she had conviction, but this sounded like something else.

"When can I tell the captain they'll be ready? With the undercurrent offline I know she's—"

"They'll be ready when I say they're ready," Zenfor growled. Her two-meter frame seemed to heave with fury.

Cas took a precautious step back. "I'm going to need more than that. Hours? Days? Weeks?"

She flashed him a glare that he thought would pierce his soul, her mouth curled into a snarl. "It's your damn primitive equipment. How am I supposed to get anything done with your ancient technology? It might as well be two Guursels pulling a cart."

Cas had no idea what a Guursel was, but he caught the general idea. "That doesn't sound promising."

She slammed her massive hands on the console, cracking it straight down the middle. Lighting flashed through Cas as for a brief moment he thought she might actually lash out at him and the crew. Everyone had stopped what they were doing, save Sesster, and were now staring at her. She took a deep breath—though Cas noticed another tiny shudder—and took two steps to the right, activating the console beside the one she'd broken and bringing up the same information as before.

"Zenfor, give me the truth. How bad is it?" Cas asked.

"The system is offline, and I don't know if I can repair it. Not with the equipment I have here." She turned to him again. "How do you deal with it? So many things going wrong. Sil ships have natural built-in redundancies. We don't experience failure on this scale. Things don't *keep going wrong*."

"The ship has some redundancies, but not enough to combat the kind of damage we suffered. The ship's armor wasn't up when the mines hit us, and they struck some strategic points which—" He'd only just now realized how surgical the strikes had been. Close to the bridge. Close to engineering. Enough to knock out their propulsion but not enough to destroy them completely. That ship that had been hiding in the time pocket had wanted to reach them, not destroy them. But for what? Threat assessment? They'd probably never know.

"This ship isn't a ship at all. It's a child's toy," Zenfor growled. "If we find suitable replacement parts, I won't be standing by idle. I'm tired of my life being in the hands of people who don't understand basic physics."

At least she wasn't talking about abandoning them. Though he wasn't quite sure what she was hinting at. "I'll tell the captain the system is down until further notice," he finally said. "Or until we can resupply."

"And rebuild," she added.

Cas thought that was about as good as he was going to get. He left her to ponder at her station. She still might find a way out of this with what little they had on-hand, but everything kept coming back to restocking and resupplying the ship with the necessary components. Sure, they'd had some replacement components on-hand, but a lot of those had been blown into space during the attack and they'd had no time to retrieve them. Which meant unfortunately it left them undersupplied and out of luck when it came to repairing a lot of the existing systems. He hated to do it, but he'd have to inform Evie right away. Maybe it would help convince her to make a decision about searching for help. Or even entertaining Vrij's "offer".

As Cas left Engineering, he caught Tyler giving him a friendly nod. Surprised, he returned the gesture and left feeling more confident than when he'd come in, despite the bad news.

***

You seem distressed. What can I do to help?

Zenfor grimaced as she stared at the console. The information wasn't going to change, the calculations weren't going to magically work themselves out, so why did she continue to watch the screen like she might see something she hadn't already been over a thousand times?

Because you don't want to let them down, Sesster said in her mind.

That's not it, she thought. It was strange communicating this way, but she preferred it to verbal communication. It reminded her of being home, where not everything had to be done manually. Talking to Sesster was easier than anything else on this ship.

Thank you, I feel much the same way. Inside, she smiled, though she'd never let it show on her face. She preferred to keep it all hidden. And now for Sesster too, she supposed. But that was okay, she didn't mind him seeing. He'd been the primary reason she'd been interested in coming on this ship in the first place. *You flatter me.*

It's true. It was why I volunteered to come aboard rather than stay on the Coalition starbase with Mil'less.

You miss her very much. His thoughts pierced her. There was a drawback to this kind of communication; little could be hidden or obfuscated. And she wasn't one who was open with others. *It is okay to miss people. I too miss my own kind.*

She hadn't considered that. *I hadn't considered your feelings about your own people. Would you like to speak to me about them?* In addition to listening to his concerns it might also keep the focus off her for a while.

You don't have to use subterfuge with me. If you don't wish to discuss your situation, please say so. No deception is required.

Inwardly she grimaced. *I apologize. I'm not used to being the focus of anything. It's...uncomfortable.*

That is alright. I will take you up on your offer as it isn't often I am able to speak of my people. Especially in the presence of other Coalition members. But you...you might understand better.

Understand what? What concerns could a Claxian have? She knew not everyone was receptive to a Claxian's thoughts, but at least a few people on board were, including Caspian and Lieutenant Tyler. Not to mention acting Captain Diazal.

The captain isn't technically receptive to my thoughts. She can't hear me unless I bring her into a shared space. And yes, while I can help her and speak with the others, it isn't the same as speaking with my own kind. You are perhaps the first person I've met I can be completely honest with.

I'm honored, she replied.

I'm unaware if you know, but Claxians do not often leave our homeworld. We are bound to it in many ways, preferring instead to allow others to come to us. This had been both beneficial and disastrous for us in the past.

Zenfor shuddered. She couldn't imagine inviting alien species to Thislea. It would do nothing but leave them open to attack or worse.

Many other species feel the way you do. But not mine. We are a race of pacifists. And when others came to conquer us they may succeed for a short amount of time, but only until we build sufficient technology to repel them from the planet. Just because we do not like war doesn't mean we won't fight for our home. So many of us stay and decide not to leave our system.

I've read some of your history. What about the humans?

The humans came to us in great need. They were dying, killing themselves really. But they were also looking for something. Reaching out. And we took pity upon them. And now a few thousand years later see what we have built together. Had it not been for the humans we never would have entered into this Coalition. But they convinced us it was in the best interest in all of our people. And no one has attacked Claxia Prime since. I can't say that they were wrong.

Zenfor sensed hesitation. Sesster was holding something back.

You're right. Even though the Coalition is a positive force in this part of the galaxy, my people are held to a higher standard than all its other members. They all look to us for guidance, wisdom, technology, innovation. We learn very young that we are an example to all other races, and we must present ourselves as such.

Is that why you're on this ship? she asked.

Partially. I wanted to help. But it was also a challenge, to see if I could leave Claxia Prime and make a life for myself out here. But it hasn't been without its obstacles.

Tell me about it.

He was silent a minute and she glanced over to his physical form, still operating many of the controls with his long tentacled arms. *There is a credo among my people: Claxians can do no wrong. It isn't a statement of pride or confidence, but instead it is a warning. It means that we cannot make mistakes, especially in front of other members of the Coalition. We hold ourselves to the highest standard. And it is one I have not been able to match.*

Zenfor returned her attention to her screens even though she wanted to reach out for him. It would look strange if she suddenly walked over to him and stood there, staring at him. Everyone would know they were speaking. *That sounds like a difficult standard to uphold.* She couldn't help but think about the camps where she was trained. Where Sil stayed there until they finished the training, even if it took years. Even if it took a lifetime.

I have made many mistakes since coming aboard. But the funny thing is, some have turned out for the better.

How do you mean?

You, for instance. Had I not assisted Mr. Robeaux in escaping in his own shuttle, it is very possible we never would have established a dialogue with your people. And you would not be aboard.

She couldn't argue with that. She'd been ready to kill Caspian and it had only been at the insistence of her brother Kayfor that she allow him to live and hear him out. *I didn't know you helped him escape.*

Yes. He figured out your ship was the same one he encountered seven years ago. But he could only do that by illegally downloading information, which I allowed. The captain promised not to tell the Sanctuary on the homeworld, but I fear the information will reach them one day.

Another strain of guilt ran through Zenfor. She too had kept information from Mil'less, specifically that she'd used Sil technology to upgrade *Tempest* after promising she wouldn't. It was an action punishable by discharge back on Thislea.

I had no idea you were facing much the same problem, Sesster said.

I feel like I've betrayed her. Like I've betrayed my people.

I understand what that means to you. Perhaps... He hesitated again.

Yes?

Perhaps we can explore our feelings together. And in this way we will no longer each be alone with our mutual problem.

She considered it. She had been terribly lonely since leaving Mil'less, even though she knew by now she had to be aware of Zenfor's actions. And she would probably not be receptive to Zenfor ever again, especially after she lost her command. And maybe that's what was really bothering her. The fact she knew Mil'less would abandon her upon her return, and all of Zenfor's actions had done nothing but ensure that outcome. Maybe if the engine upgrades still worked she could have told herself it was worth it; that they got something out of it. But now...

I think I understand. You need the engines to work in order to justify your betrayal. Just like I needed you to come back with Mr. Robeaux to justify mine.

I suppose that's one way to put it, she replied.

I don't want either of us to face that burden alone.

Neither did she. It was too hard alone, and she was tired of doing it. She decided right there to never be alone again.

This was stupid. He knew this was stupid and he was on his way to do it anyway. His conversation with Zenfor hadn't given Cas any more confidence as to the state of the engines. With both the undercurrent and Zenfor's enhancements down, there was little chance they'd survive. And the only lead they possibly had was this...prisoner with a magical map to treasure and fortune.

Fuck. Even thinking it sounded stupid. But he didn't need to commit to anything. Not yet. He was just going to listen to the man's story, and then he'd bring Evie down and let her listen. Then, after a careful evaluation, they'd decide what to do.

Cas waved to the security guard who opened the doors to the brig for him, where the alien still sat on his small bench in his room, his knees pressed together, and his entire body tensed up like a spring. Cas felt like he was waiting to launch himself at the barrier itself but holding back with barely any control. He drew a deep breath.

"Hello again."

"Back f-for more," Vrij said, his body shaking. "Back for m-my offer."

"First why don't you tell me how you came to be in this position. How did you get to be a scavenger, *borrowing* from other people's ships?"

Vrij creased his brow and gritted his sharp teeth. "Not a g-good story. Sad. Dangerous."

"Give it to me anyway. I've got the time." Cas walked over to one of the empty desks in the room, pulling the chair free and setting it down in front of Vrij's cell. He took a seat, so he was directly opposite the alien.

"Borrowing started when Laq disappeared," Vrij said.

"Who is Laq?" Cas crossed one leg. Vrij watched the movement, then mirrored it.

"Home. Laq was home and now it's g-gone. No more."

Cas huffed. It was like pulling teeth to get anything from this guy. "Okay, so you lost your home. How did you get your ship? Where do you dock?"

"D-dock? Where all Bulaq dock now. At t-the *Hub*. Outskirts. I s-stay out there. Most Bulaq a-aren't friendly. T-to m-me."

Cas wasn't sure if it was the auto-vox or if Vrij was in fact stuttering. Whatever the cause it seemed to be getting worse. "Okay, so you live on the hub now. Where is that?"

Vrij reached up with one hand held to the sky and undulated his four fingers in a rhythm. "Where the s-supplies are. Y-you can refuel."

"Right." Cas uncrossed his leg and crossed the other one. Vrij mirrored the movement again. "And as soon as we get there all your friends jump us and take whatever they want. I'm not buying it."

"I-it's the t-truth," Vrij replied, anxiety coloring the translation of his voice. "Y-you could b-bargain. Barter. Trade."

"And what could we trade that would be valuable enough to get what we need?" Vrij looked like wanted to answer but instead hesitated. Cas made a motion with his hand. "You can go ahead and answer. I know you've already scanned our ship."

"Food. M-medicine. T-the Bulaq have lots of p-parts, little food."

Cas took a deep breath. Evie wasn't going to like that. They'd decided to put everyone on rations for a reason. While it was true they had a stockpile of food at the moment, it was designed to get them at least halfway back home. They couldn't barter it away. Not unless Cas was absolutely sure they could fix Zenfor's upgrades with the materials they procured. Because if they could get back using the same system that got them out here, they wouldn't need the food.

"Okay, let's say—" The room jolted, throwing Cas from his chair and Vrij from his bench, both of them hitting the floor at the same time. Cas hit his comm. "Bridge, report!"

"They're making another run for the ship, Commander," Uuma said on the other end.

"Bulaq idiots," Vrij muttered, pushing himself up.

"Are weapons—?"

"Still down, sir, but Rafnkell has four spacewings out there engaging them right now." Cas shoved the chair aside. The rest of this could wait until later. If the ship out there realized *Tempest* didn't have any weapons they might call in some of their friends. And no number of spacewings could help them then. He ran to the door.

"Wait!" Vrij called, his hand on the barrier separating them. It was meant to provide a mild shock but Vrij held it like it wasn't hurting him at all. "Bulaq have f-fuel cells...on the tops of ships. Looks like—" He made a triangular motion with his hand, then extended it out.

"Fuel cells?" Cas asked.

"H-hit fuel cells, ships crippled," Vrij said.

"I'll keep that in mind, thanks," he replied. Cas left the brig and took off down the hall, tapping the back of his hand. "Uuma, tell Rafnkell to aim for some kind of triangular apparatus on the tops of the ship. They're supposed to be the fuel cells."

"Aye, sir," she replied.

"I'm on my way." He bypassed the hypervator and ran to the nearest access corridor. Half the hypervators were still out and there was no sense in him taking one for just one level. He'd already decided in his head he'd avoid them when he could until the ship was back up and at a hundred percent.

He scaled the ladders easily and popped out on level eight, finally reaching the bridge. When he arrived, Evie was issuing commands from the captain's chair. Cas took his place beside her.

"They're getting bolder. It's two ships this time," she said. Cas took stock of the tactical field before them. It was a straight-on dogfight and despite their superiority in numbers, the spacewings were having a hard time keeping up with the Bulaq craft. "We got a scan on one of the ships, it's construction is similar to our guest's."

"Have they managed to hit those fuel cells yet?" Cas asked. It was time to see if Vrij knew what he was talking about or not.

"Not yet, sir. They've—" A bright flash of light on the screen cut her off. Cas shielded his eyes until the automatic shade turned down the brightness of the screen for a moment before bringing it back up.

"What was that?" Evie asked.

"Checking now," Uuma replied.

"I believe it was one of the alien ships," Lieutenant Zaal said in his deep, monotone voice. He still hadn't managed to fix his personal apparatus from the attack and his robotic armature was on complete display for everyone to see, red eyes and all. Though he still wore his ceremonial robes.

"Fuck yeah, that's what you get you sons of bitches!" Rafnkell yelled through the comm.

"Chief! Don't destroy the other one, we need it for—" Another bright flash of light cut Evie off as the screen went almost white.

Rafnkell whooped again. "Sorry, Captain, what was that? I didn't catch that last order."

"Nevermind," Evie replied. She cut Rafnkell's comm and leaned over to Cas. "I guess I should have told her that *before* they went out there."

"Might have been a good idea." He smirked.

"Sir, how did you know about the triangle targets?" Uuma asked. Evie looked at Cas in anticipation of the answer as well.

"It seems our guest wants to put himself in our good graces," he replied.

Evie leaned back in her chair. "Awfully convenient, isn't it? He knows exactly how to destroy the one enemy who has been attacking us constantly? What if he wanted to get caught? He's got to be a mole."

Cas shrugged. "To be fair he told me shooting those things would disable the ships, not destroy them. If he was hoping a few more of his friends would be joining him in that brig I'm afraid I'm going to have to disappoint him."

"No," Evie replied. "I'm tired of hearing about this second-hand. I think it's time I met our illustrious guest. And see what he has to say for myself."

Cas nodded. He couldn't think of a better idea.

***

Evie stepped up to the barrier, inches from the edge. The alien on the other side did the same, getting as close as he dared, though Cas told her he'd been able to touch the surface and hold his hand there with little to no indication of pain. She couldn't decide if the plates all over his body protected him in some way or if he'd just been willing to endure the pain, but it was obvious from his behavior this was a resilient species. And she was struck just how much he resembled some of the Ashkasians. Cas hadn't been lying. There were obvious differences of course; his eyes were larger; his mouth and chin shapes were different, and the lack of a tail was probably the biggest sign they weren't the same species. But as she stood there watching his small nostrils flare and contract as if he was trying to smell through the barrier, she couldn't help but think they were related in some distant way.

"Mr...Vrij. It seems your information was helpful, so I want to thank you."

He nodded a few times, but his eyes always came back to Evie's. He wasn't someone who was shy of eye contact. "N-no more threat?"

"No, no more threat," she replied, chancing a glance at Cas. He shrugged. "My friend tells me you know where we can find replacement parts. Where we can repair our ship."

Vrij nodded. "The h-hub. Bulaq there can h-help you r-repair."

"You can't seriously think I would take my ship into the middle of your people's stronghold, do you? I'd be handing it to them on a platter."

Vrij cocked his head. "B-but your needs—"

"Are not so dire I'd risk the safety of this entire ship. So, if you were sent here to entice us into delivering a perfectly good spacecraft to your people, your mission has failed."

Vrij creased his brow. "I-I'm not on—no mission. Only *borrowing*. T-to survive. T-to stay warm."

"Yeah, I'll buy that when my ship is repaired and my crew is safe," Evie replied. "But your intel was a little too good. We ended up destroying your friends' ships."

Vrij twisted his mouth into a smile. "Good. Serves them r-right. Stupid Bulaq. Waste, nothing b-but a waste."

Evie turned to Cas again. Either he was a good actor, or he hadn't cared about the lives of the people on those ships. "Tell me more about this Hub. Who would we need to talk to in order to get the supplies we need?"

Vrij flinched. Evie wondered if Cas caught it too. "Diamant. T-talk to Diamant. H-he controls—he's been there longest. P-people know—trust him."

"Who is he?" Cas asked.

"Leader. He—" Vrij flinched again, finally breaking eye contact and cocking his head as if he was hearing a high-pitched noise. "H-he's the prophet. The o-one who survived."

"Survived?" Evie asked.

"W-when Laq was—taken f-from us. Diamant was t-there. The o-only one who c-came back. He's our last c-connection to t-the Great Ones."

Evie turned to Cas. "What the hell is he talking about?"

"I'm not really sure. Either the auto-vox is on the fritz or he's just not making sense. He mentioned that before though: Laq."

Evie returned her attention to their prisoner, catching his eye and keeping it. "Vrij. I need you to explain what you're saying. We don't understand. What is Laq? How was it taken? What happened?"

Vrij really seemed in pain now, but he pressed on anyway. "Laq was o-our home. O-our planet. T-then t-they came. Destroyed it. Destroyed o-our people. Diamant survived. He w-was the only one."

Evie stopped. "Wait. Someone destroyed your planet?" She exchanged glances with Cas. "Did they also destroy your stars?"

Vrij's eyes went wide. "How did y-you know?"

"It seems," Evie said, "we have a lot to discuss."

<u>8</u>

"So? Now what do we do?" Cas asked as they stood outside the brig.

Evie couldn't believe it: Vrij was from the planet they'd seen destroyed on the long-range telescope sensors. The destruction of his planet had been what had alerted them to the *Andromeda* threat in the first place. Now she understood why he and his people were scavengers. They'd lost their entire homeworld in the blink of an eye. And then their stars along with it, taking out any other habitable planets in the system. And while this presented them with an opportunity to learn more about the threat, it also put them right in the middle of a desperate people looking for any way to survive.

"I'm not sure," she replied. "Do you think Sesster can spare me a few minutes?" She needed to get her head straight and the only thing that seemed to work lately was her sessions with Sesster. They'd been having them up in one of the cargo bays but since he'd returned to Engineering they hadn't had the chance. There had been too many crises in the way.

Cas shrugged. "I'm sure he could spare a few minutes at least. He's a multitasker."

Evie shuddered. "I hate thinking about doing it in front of so many other people. It's hard enough when I'm not being gawked at."

He squeezed her shoulder. "Just do what I do when I want to talk to him. Go sit at a console and stare at it, pretending to work. It makes you much less conspicuous. And it isn't like you need to be looking at him while you're in that place, right?"

She shook her head. He was right, she shouldn't be self-conscious about it. She was the acting captain; she had the prerogative to go and do as she pleased as long as it didn't endanger the ship. Yes, this was something more of a personal nature, but that didn't mean it wasn't important. And if she needed a clear head in order to make decisions, then so be it.

"Get back to the bridge, coordinate with Rafnkell. I want to make sure we're ready in case they pull a surprise attack on us. I'll be there in a few minutes."

Cas nodded, but his gaze lingered on her for a moment. She was about to ask him why when he turned and headed in the opposite direction for the bridge.

Evie didn't bother with the hypervator as Engineering was only one level below them and half of them were still out anyway. But on the climb down through the access corridors she couldn't help but be reminded of her time on Sissk, into the mines where all the kids played. One of the simmilists' species was especially good at echolocation and often used the mines as a place to hide during games. Evie had still been young, but she wasn't the first child where a combination of eagerness and a desire to be liked led to questionable decisions. She had gone in looking for the other kids, only to become hopelessly lost. It had taken hours for someone to come for her and she just remembered climbing deeper and deeper into those mines with little to no regard of the consequences or a way out.

She shook off the feelings, planting her feet firmly on deck ten and making her way down to Engineering. Damage control teams littered the decks attempting to reinforce the existing bulkheads and structures. A few nodded to Evie as she passed. She needed to do right by them until Greene was back. She wouldn't let them down, even if she had to take a few more risks than she'd like.

Engineering was likewise a mess. More so than last time she'd been in here, which had been right before the life support had failed and she'd had to coax Sesster out of his cradle. If she hadn't they would have lost their chief engineer to suffocation.

She felt something like a pressure on her brain and glanced up to see Sesster had taken notice of her. A few of the other crew had as well, but most went right back to work.

"Captain," Lieutenant Tyler said, looking up from the main control station in the middle of the room. "I wasn't expecting you. Is there something—"

"No, I'm here to see our chief engineer. It's a private matter," she replied.

He nodded. "Of course. Let me know if I can help." She had to hand it to Tyler. When she'd first come aboard she never would have expected him to make it. He had been so wet behind the ears and with the added pressure of translating for Sesster she was sure his stress would have broken through before now. But he'd kept his cool during a crisis and managed to impress them all with his selflessness while Engineering was falling apart around them. She was glad he was down here with Sesster.

Evie made her way around all the smaller stations, toward the back and avoiding the large conduits that ran to the floor and ceiling which provided the ship with its undercurrent capability. Though she noticed one of the conduits was cracked. It was to be expected with as much stress as they were putting on the ship.

As she approached, she noticed Consul Zenfor standing off to the side; she'd been hidden by a console to where Evie hadn't seen her when she'd first come in. The consul only stared at the information on the screen: some kind of Sil glyphs Evie guessed. But the consul wasn't moving. Evie would have been concerned if she hadn't seen the subtle rise and fall of her back.

"Consul?"

Zenfor blinked a few times then turned to Evie with a concerned look on her face. "Captain Diazal." She glanced around the room, then back at her screen. "Two hours. That's…concerning."

"Are you alright?" Evie asked.

"Fine." She glanced up at Sesster then back at her console again. "I need a break. I'm not making any progress on the engine enhancements."

Evie gave her a sympathetic smile. "You looked like you were deep in concentration."

Zenfor glanced to Sesster again. "Something like that. The commander and I have begun a formal relationship." Evie's eyes widened. "We find it mutually beneficial."

"That's…wonderful," she replied. For once she was glad the comm towers were down. How was she supposed to include this in a report back to the Coalition? And how would they even react to a Sil becoming involved with one of the founding species? She knew it wouldn't go over well.

"You sound upset," Zenfor said. Evie wasn't about to question this woman's motives. The last thing she needed to do was upset her.

"No, just…you know what? It's none of my business. Carry on."

That seemed to satisfy her. She stood, made a curt nod to Evie, and left.

It isn't what you think, Sesster said in her mind.

She glanced up at him. "Like I said, it's none of my business. And that's not why I'm here. I need to go back in."

Are you sure?

"It gives me clarity of thought. I'm afraid without it, the hallucinations will start again." After her final encounter with her "father", she'd begun hallucinating during the day and couldn't sleep at night. All that had stopped after she and Sesster shared the *mind-space*. And she hadn't had any trouble since, but she'd also had a regular set of meetings with Sesster to continue to explore it. This was the longest she'd gone without some kind of experience and she was afraid of what might happen if she went too long.

Very well. Please take a seat and close your eyes.

Evie did as she was told, taking the seat next to Zenfor's console. This was the part that she always found most nerve-wracking: sitting here, waiting for something to happen. She closed her eyes and took a deep breath, waiting for the pull.

It was like being yanked through time and space on a tether hooked to a mark seven hypershuttle. One second, she was sitting in Engineering, perfectly calm, and the next she was standing in the middle of a nondescript desert, the horizon white in the distance against the gray sky. The ground beneath her feet was dry and cracked, as if this place hadn't seen water in years. In the distance a figure approached, wearing a standard Coalition uniform. He was completely bald, with no evidence of hair anywhere and his eyes were as white as the horizon. "Captain," he said in a soft voice.

"Commander," she replied. This was how it always started. Sesster told her the man was her personification of him if he were human and might be how her true mind's eye really saw him. She had to admit she found it easier to interact with him this way.

"How would you like to begin?" he asked.

"I think we can skip the preliminaries." The scene shifted to them floating in the depths of space. They hadn't traveled there, the desert floor had just vanished in an instant, with the two of them remaining in their places. And even though they were now surrounded by blackness and stars, Sesster still had something of an aura to him. A slight glow that was faint and powerful at the same time.

"I am glad you're able to exert more control over these visions," he said. She was too. The first few times it had been nothing but the same, she'd had to enter her old home on Sissk, encounter the visage of her father who then transformed into a creature she'd never seen before but had come to suspect was one of the *Andromeda* aliens. She didn't know quite why she suspected that, but now that she'd learned about Vrij's people she was anxious to see if she could extract any more information from the vision.

"Our new prisoner is a victim of the aliens," she said, still floating. "His planet was the one we caught on the long-range telescopes."

"Then it would be prudent to examine everything we can about what you're seeing," Sesster replied. She nodded. The next part of the vision always followed the first: they were transported to space and then shown a planet Evie had only seen here. It was like no other planet she'd ever seen before, as it was a terrestrial planet and yet it was massive enough to have rings. The atmosphere and what she could see of the surface was green and two small silver moons were locked in orbit. It was beautiful and also foreboding. She could only assume this was the alien's homeworld, yet her evidence for such a conclusion was limited at best.

"Can you see anything you didn't before? Feel anything?" Sesster asked.

She closed her eyes and concentrated, trying to focus on the thoughts themselves. Where had these images come from? And why was she always shown the same ones? There had to be a reason for this. Each time before she'd been distracted by thoughts of her father as he'd played a prominent role in the first part of the vision. But she'd since learned how to move the sequence back and forth, exert her will over it and make it show her what she wanted. But nothing else was coming to her. It was just…the planet. "I can't—"

"Quiet your thoughts. Try not to think about it too hard," Sesster replied. "It's not life or death. Just…think."

She nodded, opening her eyes again. The planet gleamed like an emerald jewel and for a moment she thought she saw a shimmer near the twin moons. "There," she said, pointing at the natural satellites. "I think I saw something." But just as she concentrated on the shimmer, she and Sesster were yanked forward again, down through the planet's atmosphere to the surface where they stood on a grassy hill, overlooking scores of the aliens. They all turned to her in unison, staring with their cold, gray eyes. "Dammit," she muttered. This was the next part of the sequence, the king of the hill as she called it.

"You can take us back, just focus hard," Sesster replied. She did, thinking back to where they'd just been. The scene changed before them and they were floating in space once more. "Now, focus on what you saw. Take us there."

She nodded, focusing her mind on the moons. Slowly they moved across the reach of space until they were in front of the moons themselves. "These resemble the moons I saw at Omicron Terminus," she said. There she'd found two moons who had been tidally locked with what seemed to be an ancient arch spanning the distance between them. Was it possible there was an arch here too, but invisible to her?

"What do you think?" Sesster asked.

"I think there's something here I can't see. And I think it might relate to how these creatures travel. But—"

They were yanked forward again at near-undercurrent speeds until they found themselves in another system. The primary star was a dark-blue O-type while the secondary was a yellow G type and the system had half a dozen planets in orbit. Evie recognized it immediately.

"Captain," Sesster said, trepidation in his voice.

"I know," she replied. "This is all new." All the other times after her time on the green ringed planet she'd been transported to Omicron Terminus before the sequence started over again. But this was different. She'd seen this system though the sensor telescopes given to them by Starbase five. Out of the corner of her eye she saw the approaching armada, all the ships identical to the one they'd seen back at Omicron Terminus. As they passed the fourth planet in the system a pair of much smaller ships approached from its surface. Before she'd realized it, the armada had destroyed the smaller ships and turned their attention on the planet. Beams of orange light erupted from the ships and converged into one solid beam, plowing into the planet's core. Within moments the surface began to crack and break apart, the entire surface of the planet shattering before smaller sections broke off. The molten core, exposed to the vacuum of space for the first time, expanded, then began to fall apart as well. It had taken minutes.

Evie caught more ships approaching from other planets in the system, hundreds in fact. This *hadn't* been on the telescopes. But instead of turning their attention on the smaller ships, the armada trained their weapons on the O-type star itself, releasing another blast of energy. As soon as their weapons had finished firing, the entire armada disappeared while the star itself expanded in an ever-increasing fusion reaction. The result was a supernova that created a shockwave, igniting a similar process in its mate, destroying what few planets remained in the system and wiping out the smaller ships all in one blast.

It was a massacre.

Evie jerked forward, falling out of the chair. She threw her palms out at the last moment to keep her face from smacking the metal but as soon as she was stable she promptly vomited all over the ground.

"Captain!" Tyler came running over along with two of the other engineering crew.

Evie wiped her mouth with the back of her sleeve. "I'm fine." She held up her hand as she gathered her bearings. The last time she'd seen that massacre it had been cold and detached, from hundreds of thousands of light years away. But this time it had been much more real, much more visceral. Like she'd experienced it in real time. She glanced up at Sesster. "What the hell was that?"

I don't know, Captain. But I suggest you take a break. You were under for almost an hour this time.

"An hour!" *Shit!* She jumped up, shaking the nausea moving through her like a wave through sand. She checked the chronometer on the closest console. Yep, it was fifteen after. She was late for dinner with Laura.

"Are you sure you're okay, Captain?" Tyler asked.

"I'm fine, Lieutenant," she said with more heat in her voice than she'd meant. He and the others backed off, returning to their stations. But she couldn't help but feel the eyes of the room on her. "I'll get someone down here to clean this up," she said indicating the mess on the floor. The last thing she felt like doing at the moment was eating again, but she'd made a promise.

I've already taken care of it, Sesster replied. *Take a break, Captain. This was much more intense, for both of us this time.*

She hadn't considered that. Sesster had seen everything as well, and if he had a mouth he'd probably be vomiting all over the place too. But she couldn't worry about that at the moment. She needed to get to her quarters. This wasn't how she wanted this date to start off.

"I'll...be back later and we can try again," she said. Sesster didn't reply in her mind, but she couldn't help but think he was fine with it. One thing was for sure, Vrij's people were in dire straits. Which could either make them the perfect allies or very dangerous. And she was going to have to decide which.

She only hoped she made the right choice.

<u>2</u>

Evie stirred, groaning at the headache that had permeated her dreams and sustained itself until she was fully conscious. She knew it was going to be a bad one and she'd have to make a trip by sickbay before hitting the bridge this morning. Even though sickbay was the last place she wanted to be. Despite her own personal bad memories of being there she didn't like being so close to the captain's unconscious body. It was creepy but why she couldn't say.

She rolled over, reaching out and feeling the cold sheets next to her. Even though she'd been expecting it, the lack of someone else there left a pit in her stomach. Laura had tried to hide her disappointment the evening before, but Evie could still tell she'd been hurt even though she said she understood. And it didn't help Evie hadn't stopped going on about the visions and what they might mean and what they should do about them. Had she even asked Laura about *her* day? How *she* was feeling? She groaned again in frustration. She'd screwed up big-time and she'd need to find a way to make amends for it.

She dragged herself out of bed, her head pounding and took a quick shower, just enough for a quick rinse before getting dressed and ready for the day. She still wasn't used to the captain stripes on her uniform and only hoped things would go back to normal in a few days. Weeks if necessary. She couldn't be in charge and still deal with these visions at the same time. In fact, she probably needed to get back down to Engineering again to go through it all a second time but there just wasn't any time today. And that was another thing. Before all their sessions had lasted maybe fifteen minutes at the longest. But this one had been over an *hour*. Had Sesster not noticed the passage of time either? Had they both been stuck in there in some kind of limbo while the rest of the ship had moved-on without them? She couldn't be sure, but she didn't like the thought of being lost in the *mind-space* forever. Next time she'd need to ask Sesster to set a timer. Or get someone else to wake them up. Zenfor perhaps.

Evie chuckled at the implications. Sesster and Zenfor. Who would have thought? Though it made sense. They were both alone on this ship, both having left their homes to help the Coalition. Both unique among all the other races onboard. But she suspected it was deeper than that. A shared kinship over something she didn't quite understand. And that was fine. She was just glad she wasn't the one who had to write the report on it. Greene would be floored when he woke up.

As she left, she took a glance at the sword hanging on her wall, the constant reminder that she was better than her father ever had been and that she was worthy to keep such an old family heirloom. At one time she'd found it something to be ashamed of, but not anymore. Now it was hers and vice versa. She planned on being buried with that sword.

Sickbay was quiet this morning as it was still early. The third shift hadn't yet finished, and first shift was just gearing up so most of the people she passed were preparing for their days. And when she entered the medical ward she was grateful to see all the other patients had finally been discharged.

"Good morning, Captain," Box said, approaching. "May I ask how your sex life is going?"

"No, you may not," Evie replied, not missing a beat. She'd gotten used to him over the past few weeks and despite assurances from Xax he was getting better with his inappropriate comments Evie hadn't seen a difference. Perhaps Xax had given up. Or, more likely, Box was only behaving when the doctor was around. "I need something for a headache."

"How bad on a scale of *I ate something spicy* to *my eyeballs are going to burst into a gooey mess?*"

"Somewhere in the middle," she replied.

"You got it." He walked over to the far wall, programming something into the computer. "Have you made a decision on the prisoner yet?"

Evie furrowed her brow. "Let me guess, Cas told you."

"He was in here drinking again last night, I had to keep him entertained until it got out of his system."

Evie's shoulders fell. Dammit. She had really thought he'd given that up at least while they were dealing with all these emergencies.

"Oh," Box said, returning with a small pill in his hand. "I'm sorry that was cruel. He wasn't drinking. But he did tell me about the guy. He sounds weird."

She sighed, exasperated. "We're all weird. Was he drinking or not?" She took the pill and swallowed it without any water.

"No, I was just disparaging his character. It's a hobby of mine."

"That's not very nice."

"I'd say I won't do it again, but we both know I will. What if I went with something less destructive, but completely within his capability? Passing gas for instance? He could have been in here farting up a storm, you never know." Box stared at her with his bright, yellow eyes. They weren't blinking today. "So, did you decide?"

"It's classified," she replied.

"Fine. Don't tell me. I'll find out from him later anyway." Evie rolled her eyes as Box returned to his duties. "I don't need to know. I only single-handedly saved everyone on this ship."

She knew he was baiting her, but she couldn't help it. "How?"

"When Engineering was about to collapse. I stood guard and made sure everyone got out in time. It was the struggle of my life, holding those bulkheads back. They could have buckled at any moment! It was only by my infinite determination that I was able to succeed."

"You stood beside the door and watched people leave," she replied, deadpan.

Box turned to her. "Agree to disagree. I'm a hero." Something clicked inside his head. "*I think he's brilliant.*"

"Is that Commander Volf's voice?" Evie asked, approaching him.

"Yep. Her first words to me. I recorded them for posterity." Evie couldn't help but laugh. Of course he did.

"Do you ever make recordings of anything I say?" she asked.

He hesitated two beats too long. "No."

"Box…"

"No, with an asterisk."

"Delete them, right now."

His eyes blinked like wild. "But they're for my research! I'm going to write a medical journal on the mating patterns of all Coalition species. It'll be a compendium like no other. I need firsthand corroborations."

"Get them from someone else," she replied.

"Ugh. Fine. You're getting to be just like him. I thought you were *cool*."

"Cool doesn't mix well with running this ship." She glanced over to the other side of sickbay, behind which the captain's body still lay. "Has there been any change?"

He shook his head. "Doc hasn't begun her procedure yet. She scheduled it to begin later this afternoon."

"Let me know how it goes, will you?"

"I will," he replied.

She left him there, heading to the bridge. Box might be a pain in the ass, but he was a good soul underneath. Or whatever the robot equivalent was. Coalition Central still hadn't come up with a classification for him when they'd lost contact, though Evie imagined it was probably low on their list of priorities what with the impending armada on their doorstep. She only hoped they could get back home in time to share what little they knew.

Although, with this new information from Vrij, they might be able to discover even more. But that wasn't the priority at the moment. Only if it was convenient. What had he said? This...Diamant had survived the destruction of their homeworld? After witnessing the destruction firsthand in her visions Evie wasn't sure how that was possible but maybe it was worth investigating. At least with a small contingent of officers.

Evie stepped off the hypervator on the bridge to find Cas already at his posting as the rest of third shift was taking their leave and first was coming on. Laura took up tactical from Lieutenant Stillwater but only shot a quick look at Evie before turning back to her duties. Yep, she was pissed. And Evie couldn't blame her. No wonder she went back to her own quarters last night. She needed to apologize but she wasn't going to do it here; it needed to be somewhere more private.

"Cas, in the command room," she said, bypassing her seat and making her way for the door adjacent the bridge. Inside she took her seat behind the desk while Cas took the one opposite her. "Any further thoughts about our...opportunity?"

"I still think it's worth the risk. We're due for another attack in under three hours and we're still not completely recovered from the last one. Though I think having Rafnkell out there helped a lot. They managed to get half the weapons systems back online overnight. But there's no telling if they'll hold. We could make it through another fight and the relays could blow again, leaving us right in the same place where we were. We can't keep going like this."

She sighed. He was right. She'd really hoped Greene would have woken up before now, he'd know what to do. No matter what he always had a plan.

"There's something else," he added. "When I got on the bridge I overheard Commander Volf saying something about you. I didn't catch all of it because she stopped as soon as she saw me, but I heard your name and a few other choice words I won't repeat."

She couldn't say she was surprised. After their tiff on the shuttle and Evie's dressing down of her publicly on the bridge as they were trying to escape the minefield, she'd felt like Volf'd had it in for her ever since. "I don't care about that," she lied. "If she has a problem with me she needs to bring it to me in private, not gossip on the bridge. And you need to call that behavior out when she does."

"I almost did..." he began. She sensed a lot of hesitation there. What was going on with him? Usually he didn't have trouble confronting people. She waved it off; they had bigger issues.

"My experience with Sesster last night was...illuminating. I think the Bulaq could be good candidates for allies, but only if they can show they can control themselves. We need these attacks to stop."

Cas leaned forward. "Agreed, and we'll need to establish some ground rules with them before we agree to anything. If Vrij is telling the truth and this friend of his really survived that attack, we need to know everything he knows. It could be more important than the supplies themselves."

"Not if we can't do anything with the information. Either we find a way to transmit it back or we fix the engines so we can return home. That's priority one. Priority two will be to gather information about the threat from this Diamant or whoever he is. Get with Rafnkell and take a shuttle to this hub. See what they're offering. Then we'll take the next steps."

He nodded. "What changed your mind?"

She drew a deep breath. "A lot of things. We need to find a way to survive out here and it's obvious we can't do it alone. But we also can't be stupid about this. I'm not thrilled about taking this step but maybe Vrij was a happy accident instead of saboteur."

He eyed her. "You don't really believe that, do you?"

"It doesn't matter what I believe. It's what is best for the ship."

He nodded. "Okay. I'll get right on it. Anything else?" he asked, standing.

She smirked. "Yeah, try not to get yourself captured or killed. We're short on personnel as it is."

10

"You're not coming."

"I am too coming, and if I don't, the whole ship is going to get a shot of your naked ass on their screens in the morning," Box said, his tinny voice coming through the comm.

"Do it and you won't live to regret it," Cas replied, double-checking to make sure he had all his equipment.

"Drastic times call for drastic measures!" Box yelled.

"Oh yeah? Let me talk to Xax."

"That's not necessary," Box replied too quickly.

"Uh-huh." Cas turned and motioned for Ryant to load the rest of the cargo containers on the shuttle. It had been Cas's idea to take a sampling of food with them to show good faith, though he wouldn't be using it unless necessary. "The fact is you have a responsibility here now and you can't go off globetrotting with me whenever you feel like it. Xax may need you for the procedure later."

There was an inaudible grumbling on the other side of the comm.

"What was that?"

"Have a good time," Box said, his voice forced and low. He cut the channel. Cas chuckled and turned back to the shuttle. He'd be done sulking by the time they got back. Jann was already aboard running through the pre-flight sequence. Vrij had said the Hub was a day's journey away, which meant they'd need one of the larger shuttles complete with full crew quarters and cargo bay. They'd already packed all the supplies they needed plus some extra and what Cas hoped to barter. Even though they were on one of the largest shuttles *Tempest* carried, he felt it might get a little cramped. Not only were Jann and Ryant providing their much-needed muscle, but also Uuma was coming along to guard Vrij, who would need to be kept on a short leash until they got there. Speaking of which, Cas glanced toward the Bay's entrance, looking for Uuma. She hadn't reported in with the prisoner yet.

"Have you heard from the lieutenant?" Cas asked Ryant and Jann.

"Nope," Jann replied from the front, even though Cas couldn't see her since she was two sections up.

"Sorry, man, nothing yet," Ryant replied, setting down the last of their bartering crates in the shuttle's hold.

"I need to go check—" As Cas spoke, he turned to see Vrij being led through the main connector into the bay by Lieutenant Yamashita. He trotted over to her. "Where's Uuma?"

"I volunteered to go instead," she replied.

"Oh. And the captain was fine with it?"

"She was."

Okay then. Cas wasn't about to argue with the young woman. He motioned for her to follow him over to the shuttle, dragging Vrij along on a set of cuffs that had been pulled taught. He suspected there was something going on between Evie and Laura, but he wasn't about to butt in. "Guess it will be like old times," he replied.

"Just as long as you're not flying."

He chuckled. "No, Captain Jann will be taking care of that today. She and Ryant will be our backup when we get to the Hub."

"N-no backup. It's s-safe," Vrij replied from behind. Cas leaned around her.

"We don't go into unknown situations without backup. How stupid do you think we are?"

"G-guards will g-give Diamant the w-wrong impression."

Cas glanced at Laura. "Well, then we'll just have to be discreet. And if it turns out to be a trap, you're going to wish you never *borrowed* from this ship, understand me?" Vrij slapped his chest twice. "I'll take that as a yes. Get him aboard and settled. He's on the bottom bunk."

"W-what's bunk?" Vrij asked.

"Where you'll be sleeping. You do sleep?"

"Yes."

"Lying down?"

"Yes."

"Then you'll be fine." Laura led him up the ramp in the back around all the crates Ryant had stacked inside, and maneuvered him into the small crew quarters that were partitioned off between the cargo area and the shuttle's command deck. "Anything else?" Cas asked as Ryant finished securing all the containers to the walls.

"I think that's it, though I really wish we could take our spacewings."

"Me too. I'd feel better with the extra firepower. Speaking of which—" He patted under his armpit.

"Already got it." Ryant slapped Cas's boomcannon in his hands. It was his custom-designed weapon and had been in storage ever since Cas had come on board. He'd missed his old companion.

He shoved the weapon into its holster under his jacket. "Just like old times."

"When we get back I want you to show me how you designed that thing," Ryant said. "Could be useful if we could get a couple more of those." The boomcannon was unique because it fired not only plasma bursts as most traditional weapons did, but also projectile rounds as well. You could set it to fire both at once, or in a pattern depending on the type of enemy you were facing. Cas had rarely used it, but when he did, he always found it more than effective.

"We've got a day of travel and not much to do with it, I'll show you as soon as we take off."

"Deal," Ryant replied. "Guess that's it then. Everybody good to launch?" A round of different affirmations came back to them. Ryant wiped his hands and tapped the button beside the cargo door. At first, it illuminated with a blue glow and then the door slid down, locking them inside. Cas couldn't help his heart rate from jumping, but he pressed the sensation down, ignoring it as best he could. The blue glow disappeared. "All sealed, Commander."

"I told you, you don't have to call me that."

"Yeah, I know. But once Rafnkell started doing it we all did. Just makes things easier."

Cas shook his head. "I'll be up there in a minute." Ryant nodded and took his leave, passing through the cargo doors. Cas took a deep breath and tried not to think about how long he'd have to be on this shuttle. Thankfully it wasn't the same size or model as the one Suzanna had been on, but still, it was a shuttle. And even though it had gotten easier, he still wasn't over his phobia. He wasn't sure it would ever completely go away. He tapped his personal comm. "Captain?"

"Diazal here."

"We're ready to go. Everything set on your end?"

"We're good up here. Best of luck." He wanted to ask if everything was alright with her and Laura, but he promised himself he wouldn't interfere and so he kept his mouth shut.

"Thanks. See you in a few days." He ended the comm and made his way to the front, passing where Laura had locked Vrij down to his particular bunk. His arms hung down from the bar on above the ceiling but otherwise he looked comfortable enough lying down.

"N-not a trap," he said as Cas passed him. "I-I'd never do that."

"See, there's the problem, Cas replied, stopping. "I don't know if you'd do that or not because I don't know *you*. And until I do, this is how we're going to do things because I don't like getting jerked around. Cool?"

"N-no, I'm quite warm."

Laura stepped back inside the crew quarters, keeping near the door, observing. Cas noticed her but said nothing, instead kept his attention on Vrij. "I need to know what kind of man this Diamant is before we meet him. What should I expect?"

Vrij sucked in a breath of air. "H-he's our prophet. H-he survived. Gives Bulaq s-safe harbor. I've traveled a-all over, n-no one else helps us. All afraid of us. A-afraid ghosts w-will come for them if they help us."

"Ghosts?"

"T-those that destroyed Laq. They d-disappeared. Ghosts. Other s-species think we're marked for d-death. That the Great Ones d-didn't protect us." He shuddered but Cas couldn't tell if it was involuntary or not. "But Diamant s-survived, the Great Ones k-kept him alive to l-lead us."

Cas took a seat opposite Vrij on one of the other bunks. "So he's generous. Willing to help those in need."

Vrij hesitated too long for Cas's liking. "Y-yes. Helps. Bulaq are s-scattered all over. Probably—maybe less t-than fif-fifty-thousand of us left. Many factions. Many t-tribes."

"So you're saying he may not have control over the ships attacking *Tempest*," Laura said.

Vrij turned to her. "R-right. M-my people are getting d-desperate. Diamant controls the h-hub. W-what few resources are concentrated there."

Cas rubbed his forehead in frustration. Feuding factions and people desperate for a solution to their problems. No wonder they'd been attacking *Tempest*. "What does he want? Above all else?"

Vrij cocked his head as if he hadn't understood the question. "T-to save the Bulaq. To p-preserve what is left."

Cas shifted on the bunk. "And what is your relationship with him?"

"I-I…" Vrij hesitated again. "I know him. Worked t-together in the past."

"Doing what?"

"Borrowing."

Cas dropped his gaze. "That's why you were on our ship. He sent you there." He'd been right. This whole thing was nothing but a trap. He stood, turning his attention to Laura. "Tell Jann to turn us around, this is nothing but a trap."

"N-no," Vrij said, agitated. "Not a t-trap. Genuine. I w-wasn't working for him when I f-found your jewel. On my own. Have b-been for a long time."

"Why?" Cas asked. "Why leave the security of this hub if it's so great? And why break off a relationship with Diamant if he only wants to help people?"

Vrij turned away, staring at the far side of the wall. Cas nodded to Laura. "Tell Jann. And comm *Tempest* if we're still in range of the short range transmitters. We'll have to figure some—"

"Because I am *different*," Vrij shouted, sitting up. Cas stepped back, his hand immediately going to his boomcannon. He watched Vrij for a moment, the back of his jacket expanding like there was a balloon there, until what he could only identify as two sharp mechanical arms ripped through the fabric, wrapping themselves around Vrij.

"What the hell?"

One arm reached out and on the end Cas could see it split into two dangerously sharp blades, opening and snapping closed like a crab's claws. One of the claws reached up to where the cuffs had been affixed to the bar above him and snapped the air beside them, but then retracted again, folding back through the tears in Vrij's jacket and disappearing from view.

"Did you know about those?" Cas asked Laura, his hand still on his weapon.

"They weren't in the log."

"Do you mean to tell me you could have broken out of those restraints at any time?" Cas asked. Vrij pulled up and slapped his chest twice with his forearms. Cas took that as his culture's gesture of a yes. "Then why didn't you?"

"P-prisoners aren't supposed to escape," he said.

"What are those things?"

Vrij concentrated. "M-my people are b-born with t-their own mandibles. T-they grow from our b-backs and h-help us complete tasks or are f-for defense. I…I lost m-mine when I was young."

"What does that have to do with Diamant?" Laura demanded.

"When Diamant f-found out—banishment." Vrij turned away again in what Cas easily recognized as shame.

"But you got them replaced. Aren't yours as good as anyone else's?" Cas asked.

"No. Mandibles are a p-part of a Bulaq's nature. To l-lose them is a g-great dishonor."

Cas released the butt of his gun. He was pretty sure if Vrij had wanted he could have killed every one of the spacewing pilots that brought him aboard, as well as anyone else within a one-meter radius during any time of his incarceration. He also could have removed his restraints at any time, or kept the mandibles secret. But instead he just laid there, staring at the ceiling of his bunk and chained up when he didn't have to be.

Laura leaned over. "So, if they're not on good terms, how is he supposed to get us to see Diamant?" she whispered.

11

"Sir, wake up."

Cas was jostled from a dreamless sleep back into the reality of the shuttle's crew quarters. It took him a moment to gather his bearings and for a second he thought he was back on the *Reasonable Excuse*. He glanced over to see Laura standing beside the high bunk, her head barely visible over the top where he lay. He drew a deep breath. "You don't have to call me sir."

"Fine," she replied. "I think we're almost there. Jann told me to come get you." She turned and left the crew bunks. Cas oriented himself and dropped his legs over the edge and hunched out of the cramped bed. The bunks were really horizontal alcoves that could be shut if the occupant wanted, but they didn't leave a lot of room for comfort. They weren't more than a meter in height in order to maximize the number of spaces in one shuttle which made getting in and out of them a challenge. Especially the top ones.

Cas hopped down and bent to check on Vrij on the bottom bunk, still in the same position he'd left him in. He didn't expect the alien to go anywhere, or to even break his restraints. If Vrij was planning something, he wouldn't act until they had disembarked. Though Cas couldn't help but think he still hadn't gotten over his shame from admitting to them his "disability", if you could call it that. If Cas had two-meter-long bladed scythes tucked into the folds of his back he certainly wouldn't consider them a disadvantage.

He made his way to the front of the shuttle where Jann and Laura sat in the pilot and co-pilot's seats, respectively. Without turning to acknowledge him Jann nodded toward the structure ahead of them. "That's it. Right where he said it would be."

"Seems kinda...plain." It looked like nothing other than a massive rectangle floating in space. Though the outside had markings and other indications it was more like a massive cargo container. "I don't see any ports or any access areas. How are we supposed to get in?"

"It's like Takar," Jann said.

"What's Takar?"

"Training mission," she replied. "A couple years back we had a training exercise in the Argolis system. Takar is the asteroid belt which makes up most of the system; it's huge. But our training involved dogfighting in an area with a lot of obstacles. Dorsey, Grippen and I, we'd hidden out behind one of the larger rocks, waiting for the autoprobes to come find us when Grippen gets this insane idea we needed a window."

"A window? Cas asked.

"Yeah. So, she starts blasting away at the rock, burrowing a tunnel straight through it with the weapons. Ryant and I joined in and a few minutes later, we had a two-meter square tunnel we could stare down the barrel. As the autoprobes approached, Grippen shot straight through that tunnel, taking them out easy."

Cas screwed up his face. "You want to blow a hole in the side to get through, is that what I'm hearing?"

"Maybe we should just ask the resident alien. I'm sure he knows," Laura said.

Cas nodded and returned to the crew compartment. Vrij looked up when he entered and Cas reached over, unlocking his restraints from the bar holding them to the ceiling. "We're here," he said. "I figure you could have done that at any time, and you didn't, so I want to thank you for that. But no sudden movements."

Vrij touched his palms to his chest, tapping twice and moved to stand up. When he was up Cas could clearly see the holes in the back of his jacket where the mandibles had punched through.

"Were you ever going to tell us about those?" he asked.

"N-no. I thought I m-might need them to escape," he replied. "I didn't e-expect...trust."

"You mean you didn't expect us to take you up on your offer to come here," Cas replied. Vrij touched his forehead with two fingers. "I don't know what that means."

"I didn't expect it."

Cas surveyed the small room. "Neither did I. But both our people need help. And maybe we can help each other. Head up to the front, I think we're here."

Vrij made his way past Cas, careful not to touch him and Cas followed, trying to see the outline of the folded mandibles on his back, but the jacket hid them well. Rafnkell was going to have a fit when she found out he'd been harboring dangerous weapons and her people hadn't searched him.

"It this it?" Laura asked as Vrij stared out the main window of the shuttle. He tapped his chest twice. "What is that? Does he mean yes?"

"Yes," Vrij said, his gaze locked on the rectangle.

"This is all that is left of your people?" Cas asked.

"T-this is where m-most of us are," he replied. "Others, still s-scattered." He pointed to the large rectangle. "We u-used our l-largest cargo holds—s-stitched them together. Built w-what we could."

"Your people, you excel at engineering, don't you?" Cas asked. Vrij tapped his chest twice again. "Pulling those power converters off the side of *Tempest* was delicate work. I'm not even sure we could have done it from that side. And certainly not as fast."

"Experience," Vrij replied.

"It's something I can appreciate. How do we dock? I don't see any ports."

"You d-don't dock. No ports. Land."

"Did he say *land?*" Jann asked.

Vrij pointed to the port side of the rectangle. "Over t-there."

"Bring us around, see what he's talking about."

Jann swung the shuttle around to the side where Vrij had pointed and his reason became clear. This side of the rectangle was open to the inside, which was nothing short of breathtaking. The Bulaq may have repurposed old shipping containers, but the inside was a fully functioning city. Cas could tell where other, smaller ships had been repurposed and retooled into buildings that now peppered the "floor" of the cargo containers. Some were stacked on top of each other and some had been disassembled and reengineered to create brand-new structures. The far side of the container was closed, and scaffolding climbed all over that end of the structure while the entire "ground" of the massive container was covered, with the exception of maybe a dozen different landing sites. The walls had been reinforced with skeleton structures and some of the "buildings" had begun to climb up the sides, acting as additional supports. Cas also noticed large pipes running through the "streets" between the buildings from one end of the structure to the other. He took note of the high number of spired buildings inside. Could those be shrines of some kind?

"Vrij, this is the Hub?" he asked.

"Yes."

"And how long did it take your people to create this?"

He seemed to be doing a calculation in his head. "Ninety-four Vrij stays."

Cas furrowed his brow. "Vrij stays?"

"I think he means the length of his stay on *Tempest*," Jann offered. Vrij tapped his chest twice.

"But you've only been on the ship two days. You mean to tell me your people did all this in a hundred and eighty days?" Cas gawked at the structure. Had he not known better he would have said it had been there for centuries, not barely more than two seasons. What had their home *planet* been like? "You really do have an abundance of building materials."

"The b-best," Vrij replied.

"Jann, patch into the auto-vox and send them a message requesting to land." Cas understood why they needed food and medicine now. They could literally build whatever they wanted but without a constant supply of food their people would all die out, great structures or not. The destruction of Laq had probably destroyed what food-producing facilities they had.

"This is the shuttle *Hymettus*, requesting permission to land on the Bulaq structure Hub," Jann said into the system. The comm was silent for a moment as they waited on the response.

"Sometimes—t-takes a minute," Vrij said, tapping the small device on his neck.

"Approved, please follow the appended coordinates," a voice very unlike Vrij's said on the other end. Cas was surprised but tried not to show it. He thought Vrij's stutter might be a natural affliction of the auto-vox not being able to properly translate his words. But that might not be the case after all.

Jann brought the shuttle down and as they passed the terminus into the "city" there was a slight bit of turbulence. "P-pressurization," Vrij said when Cas glanced at him.

"Are we—holy shit!" Ryant said, emerging from the back. "This place is huge! The way he was talking I thought it was just going to be a bunch of ships tethered together floating out in space. This thing is probably as big as Starbase Eight! If not bigger!"

"They're builders," Cas replied. He noticed as they were setting down on one of the pads a number of smaller ships coming and going through the space. Many were headed off toward the back of the container. "Vrij, what are those?"

"S-supplies. To b-build the t-temple."

"Is that what all the scaffolding at the back of the structure is for?" It seemed like whatever this "temple" was it would be massive when it was finished.

"Yes. It w-would have been—already f-finished but slow since…"

"Since you're having trouble feeding your people," Cas finished. Vrij tapped his chest twice.

"Contact," Jann said as the shuttle set down on the pad. "Keep it hot or shutdown?" She turned to Cas.

"Keep it hot. We don't know what we're walking into here. In fact, I think you should stay with the ship, just in case."

Jann eyed him. "You're sure? I came along to be your backup."

"I know. Just keep an eye out and let us know if there's anything funny going on while we're meeting this Diamant. We do have valuable supplies on board after all." She nodded and drew a pistol from a hiding spot Cas hadn't even seen, placing it on the console where she could reach it quick. Cas turned to Ryant and Laura. "You two, equip force barriers and light weapons. I don't want to go in guns blazing but I also don't want to get jumped. Use your best discretion."

"Y-you don't n-need weapons," Vrij said after them.

"Look, if all your people have these 'mandibles' on their backs which can kill us in an instant, we're not going in there without some protection, I don't care how peaceful your people are. Not to mention every encounter we've had with them so far have been hostile."

"Outliers," Vrij replied. "N-not like the rest."

"We'll see."

***

Ten minutes later the four exited the shuttle, leaving Jann inside by herself. Cas gave her a reassuring wave as they approached the two Bulaq standing on the edge of the landing pad, their hands crossed in front of them. One of them spoke to Vrij as they approached and he spoke back, though Cas couldn't understand either of them. He didn't like being in the dark especially in a situation like this.

"T-they want to know our p-purpose here," Vrij said.

"Tell them trade. And to see Diamant," Cas replied. Before stepping off the *Hymettus* he'd taken stock of himself. He hadn't been out of the Coalition in seasons, the last time being when he was on Zenfor's ship. But before that, the last place had been Devil's Gate. And this place felt more like there than anywhere else he'd been lately. It was dirty, crowded, noisy and Cas got the distinct impression everyone was out for themselves here.

"He won't want to see you," one of the Bulaq said in perfect standard after Vrij had relayed the message. Cas caught sight of small translators on their necks as well. Either they had synced up with Vrij's, or the few words he spoke had been enough for them to translate.

Cas stepped forward. "We are here to make a deal. We were told he needed assistance."

The Bulaq stared at Vrij before turning his attention back to Cas. "What kind of deal?"

"That's for us and him to work out." Cas's eyes widened as from behind the Bulaq two large mandibles extended, their ends snapping and clicking. They were greyish-green in tint, much different from Vrij's mechanical ones. And by *Kor* they looked sharp. Cas instinctively reached for his gun. "We didn't come here to hurt anyone. We may have supplies you need. But if Diamant doesn't want to talk, we'll be on our way." He made a motion for Laura and Ryant to step back, which they did while all three kept their eyes on the guards.

The mandible retracted behind the man and he glanced at his counterpart. They both tapped their chests twice. "Follow me," he replied.

12

As the guards led them through the narrow streets between what were once shuttles, repair craft, pleasure vessels, and several other kinds of ships Cas didn't recognize. He felt an overwhelming sense of déjà vu. Many of the buildings they passed had no windows or doors, and the ones he could see into were filthy inside. Cas could only assume this was residue from all the construction, though cleaning was probably on the bottom of your priority list if you were just trying to eat and feed your family. Small Bulaq children without shirts skirted around their feet, playing games and oblivious to the dire nature of their world. Though Cas did get a good look at how their mandibles folded up on their backs. They were like another set of thin, compound arms which scissored in and locked behind the Bulaq shoulder blades. They blended in so well they were almost invisible unless you looked hard. Cas could only imagine it had been a contributing factor as to why the Bulaq evolved as the dominant species of their planet.

Almost every corner they turned they were confronted with another unique smell. While most were tinged with sulfur, a few he didn't recognize, and were completely foreign to his palate. He was glad he'd ordered everyone to wear the force barriers. There was no telling what kind of diseases these people might be unintentionally carrying. He glanced over at Ryant. "You ever heard of Grum?"

Ryant furrowed his brow. "Border world? On the far side of Sargan space. Past Tau Hydrae?"

"That's it. I went there once on a courier job. I was one of the last non-Grum ships to leave the planet. The Sargans had cut them off, forced them to become self-sufficient. This place reminds me of what little I saw. Cut off from the trade routes and influx of goods and exports off the planet, the people were starving."

"Why were you there?"

"To pick up some last-minute diplomats from Cassiopia," Cas said, stepping over a man slumped down on the wall, his head hung between his knees. "They were delivering the final edicts to the Grum. A hundred years of banishment. Then, if anyone was still alive after a century, they'd be admitted back into the Sargan way of life with a clean slate."

"Seems kinda harsh," Ryant said.

"It was designed to act as a message. The Grum had rejected the Sargan edicts, and in a move of sheer lunacy, had tried to emulate the Coalition. I heard about it from one of my courier buddies. The Sargans weren't pleased."

"So, they cut them off entirely?"

Cas nodded. "To show everyone else in the Commonwealth what would happen if they didn't maintain loyalty. I can tell you not many people in the Commonwealth are what we would call happy, but they sure won't be rejecting the edicts anytime soon."

"Sounds like a shitty place," Ryant replied, tenderness in his voice. "I'm surprised you could stay there."

"It wasn't like I had a lot of choices. And it has its positives. But yeah, the Grum didn't deserve that. Just like I suspect most of these people don't deserve this. Can you imagine, having your entire system destroyed? Think about what that would do to the Coalition."

He screwed up his face. "Earth and Claxia Prime would be gone immediately. Valus too. The defense grid. Outposts Alpha, Beta. Maybe even Gamma. That's a lot right there."

Cas nodded. "Enough to cripple us. This could very well be us if those aliens reach home. We have to do everything we can to stop that from happening."

"How long ago were you on Grum?" Ryant asked.

"Three years."

"And what's it like now?"

"Last I heard they'd lost sixty percent of the population to starvation."

"God*damn*." Ryant looked like he might be sick. Maybe Cas shouldn't have relayed that story so close to meeting Diamant. That probably could have kept until they were back on the shuttle.

The guards continued to lead them through winding alleys and roads. One thing Cas noticed was there didn't seem to be a defined thoroughfare anywhere. The roads seemed to follow the shapes of whatever ships were being used as buildings with little thought to spatial planning. The only way he could keep his bearings was by keeping an eye on the large pipes that criss-crossed above them in different directions. As best he could tell they were moving further toward the back of the structure but had barely reached a quarter of the way so far. Now he really had wished Box had come; he could have built a mental map of this place in an instant. Cas wasn't feeling too good about their ability to escape this maze back to the ship unscathed.

Finally, the smaller ships opened up to a much larger structure. Cas could tell it had once been a medium-sized ship of some kind, but so much of it had been dismantled and repurposed it was hard to see exactly what its purpose had been. It was as if the Bulaq had taken this particular ship and turned it into one of their shrines. A large dome sat on the top, capped by a spire reaching high into the space. In front of the ship, a grand staircase had been constructed leading up to the access port as the landing gear of the ship itself was still deployed. How could these people spend so much time building and expending energy when they had little to no food available? And how many had they lost in the process? Cas wasn't sure he wanted to know.

They reached the top of the staircase with Vrij in front, Laura right behind him with her hand on her weapon and Cas and Ryant bringing up the rear. Cas could sense the tension among them, much of it emanating from Laura. Evie had told him she'd been in the tactical simulator a lot lately, though he suspected that was more for the tactical station itself rather than hand-to-hand combat. He hoped he didn't have to find out how much training she'd been through.

The guards led them through the narrow corridors of the ship/shrine until they reached what had to be the rear where it opened inside. In what was probably once the engine room, the entire area had been repurposed into what looked to Cas to be a refugee camp. Beds of all sizes littered the floor and swung from apparatus bolted into the walls, while Bulaq of all shapes and sizes milled about. It had become a place of refuge for these people. Cas noticed other Bulaq moving through the crowd, handing out supplies and rations, taking special care to make sure each Bulaq child had something.

"It's a sanctuary," Ryant whispered as they all looked on. One of the Bulaq guards who'd escorted them made an unusual noise in his throat that sounded to Cas like a cough combined with a click. Half of the people down below glanced up but one in particular stood out. He was larger, more muscular than the others and Cas could tell he'd been fed better, despite the fact he was one of those handing out rations.

His face was similar to Vrij's, though a few scars ran across his cheeks and over his bald head. Cas had no doubt he was the man they were here to see.

He handed the rations he was holding off to another helper and made his way up a side staircase to them, motioning they follow him through another set of corridors. The guards indicated it was okay but Vrij held back as Cas took the lead, wanting to make the first impression. He couldn't help but wonder just how dire these people's situation was. As they walked, he tapped the comm embedded in the back of his hand.

"Hey, Saturn, everything good?"

"Still good here," Jann replied. "They haven't even come close to me yet."

"Good. Keep me informed."

"You got it." He cut the transmission.

After a few more minutes the corridors opened into another large space, though not as large as the one they'd just left. Cas recognized it as the control center for what had been the ship, though many of the components had been cannibalized or removed. The only indicator this had been the bridge was one large chair in the middle of the room, where the man they'd followed now stood. Each of the guards touched the small black devices on their necks as he picked one up from the chair, affixing it in the same place.

Cas glanced to the others. Ryant seemed alert, but relaxed. Laura's eyes were darting around the space, as if looking for a way out in case there was trouble. While Vrij remained completely immobile, his focus on the floor in front of the other Bulaq's feet. Feet, Cas noticed, adorned by quality boots. Much better than Vrij's scraped and tattered versions. The man they'd followed in here tapped his chest twice and the two guards approached Cas and the others.

"No sudden movements." They each held up a small device and moved it up and down in front of each of them. "They're armed," one of the guards said.

"Leave them be," the man said, his voice strong yet slightly raspy. "They didn't come here to kill us."

The guards exchanged glances then dropped the devices and took up positions behind the group.

"Or am I wrong? What is your purpose here?"

Cas stepped forward. "My name is Caspian Robeaux. I come from what is known as the Sovereign Coalition of Aligned Systems, a confederacy far from here. We were told you needed help."

"You were." The man's eyes darted to Vrij and remained fixed on him. Vrij seemed to shrink under the gaze. "I must admit, we are the recipients of some very bad luck, but we are not as destitute as some might have made it seem."

"Are you Diamant?" Cas asked.

"I am. But I'm sorry if you were led to believe I'm some kind of influence here. I am merely a humble servant of the Bulaq people." Vrij made a noise and Diamant shot him a look, causing the smaller Bulaq to shrink away.

Cas glanced back to the guards, then took in what had once been an opulent bridge. "Doesn't look that way from where I'm standing."

Diamant cocked his head, much in the same way Vrij had done when he didn't understand something. "Caspian, I was given the gift of a second chance. I can't *waste* that on anything other than service to my people. They may hold me in some high regard, but I assure you, I'm little more than a man of my people."

Cas sensed Laura shift uncomfortably beside him. "Will you at least allow us to make our offer?" he asked. Diamant tapped his chest twice. "Thank you. My ship needs building and repair materials, which I can see you have an abundance of. We have food, medicine and other supplies to trade. We can help each other."

A crease formed across Diamant's considerable brow. He took a few steps to the right, his head bowed in contemplation. "Caspian, would you consider yourself a trusting person? Do you find you're generally a good judge of character?"

The question put Cas off. He wasn't sure what the man was getting at, but he felt like they were being toyed with. And he didn't appreciate it. "Those are two different questions. And I don't really think my answer would make any difference to you."

Diamant made a sound which Cas assumed was a laugh, from the amused look on his face. "I can't fault you for that. But I must ask, why have you taken the word of a known outcast? Someone who is a disgrace to our people and our heritage?"

Cas glanced at Vrij. "Look, I'm not concerned with your internal politics. Vrij told us of your…history. We thought it was worth the risk."

"You must be in quite the need if you're willing to trust the word of a criminal. How did you know he wasn't leading you into a trap?"

Cas felt like he was being teased; as if this was an elaborate dance. And he didn't like where it was going. "He assisted in the defense of our ship. And I don't need to justify my decisions to you. All I need to do is negotiate a trade. Then we'll be on our way."

Diamant's gaze landed on Cas. "You are straightforward. I can appreciate that in a man. But I have one more question for you. Why would you trust a man whose people are so desperate they would do anything to survive? Why would such a man not do whatever is necessary to accomplish his own goals?"

Cas turned to Vrij again who had seemed to shrink down even further. "Sometimes risks are necessary. We don't have the luxury of playing it safe." He turned back to Diamant. "And neither do you. At least from what I've seen."

Diamant puffed air through his nose, though Cas couldn't tell if he was amused or annoyed. "Very well. Let us make a circle. And we can discuss your offer."

13

Evie strode down the corridor, her heart beating a hundred beats per second. She'd been in the middle of helping Zaal reset some of the control units on deck six before they lost all power for half the ship when Xax had called. The urgency of her voice had done little to assuage Evie's fears. And the hypervator had taken forever to get up to six. But now that she was only a few meters from sickbay she wished it had taken longer. She wasn't sure she was ready to hear what the doctor had to say.

The doors moved aside for her and the first person she saw was Box. He glanced up when she entered but when he didn't make some kind of crack she knew something was wrong. She glanced over to Xax who had stood from her desk in the adjoining section and made her way out to Evie.

"Before you say anything," Evie said, "Just give me a minute to breathe, okay?"

"I could provide an anti-anxiety drop," Box offered from the other side of the room.

"That won't be necessary," Xax replied. "The captain can handle it. Let's go in my office." Evie didn't want to go in the office. Plus, all the other patients had been discharged. It was only her, Box, the doctor and a few nurses milling about.

Everyone in this room already knew except for her, so why the need for propriety?

"No, just tell me here."

"Captain, I really think you should—"

"Stop calling me captain." Evie hissed. "I'm not the captain, Greene is. And until—" But she didn't need to say another word when she saw Xax's face. Even though she had six eyes they were all filled with sadness and pity and Evie hated it when people looked at her like that. "No."

"Box and I began the procedure a few hours ago," Xax said, her voice hushed. She reached out with two of her hands and placed them on Evie's arms. "The new technique I developed showed the damage was far worse than we'd originally thought."

Evie winced, tears welling up in her eyes. "*No.*"

"Here, come on," Xax said, leading her into her office. She helped Evie take a seat while she pulled something up on her display. She flipped the image, so it was visible from the other side. "This is Captain Greene's normal brain scan. We take them every three seasons. His was made not more than sixty days ago."

Tears were already running down Evie's face, despite her furiously wiping them away. The image was blurry, and she couldn't seem to clear her eyes to get a good look.

"This is a scan I took this morning, using the deep tissue micros. See all this here?" She pointed to an area around the middle where the two halves of the brain connected. It was a deep red in the middle surrounded by an orange aura.

"Is all that from the attack?" Evie asked, trying to retain her professionalism.

"No. But the attack was the catalyst. His brain has a genetic anomaly we hadn't previously detected, and when he was injured it only exacerbated an existing condition the captain has been living with his entire life. I'm afraid he's down to two percent brain function. He won't wake up from the induced coma."

"Won't or can't," Evie asked.

"Either. If we used our equipment to bring him out of the coma, he'd have no bodily control. He wouldn't even be able to breathe on his own. The brain is a husk at this point, and it's only getting worse. This disease is will tear it apart, piece by piece. Once this specific anomaly is active, it's like a parasite that feeds on brain matter."

Evie put her head in her hands for a moment then withdrew them, wiping the tears at the same time. She took a deep breath. "What do we need to do?"

Xax folded her top set of hands in front of her. "I suggest cutting all life support. I don't believe any of him is in any way conscious, though if he is, it isn't pleasant. My hope is he's already gone. And while I can still detect some very light brain activity, that could just be the anomaly at work, lighting up his brain centers as it consumes."

"You want to kill him," she replied. "You want to kill one of the most decorated captains in the fleet."

"Evelyn," Xax said. "He's dead already. There's nothing we can do but end his suffering."

"But that can't be *possible*," she hissed. "He needs to take command of this ship. Of this crew. He has to get us out of this." She could feel the desperation clawing at the edges of her mind, but she didn't care. What good was all this technology if it couldn't save the captain's life? Why did they even have a sickbay if some random anomaly could kill any of them at a moment's notice?

"I know you don't want to hear this, but that's your job now. This clearly falls under the Coalition's battlefield promotion statute. You need to formally take command of this ship because there is no one else who can do the job."

She pulled her tight ponytail over her shoulder, feeling the familiar wrap in her hand. Wiping her eyes one last time to make sure she'd cleared any remnants of tears she stood. "Do you need my authorization?"

Xax nodded. "As the chief medical officer of this ship I can elect to do it alone, but I'd prefer your signature on the documents as well."

She drew in a deep breath through her nose. "I need some time. To make sure everything is in order."

"I understand. But please don't take too long. If there's even a chance he's conscious, he could be in agony."

Evie nodded, pulling her lips between her teeth. She squinted at Xax. "Anything else?"

"Not right now."

She left the doctor there, passing Box without a word and launching herself into the corridor. As soon as the doors were closed behind her she slammed the base of her fist into the wall. "*Goddammit!*" Heaving breaths almost overtook her, but she wasn't going to pass out. And she wasn't going to let this get her. But she wasn't ready to lead this ship. She wasn't ready to do this all alone. Especially not after everything she'd been experiencing lately. How was the crew supposed to count on someone who was seeing hallucinations and couldn't tell the real from the imagined? How was she even fit to command in that sort of state? Sure, things had stabilized but there was no guarantee they'd stay that way. And she wasn't sure she could risk the safety of the crew.

It should have been her. If she'd hadn't been out on that shuttle, she never would have seen that stupid arch and would have been on the bridge when the mines hit. She could have saved him but instead she'd been in Engineering going through mental therapy with Sesster.

She couldn't think like that. It would only make things worse. She really wished Laura hadn't gone off on the mission. When she'd come to her and asked, Evie hadn't been sure if it was because she wanted to prove herself, or if she was just upset about what had happened the other night. She hoped it wasn't the latter because until then things had been pretty good. And if something little like that could get between them how were they supposed to navigate the really rough stuff?

How was she supposed to do this by herself? Without his guidance and wisdom? Was it even possible?

Evie pulled her hand away from the wall, noticing a dent where she'd hit it. She furrowed her brow. Normally these bulkheads were reinforced galvanium. Maybe one of the maintenance teams had replaced some of these with less sturdy materials. Right now she really didn't care. She had a lot of paperwork to do. Officially transferring command of the ship required a lot of prep work. And she'd better get it done before the next attack came. The last thing she needed was to issue an order to the computer, only for it to refuse or spit back an error because she'd forgotten to change the command controls.

Sighing, Evie left the corridor and headed back for the bridge.

14

When Diamant said they'd make a circle, Cas thought he was being cagey or perhaps the auto-vox malfunctioned. But no, he had meant *a circle*. He'd gathered them all around a central point in the room and had them crouch down, though he'd stared daggers at Vrij who had excused himself back to the other side of the room with the guards.

In the middle of the circle Diamant had placed a small disc about half a meter in diameter on the ground. It was thin, seemed to have some heft to it and the top was covered in a shimmering material. Cas couldn't help but consider the absurdity of the situation, the four of them crouching on all sides of the "circle" in this decrepit old room that had once been the command center for a large and powerful Bulaq ship. He also realized he wouldn't be able to hold this position very long as he'd yet again neglected Box's advice and skipped all of his gym times. Though with everything that had been happening the past few weeks he doubted anyone had time to get down there. But his legs were going to get sore, fast. He suspected that wasn't the case for Diamant or any of the other Bulaq. With their powerful hindquarters Cas bet they could probably spring ten meters in the air if they really wanted to.

Diamant glanced at each of them in turn, then tapped the top of the disc. It glowed bright blue which then transformed into blue plasma. It wasn't hot, but it lit up the room in a way the natural lighting couldn't. The walls seemed to react to the flame, glowing with energy themselves.

"Wow," Laura whispered.

"This is what's known as a seeding circle," Diamant said. "It is where my people come together to speak of our days, to work out our problems. And to pray. I have invited you into my seeding circle so we may discuss your offer."

Remembering Laska's lessons, Cas took the initiative. "Thank you for your hospitality, we're honored you've included us in this...ceremony."

Diamant tapped his chest twice. "You are most welcome. However, I must insist on the seriousness of what you have entered, Caspian. The seeding circle is sacred and shall not be disrespected. Do you understand?" Cas nodded, then remembering the Bulaq might not understand he tapped his chest twice as well. Diamant smiled. "I am glad to see you know how to respect potential allies."

Why did he feel like everything Diamant said came with a heaping of sarcasm? He needed to get this moving. "Vrij has told us of your plight. What happened to your world. To your system."

"To all of us," Diamant said. "None were immune. We are a proud people. To see this happen...it's heartbreaking."

"What are your current needs? How many people do you have here? And can you feed them all?"

"Our needs are numerous. Surely too much for you to satisfy. But I'm willing to listen anyway." Diamant was still as a stone but Cas could already feel his legs getting tired in the crouch. He shifted.

"You're right, we can't provide enough food for everyone, but we can provide some. Along with medicines and techniques for growing more. Our civilization depends on growing and making food in space. I don't know if yours—"

"We're quite capable of making our own food," Diamant said. He dropped his head. "Though I admit we could use assistance in certain areas. How much are you offering?"

"First let's talk about what we need," Cas replied. "Our ship was damaged recently. We have the ability to refine parts and components, but we need the materials. We can't just make them out of thin air."

"You're in luck, Caspian. Materials we have," Diamant said. "We are a race of builders, after all."

"We saw your...temple? Under construction. Is that for—"

"To honor our Great Ones." Diamant made a sweeping gesture with his hands. "The ones who have kept us alive during this time of trial. We all must endure hardships but, in the end, our people will thrive again." Cas glanced over his shoulder at Vrij, who had pressed himself up against the far wall.

He turned back to the group. "Vrij mentioned your...Great Ones. Were they your spiritual leaders?"

"In a sense. They protected our world and our people. But when Laq was destroyed, the Great Ones perished with it. Those of us who remain decided a memorial in their honor was the best way to immortalize them."

"But aren't your people starving?" Ryant asked.

"I think what my friend means is how can you afford to continue to build if people can't eat?" Cas added, shooting a look at Ryant.

Diamant narrowed his eyes. "Trust me. We manage." His tenor changed. "I will need food and supplies for at least five thousand. Anything less and I'm afraid we're wasting our time."

That was out of the question. Even if he wanted to, they couldn't provide that much. *Tempest*'s crew was barely over a hundred people. He could maybe provide enough for five hundred for a couple of weeks, but that would put a real strain on their own survival. He needed to switch tactics.

"There is something else we're interested in," Cas said. "Vrij told us you were the only person to survive the attack on your world. I'd like to hear that story." He could feel Laura tense beside him. Diamant probably had little to no idea how important his information was, and Cas didn't want to show his hand for fear of Diamant asking for even more in trade.

"I was lucky," he replied. "But it *is* a harrowing tale." Out of the corner of his eye, Ryant dropped from a crouch to his knees, wincing at the pain. Cas knew exactly how he felt, though Laura seemed not to be bothered by it. "You say you're from a faraway place."

"That's right," Cas replied.

"Then I propose a tale for a tale. Perhaps afterward we can discuss more…tangible arrangements."

Panic ran through Cas's mind. Was there any downside to telling Diamant about their situation? He didn't need to mention they were looking for the *Andromeda* aliens, he could just say they were on an exploration. And if they got the information they required, why not? It might also loosen him up to negotiation.

"Okay," Cas replied. "A tale for a tale."

Diamant clapped his hands once over his head. One of the guards left the room, though no one else moved. Cas couldn't take it anymore; his legs were killing him. Diamant hadn't seemed to take any offense to Ryant resting on his knees so Cas did the same, relishing in the brief sensation of relief in his legs. He'd be feeling that tomorrow. He watched Diamant's face for any indication it was a problem but saw no change.

The guard returned with a large bottle of green liquid which he handed off to Diamant before returning to his post by the door.

"You should feel honored. This is one of the last bottles of *Ossak* from my world. It is imbibed when important information is being discussed. It...peels away the distractions." Diamant smiled, grasping the neck of the bottle and uncorking the stopper. He tipped the bottle and a drop of the viscous liquid fell into his mouth. To Cas, it resembled tar inside and he wasn't sure about sharing in it. There was no telling what its effects could be on a human body. Diamant offered the bottle but Cas hesitated. Whatever was in there could be poisonous for all he knew. They had zero information on the Bulaq digestive and blood systems.

"Here," Ryant said, holding his hand out for the bottle. "In our culture we drink counterclockwise."

Diamant glanced at Ryant, then back at Cas as if he suspected this might be a lie, but he handed the bottle off anyway. Cas made a subtle shake of his head for Ryant not to drink it, but the larger man ignored him. And before Cas could attempt to convince him further, he tipped the bottle back and one drop hit his tongue.

Ryant smacked his lips, running his tongue around the inside of his mouth. "It's sweeter than I expected," he said. Cas watched for any signs he might get sick or otherwise show an adverse reaction but there were none. "I hope that comes around more than once."

"Then you're in luck. Traditionally, if the conversation lasts until the bottle is empty, it is considered a successful meeting," Diamant said, a smile on his face.

Cas eyed the bottle as Ryant passed it to Laura. She stared at it a moment with genuine interest, then smelled the opening. Without looking to Cas for confirmation she tipped it back and a drop fell on her tongue. A small smile appeared on her lips as she passed the bottle over.

It was slightly warm in Cas's hands and the liquid inside moved slow and with purpose as he inspected the bottle. He almost had to laugh; after all the poison he'd drank over the years he was squeamish about this one unknown substance. If only Evie could see him now, hesitation and the unknown clouding his judgment. But Diamant was watching him intently and Cas got the distinct impression if he didn't comply, there was no chance of making a deal.

He tipped the bottle back.

***

"That's quite a story," Diamant said.

Cas blinked; his head foggy. The *Ossak* either had hallucinogenic—or at the very least—alcoholic properties. Not only did he feel supremely good, but he also felt his lips loosening. Was this what Diamant had meant when he said the it stripped away all the distractions? He glanced over at Ryant and Laura, both who looked about as well as he felt. Their eyes were glazed, but not to the point where they were out of it. He could see them struggling to maintain their grasp on the situation. But they swayed and every few minutes had to retrain their focus on the flame in the middle of the circle.

The only good Cas could see was Diamant seemed to be having just as much trouble as they were. His eyes had gone glassy and he'd straightened into an unnatural position, as if attempting to assume dominance. But his attention had remained rapt on Cas as he told him how they managed to find themselves so far away from the Coalition. He'd done his best to stay light on the finer details, attempting to craft a plausible story about a group of explorers, though he hadn't been able to keep from mentioning Suzanna and his sense of loss.

"I must say, I'm sorry to hear about your crew." Diamant leaned forward, his focus completely on Cas. "How are you handling it, Caspian?"

He shrugged. "As well as we can. I miss her, though."

"Of course you do. After all, how were you to know this creature would kill them so mercilessly?" Cas winced. Diamant had just taken a drink and passed the bottle. "But you shouldn't blame yourself."

He could almost feel the tears welling up inside him, but he kept them hammered down. If Diamant saw he'd gotten to something precious, he'd use it for all it was worth. He was testing Cas for weaknesses. "I've lost a lot of crews in the past. You get over it," he said with a certain amount of disdain in his voice, hating himself for disrespecting her memory.

"So," Diamant said, his voice lighter as if they hadn't just been talking about one of the worst experiences of Cas's life. "Then you found yourselves in the system with the three suns," Diamant said.

Cas nodded, taking a measured breath. The bottle was still with Ryant who had yet to pass it on to Laura again. The blue flame danced in front of them, its energy taking on a life of its own. "We did. And found ourselves in an ambush." Here was where he needed to be careful. He wanted to move on to information about the aliens, but he couldn't tip his hand. He'd already taken this farther than he'd meant to. "A ship…appeared. As if from nowhere. And it controlled these mines. If not for our navigator, we never would have made it out of there alive. But we sustained damage. Which is the whole reason I'm—we're here."

"Out of nowhere, you say." Diamant rolled the words around in his mouth. Laura took the bottle from Ryant and with what seemed like a will of strength, tipped it until another drop fell on her tongue. For a second her eyes rolled into the back of her head before she focused again and held the bottle for Cas, her arm shaking. Cas noticed it was only about half empty. Any hope of finishing it was out the airlock; they couldn't last that long. But maybe they just needed to get through Diamant's tale. He glanced behind him; the two guards hadn't moved and Vrij remained beside the wall, though he'd slunk down and was clicking his finger claws together in a strange rhythm.

"This ship, that came from nowhere. What did it look like?" Diamant asked.

Cas held the bottle, prolonging the next drink. "Black, with kind of a plow on the front. Sweeping wings to the sides. I saw no windows." He wasn't about to mention he'd been aboard; that would only invite unwanted questions.

Diamant nodded. "I too have seen this ship. And others like it. They are the ones who attacked my homeworld. We call them the *Cho'ju'itsa*. It means Destroyer of Worlds."

"What can you tell me?" Cas lifted the bottle and another drop fell on his tongue. It was having a cumulative effect. He wasn't even sure he could stand if he wanted to.

Diamant took the bottle. "My illustrious career came to an end that day. I used to be a Second Qyall in the military. It was *my life*." He paused, taking a drink. "Or that's what I thought before I found...this." He motioned to the room around him. "My ship was on patrol on the other side of Laq when they came. We received a general alert to unknown ships entering the system." He paused again and Cas couldn't help but think it was for nothing more than effect. "There were so many. We had no idea. Thousands. Like little bugs, filling up space." He tapped at the air with his fingers. "When our scout vessels attempted to contact them all their ships stopped, turning to face our planet. They each initiated a forced plasma beam which entangled itself with the beams from every other ship in formation." He stopped; his eyes having glazed over as if he were living it all over again in his mind's eye. "They gave *no warning*. The blast hit the northern continent, where many of our larger cities were. At first, I thought it was nothing more than orbital bombardment. And I was furious, demanding we return fire. But before our commander could give the order, we got word the planet's crust was breaking apart." He paused again, letting it sink in. "Imagine that for a moment. Watching your home, watching everything you love, break apart in front of your eyes." He drew his hand into a fist, his claws cutting into his palm. "I thought the readings must be false, but there was no disguising what we saw with our own eyes. In that instant everything changed for us.

"As soon as he saw what was happening, the commander ordered us behind one of Laq's three moons. The concussive blast of the planet breaking into millions of pieces at once destroyed or crippled most of our fleet surrounding the planet, and threw the gravitational pull of the moons out of sync. We were saved from the first shockwave but hit with debris from the moons breaking apart. It was a miracle we survived as long as we did." He paused.

"But that wasn't the end of it," Cas said. The story'd had a sobering effect on him. He didn't take his eyes off Diamant, only willed him to continue. Any firsthand accounts of what the aliens were capable of was perhaps *more* valuable than the building materials.

"No. The ship was in chaos. Our commander ordered us to begin an assault on the aliens, but our propulsion was down, and we were being pulled along with what was left of the moon, being thrown from orbit. Our ship was disabled, and we lost all control. People were thrown all over the ship. I lost consciousness."

"You didn't see what happened next?"

Diamant touched his forehead with two fingers, the movement slow and deliberate. "Odan. Our lifegiver. I can only assume they used their weapons on him. I've heard from others the fusion reaction inside Odan became so great that he expanded, then collapsed, creating a *do'shan*. An ending to everything."

"A supernova," Cas replied.

"The resulting explosion caused a cascade reaction in Arla, Odan's mate. Together their destructive power destroyed the system, all the planets, all the moons, everything. When I awoke, my entire crew was dead, and the system was decimated. My ship was in pieces, but somehow...I had survived."

Cas leaned forward. "Do you know how? Or why?"

A smile played on his lips. "The why is easy. To lead my people into the next era of our society. How I survived? I do not know. I can only assume it was the protection of the Great Ones and their choices to bestow upon me the burden of leading our people. They knew I was the only one strong enough for it." He took another drink from the bottle and stared at the ground for a few minutes. He looked up with clarity in his eyes. "Now that we've exchanged our tales, shall we continue our negotiation?"

15

Zenfor stared at the ceiling of her quarters, barely visible in what little light filtered in from the stars through the window. She'd modified the bedding they'd provided her with as soon as she and Mil'less had boarded, but it had never really felt right. The bed itself was too…static. Not only was she not used to sleeping, but the idea of being fully unconscious pushed an undercurrent of fear through her. And for the first four days on their trip back, she hadn't slept, instead attempting to fight it off as she might a childhood disease. While Mil'less, however, hadn't had trouble with it. Then over the next "days" (a Coalition term) she'd found she could fall unconscious for short periods of time. A few squirms here and there. She became more accustomed to the accommodations and setting her body in a routine, and found she could sleep for hours at a time. When *Tempest* had arrived at the Excel Nebula, she'd managed to work herself up to six hours a night, which she felt was more than enough. Any longer and she was doing nothing more than wasting time she could be working. And she couldn't help but wonder how Mil'less was spending her time on Starbase Eight. That was her unique property, large problems never seemed to bother Mil'less. Not like they did for others, especially Zenfor.

But ever since those first few weeks on the ship when she'd acclimated to normal bodily functions again she hadn't had as much trouble sleeping as she was having now. It was as if her mind couldn't shut off to allow her to rest. In some ways she saw this as a triumph of her iron will: that her mind was refusing to cooperate with the limits her body imposed on her. But on the other hand, it was infuriating as she knew she had to be up at a certain time and if she did not get her required sleep her performance would suffer the following day. Returning to the sanctity and stability of a Sil ship couldn't come soon enough.

Frustrated, she pushed herself out of bed, still fully dressed, and left her quarters. It was the middle of third shift, but a lot of crews were working overtime to try and repair all the damage from their time at Omicron Terminus. She passed two maintenance crews on her way from her quarters to Engineering.

Once she arrived, she realized this was one part of the ship that probably rarely saw downtime. Humans buzzed back and forth, so busy with their own work they didn't even notice her. The only person who seemed to realize she was there was Sesster, at the far end of the room in his cradle. One of his appendages extended upwards as she entered. Zenfor averted her eyes to avoid the rest of the crew as she made her way to the back of the room. If there was one thing humans were annoyingly good at, it was asking you how you were when you made eye contact with them. She'd learned the best way to get through the days wasn't to look at anyone. Ever.

Hello, Zenfor, it's a pleasure to see you this late.

She took up her position at her console, without bothering to turn it on. Even though her gaze was on the computer, all her attention was on the Claxian in the room. *Good evening. That's what you say, right? Morning, afternoon, evening.*

It is what many humans say. On Claxia Prime we greet in many ways. One of which is to say, your presence honors me.

That's very appropriate. She'd much prefer that to "how are you today, Consul?" or "have a wonderful afternoon". Humans were so concerned with what could be they forgot to focus on what *was*.

You are right. They are forever chasing what is next and longing for what has already passed. It is in their nature. He paused. *What can I do for you this evening?*

Zenfor took a measured breath. She'd thought about this over the past few days but had kept it guarded. In some ways it seemed like too much to ask, like she was invading something private. But at the same time she felt she owed it to herself to try. *I've enjoyed our time and discussions together. However, I want you to bring me into the* mind-space. *Like you do with our acting captain.*

Sesster hesitated. *Why?*

Because I want to speak with you face-to-face. I want... She paused. It was too much. She couldn't ask this of him.

Please. Continue.

I want to interact with you. Physically. Being here...alone. It is difficult.

I see. More hesitation. She shouldn't have asked. She'd reached out and was about to be slapped away. She should have just stayed in her misery. At least then she would have known it couldn't get any worse. The risk of this was excruciating.

Please focus your thoughts, Sesster said.

Does that mean you agree?

Of course. But I have never done this with a Sil before. It may take...adjustments.

Trying to keep her heart from thundering out of her chest, Zenfor closed her eyes and focused her mind. She thought of her time back on *Renglas*, where she was in control and connected to the ship itself. They all were, in a way.

The world around her fell away and she found herself on a dark gray landscape, infinite in all directions. Above her stars filled the night sky, to every end of the horizon. She was clad in garments from her homeworld, though not the suits they wore on the ships. If she thought hard enough about it, this could be Thislea at night. Though the air was warm, warmer than she'd ever felt it back home. Scents of tessimon and yeslac filled the air, the smells of home. So this was Thislea after all—or at least her perception of it.

She turned to see a figure approaching her dressed in robes, his skin was light but with a blue tint, though she'd never seen a Sil so pale. And his eyes were devoid of any pupils and were black instead. He stopped a few steps from her, observing the scene, taking it all in. "Is this your home?"

Zenfor narrowed her eyes. "Sesster?"

He glanced down, examining his form. "Your people are handsome. I feel honored to represent one."

"Did I create this?" she asked.

"In a way. It is the merging of our minds, and thus you see and experience what is familiar to you. Is this your home planet?" He gazed up at the sky, then to the horizon.

"I think so, but not completely. Thislea isn't this flat anywhere on the planet to my knowledge. And it isn't this dark. One of the two suns is usually in view. On the rare occasion neither are, we call it 'true dark' but I've never experienced it." She looked to the horizon but couldn't see even the hint of twilight.

"This may be what you have always wanted to see, or your own personal representation of home. A place you feel comfortable." Zenfor turned to him and studied his features. He hadn't taken the face of anyone she knew, so some of it must be him. "Is this what you wanted?"

"Are we still in Engineering?" she asked.

He nodded. "To everyone else, nothing has changed. You are at your console and I am in the middle of repairing the microfilament centrifuge."

She sighed. Sesster mentioning the engines only brought everything back. She'd wanted to get away for a few minutes. But she didn't want to be rude, not to him. "How goes your work?"

"Slow. But I believe it should be finished within the next few hours. But that isn't why you wanted to come here." He approached her. She stood her ground, but at the same time felt the desire to touch him bloom somewhere deep within. She reached out, not knowing if her hand would pass right through him or vice versa. But her fingers gently brushed against his shoulder and she laid her hand there, feeling the softness of his robes and the curves of the muscles underneath.

"You're real. I can—" He reciprocated the gesture and as he held her shoulder she shuddered, pleasure flowing through her. It had been too long. She'd been away much too long. "Sesster, I must confess something to you."

The features of his face softened, a small smile tugging at his lips. "I'm here. You can tell me."

"I...can't fix the engines. Not without rebuilding your entire undercurrent drive. The damage—" She faltered. Never before had she failed so spectacularly. And to admit her failure to anyone other than a Sil was paramount to treason. But she'd been working on it all hours of the day for weeks and each time come back to the same inevitable conclusion.

"You haven't failed," Sesster said, his tone gentle. "As long as you breathe, you haven't failed."

"The amount of time it would take to repair; it could be years. And we don't have that long. Neither of our people do." She stared into his eyes, wondering if he could see her back. If he could really "see" her in this place. It all felt so real and yet she could also sense the real world beyond the edges. Like she was in a protective bubble, if only for a short time. It reminded her of her bio-suit, only infinitely more complex.

"If that is the case then we will have to make the journey without it. But that is not your fault. You have already helped us more than you should have."

She stilled. Could he sense the guilt in her mind or was this something else? "Explain," she said.

He reached up and placed his hand on hers holding his shoulder. "You have used your own technology, or at least your own knowledge to enhance our mission. Had it not been for you we would have died in that nebula. And our ship would have taken an extra hundred days or more to reach Omicron Terminus. Without you, we wouldn't know of *Andromeda's* ability to obscure themselves in time. I know it is against your culture to share information. But in our case the information has saved our lives. We are forever in your debt."

She hadn't expected that. She'd expected him to call her weak for not upholding her principles, as a Sil would. "I have a question."

"Please," he replied.

"If I tell the others about the engines, what will be their reaction? What will happen?"

He kept the black orbs that acted as eyes pointed directly at her. "What do you expect will happen?"

"I expect no one will trust me for any future involvement. I will be confined back to my quarters, as we were when we first boarded. I expect I will have become nothing but an observer."

He leaned close. Close enough that she could feel his soft breath on her skin. "We're not like that here. You will receive no punishment for not completing your task. Failure of your task does not mean failure as a person." His words stuck with her. Despite the lack of formality surrounding it, she'd been given a specific job on this ship, which was to maintain the system she had implemented. She was the first Sil in a thousand generations to have a task outside the one for which she was bred. Every day, as she stared at the information on the screen telling her completion of her task in the given timeframe was impossible, it chipped away at something in her. Part of her wanted to rise and say "see, this is why Sil only do one job their entire lives" while another part wanted to destroy the whole system; forget it ever happened. But the last part of her, the smallest and yet also the strongest, internalized that failure. And all she could think of was Zakria, and her failure at becoming a consul. And that failure terrified her. She wasn't used to being terrified.

"You don't have to be afraid here," Sesster added. "You are among friends."

Something inside her cracked and she reached up, touching Sesster's "face". "We must bond."

He smiled, comfort radiating from him. "Show me your way. I am eager to learn."

16

After hearing Diamant's firsthand experience with the aliens, Cas was even more on edge. Any sense of inebriation had left upon hearing the gruesome details of what had happened. And if it happened as Diamant said it had, it was something of a miracle he was there talking to the man. But he couldn't be taken in by something he only perceived. He'd known men back in the Sargan Commonwealth to embellish their tales to increase the size of their influence and Diamant might be no different. But he'd seen the destruction of Laq and its stars for himself via Starbase Five's long-range telescopes. Which meant he was more likely to believe the man. But coming to an agreement was a different matter.

"We don't have enough supplies for five thousand of your people," Cas said, rocking back on his legs again so he was crouched as Diamant was. "Not nearly that much. But we can provide you with what we have. Surely something is better than nothing."

"Caspian, you know better than that. Something worthless to me is not better than nothing. It is worse because now I have *spent time* on something when I could be doing other, more important tasks." Diamant creased his brow, turning his attention to each of them in turn. Ryant looked like he might topple over at any second, though Laura was holding her own, even if she was perspiring a lot to maintain it. Cas glanced behind him, Vrij had curled against the wall, like he was afraid of something in the room. Even though he said he and Diamant hadn't gotten along Cas had only seen the barest dislike on Diamant's part. If it was there, it was subtle. "Unfortunately, I don't think we've done anything but waste each other's time here."

Cas winced. "We can provide enough food for two-hundred and fifty, along with medical supplies. And perhaps even some new techniques for growing food, though I'll have to clear that with my captain."

Diamant touched his forehead with two fingers. "It isn't enough."

"You don't even know what we're asking for," Laura croaked. Her voice had become hoarse.

Diamant turned to her. "It doesn't matter. Two-hundred and fifty is a pittance. You've seen my people. That will barely feed a fraction of the population."

Cas shook his head. "I'm not sure we can do more. I can show you what we brought with us, it is high in nutrients and high in calories. Surely there must be some value?"

Diamant was silent for a moment. "Because I like you, I'm going to give you an offer lower than I would for some of our other 'allies' who have since left us. I recognize you are in a very vulnerable position, and I want to help. Four hundred. And if we agree, I set the terms."

Cas mulled it over. Four hundred was pushing it. But if they got all the supplies they needed and Zenfor could get her advanced drive working again, they could be back in Coalition space in several days, and it wouldn't matter how many supplies they had. But there was no guarantee. And every day they hesitated was another day *Tempest* was under attack. "I can do four hundred. We can leave what we have here with you now and then bring the rest when we come back for what materials we can't carry in our shuttle."

"Your material requirements?" Diamant asked.

"Two-hundred kilograms of galvanium. Six hundred of cyclax. And fourteen thousand beams of ursanomium. I have the molecular composition and the conversion factors." Cas pulled a small black bar from his jacket pocket, handing it over to Diamant. When Diamant pressed the button on the side a holographic list of their items came up, complete with all the technical data.

"We have these materials on hand, though we have different names for them of course," he replied. "Very well. We can make this trade." He handed the bar back to Cas. "But there is a condition."

Cas tried not to let his concern show. "Okay."

"We cannot allow you to leave and return. My people are desperate. I'm not saying this is the case, but what if we gave you these materials and you never came back?" There was that teasing tone again. "I can't take that kind of risk with something so important."

"We wouldn't do that," Laura said, forcefully. "That's not what—" A look from Cas cut her off.

"What my colleague means is we honor our agreements."

"It isn't that I don't trust you, Caspian. But how am I to know that? I propose another solution. We accompany you to your ship." He eyed Cas carefully, perhaps looking for any sign of surprise or argument. But Cas wasn't going to give it to him. "This way, you will have all the materials you need in one trip and we can transport our food and other goods back." He paused again. "Without inconveniencing you."

"It's no inconvenience," Cas said, though in reality it was. It would require another two days in transit for another round-trip to the hub and back which was that much longer they could be under attack. Diamant's proposal would be more efficient and better for them in the short term but allowing him access to the ship was something he hadn't cleared with Evie. If he were in command, he wasn't sure how happy he'd be about his first officer bringing an unscheduled guest to the ship.

"Call it, *compensation* for not being able to provide for all our needs. We'll give you everything on your list, but I want to see this miracle ship that can travel great distances in such a short amount of time. Such a wonder something like that must be."

Inside Cas's better judgment was screaming at him not to take this deal. He glanced at Laura and Ryant. Her face was impassioned, focused on him. She knew it was a bad deal too. But Ryant was just about out of it. He wouldn't be any help if they had to make a quick exit. By drinking that *molasses* Cas had inadvertently allowed them to become compromised. If they said no now what would happen? Would Diamant let them leave or would he try and capture and imprison them? Hold them for ransom for the rest of *Tempest*? And what other choice did he have? It wasn't like there was another source of materials close.

"Agreed," Cas replied. "Though you understand our ship is over a day away."

A smile formed on Diamant's lips. "Very good. That's no problem at all. We can spare a small ship to carry the rest of your goods. And in the spirit of cooperation, I suggest one or two of your party accompany my men on our shuttle and we'll do the same."

Cas tried to keep the concern off his face. "How many men do you need to bring?"

"Only a few. Half a dozen at the most. But because you're being so accommodating, I'll even sweeten this deal. We'll help you with your repairs when you arrive. You've seen what we can do, surely we can repair your ship faster than you could."

Heat rose in Cas's cheeks and he was sure it was on full display. But he wasn't about to lose it with this man. Diamant was a seasoned manipulator, and he was such a figure of influence in Bulaq society, but he couldn't let that concern him. The plight of the Bulaq wasn't their main focus; he had to keep his mind straight. Fix the ship, get back home. But it also opened up an opportunity that might not otherwise be present: with Diamant along he might have the chance to learn more about the *Cho'ju'itsa* as he called them. The more information they could bring back to the Coalition the better. "Fine," he said, keeping his temper in check.

"And to prove I'm not as bad of a person as *some* might have made it seem," he added, his eyes on Vrij. "Why don't you bring our mutual acquaintance back with us? He wouldn't be happy here; I know how much he enjoys his solitude on his own ship."

Vrij looked ready to argue but the words died in his throat as he turned away from the circle. Cas couldn't see the harm in bringing Vrij back; to be completely honest he wasn't sure what he'd planned on doing with him. He half expected this to be nothing more than a farce in which case he might have advocated to shoot Vrij out into space, but since he'd actually fulfilled his promise he didn't see any problem with taking him back and allowing him to go on his way, provided he didn't try to steal any more parts.

"There's one last thing," Cas said as they moved to get up. Diamant glanced over. "We've been under attack by some...renegades. They're Bulaq but Vrij tells us they're of a different faction."

Diamant creased his brow. "Yes. After the destruction of my world, many Bulaq went off on their own instead of doing the proper thing and staying with their own people. Usually it is a death sentence as no other species will have anything to do with us, but it sounds like you might have run into the scavengers. They're a well-organized but small group of Bulaq who prey on passing ships, wearing them down over time before sinking their teeth in." He regarded Cas for a moment. "I will see what I can do for you, Caspian. After all, you have been very accommodating to us. My influence is far-reaching. They may listen."

"Thank you," Cas replied.

Diamant retrieved the bottle of *Ossak* from Ryant's slack hand. He looked almost asleep, though he was still on his knees. "Only half the bottle," he said. "Let us hope this isn't a reflection of our agreement."

He smiled, but there was something hidden behind there. Something Cas didn't like. What had he just gotten them into?

17

Evie sat behind the desk in the command room, staring at the set of instructions on the screen in front of her. They were the final set of commands necessary to transfer full control of the ship over to her. She'd been staring at them for over twenty minutes, trying to gather up the courage to make the final call. Instead, she'd stared into space.

"Ugh." She pushed the chair back and stood, clasping her hands behind her back and glaring out the window to the nothingness beyond. How was she supposed to get them out of this by herself? There was no guarantee Cas would be successful, or even come back, though she really didn't need those images floating around her brain. Losing Laura and Cas in the same day would be too much. She'd resign right then and there. But then who would take command after her? Sesster? Volf? Maybe it wouldn't matter. Maybe they were all dead anyway. Who was to say after they repaired the ship the *Andromeda* aliens weren't already out there waiting for them, just biding their time until they saw *Tempest* try to head for home? Maybe the best thing they could do was point the ship in a direction away from the Coalition and go. Cas might have had the right idea all along.

No, she wasn't going to abandon them, not after spending a lifetime trying to get to this point. She was now officially a starship captain. And it was her duty to protect the Coalition and its citizens from all threats, whether they be internal or external. It was her duty to sacrifice her life and the lives of those under her command for this purpose if necessary. And the one thing she could not do was give up.

She tapped the comm on the side of the desk. "Volf, report to the command room. Immediately." A few seconds later the chime on her door rang. "Enter."

"Yes, comm—I'm sorry. Captain." Ever since the attack, personal hygiene had taken a backseat to more important matters, which meant her normally spiky pink hair hadn't been up for a while and she wore it loose now. A large crop of it came down on her forehead at almost a point, but Evie thought she liked it better that way.

"You're a senior bridge officer. I need a secondary input authorization before I make these changes final." Evie tapped her monitor, so the same image was displayed on the other side. Volf took a moment to read them.

"The transfer codes. I'm guessing this means—"

"The captain won't be recovering," she said. "I know you and I don't always see eye to eye, but it's my responsibility to see this ship and her crew gets home and report what little we've learned. Maybe it will help and maybe it won't make a difference, but it's our duty to try."

"Hey, you don't have to tell me," she said. "Lifelong military brat here. I know the stakes." She pressed her hand to the screen. "Authorization Volf, Delta, Sigma, Epsilon four-two-five."

Evie pressed her hand to her side of the screen as well. "Authorization Diazal, Tau, Gamma, Alpha nine-six-one."

The screen flashed *"Confirmed. Command transfer complete."*

"I guess that's that," Evie said.

"Congratulations," Volf replied. "Despite the circumstances."

"For what it's worth," Evie said as Volf turned to leave. "I'm sorry about what happened on the shuttle. I wasn't in my right mind and I had no right to hold you like that."

Volf shrugged. "You turned out to be right. And you got us out of that mine field. I may not always agree with all your decisions, but I don't question your motives."

Evie set her face. "The next time you disagree with my decisions, I expect you to bring the matter to me, instead of speaking to others behind my back."

Volf's face went red and she opened her mouth to reply, but instead shut it again.

"Dismissed, Commander." Evie nodded. Volf hesitated, then left her alone in the command room without another word. If there was one thing she wasn't about to stand for it was insubordination.

Transferring all the codes had been the easy step. But what came next was near impossible. Evie sighed, thinking maybe she should stop by her quarters before heading to sickbay. She could hold her grandmother's sword, look for a little comfort in what little connection she had to her family. It was too bad she couldn't carry it around the ship all the time; maybe she'd open up the rules about personal weapons, she was in charge after all. And they were on the frontier. She felt a lot better with it within reach at all times.

Evie double-checked her uniform to make sure she'd properly affixed the captain's rank. When she'd put it on the first time it had been a temporary measure and thus hadn't been secured well. But now the bar was straight and aligned with the rest. When they were back up to capacity, she'd make a full new uniform with all the appropriate trimmings but for the time being this was good enough. She just hated how it had come about. Looking around, she reflected on how solitary this moment was. Greene wasn't here, neither was Laura, or Cas, or even Box. It was just her alone with what was probably the most important promotion of her career. And she'd essentially given it to herself.

She took a deep breath, straightened her uniform and strode out the door onto the bridge. "Report," she said.

"All quiet," Lieutenant Uuma said. "But it's been almost twelve hours since the last attack."

"Are Rafnkell and her pilots ready?"

Uuma nodded. "They've taken up new positions. Ever since Vrij gave us the info we've destroyed every fighter that's approached us. But there's no telling what else they've got out there. She's not taking any chances."

"Good," Evie said, glancing around at the rest of the bridge crew. They were all visibly tired, except for Zaal of course, but everyone had been pulling extra shifts to cover the loss in manpower when so many of the crew had died at Omicron Terminus. "Maybe if we're lucky they'll decide we're not worth the trouble anymore and go pick on an easier target."

"Hope so," Uuma replied.

"Commander, you have the bridge. I have something to take care of in sickbay," Evie said. The air on the bridge went still. A few people at their stations glanced at her, but most kept their eyes on their duties. She hoped someone would come out and say "No! You can't! There still might be a chance he's going to be okay!" but no one did. Evie hadn't made it public just how dire Greene's condition was, but she had informed the crew he wouldn't be recovering. Now instead of twenty-two funerals they were going to need to have twenty-three.

"Yes, ma'am," Volf said from the engineering station. She stepped forward and took the command chair while Evie retreated to the main hypervator, her heart thundering in her chest. If Volf was upset about their prior encounter only moments ago she didn't show it. Evie wished Xax could have made this call without her. Even though she knew it was the right thing to do it didn't make the actual act of telling Xax to cut the life support any easier.

On the way down in the hypervator her grief mutated into something closer to anger. This was how it should have been with her father. She should have had to make the call for *him*, not her captain. But he'd denied her that in his insanity. She hadn't looked forward to ending his life but she'd always thought doing so would have given her a sense of closure that was otherwise missing from her life. And now she had to make the decision for someone she felt much closer to; someone she respected. *Damn* her father. And *damn* Captain Greene for leaving her in this position. She wasn't ready to say goodbye to him. He'd been the perfect captain and mentor, the one who upheld everything about the Coalition, despite what he knew or suspected. He always believed humans could be better when they worked with other species and he hadn't been wrong. This crew had done remarkably well under his guidance and now she had to find a way to rise to his level. To become as good a captain as he was, if that was possible.

Evie stepped into sickbay, swallowing the lump in her throat. It remained empty of patients just as before. Good, less people to watch. Box glanced up from one of the beds on the far side of the room and walked over to her. "Hello, Captain. Are you ready?"

Evie nodded. "Let's get this over with. I don't want him to suffer any more than he already has."

Box led her into the second compartment and then into the surgery room where Greene was already out on one of the surgery beds. His eyes were closed, and he was attached to several devices via hoses or electrodes, all of which she assumed were keeping his bodily functions going. Xax approached from behind, her steps soft on the hard floor. "Captain," she said softly.

"What do we need to do?" Evie asked. She'd never had to go through this process before. Greene's normally clean face was now covered in a salt and pepper beard, though it was short. She'd have to make sure he was given a good shave before the funeral.

"I need your approval on this form," Xax said. "Right beside my own." She held out a small bar that when activated showed the authorization form to end a human life. Xax had already provided her approval. As Evie's finger hovered over the pad she reflected at how similar this was to what she'd just gone through with Volf in the command room. *One thing begins and another ends.* She touched the pad, providing her personal authentication. "Okay," Xax whispered. "Box, let's go ahead and start."

Box nodded, moving around Evie as he and Xax went to work turning off all the machines. One by one they stopped what small noises they were making. Greene's chest rose and fell, though with each breath it seemed to become shallower.

"It won't take long," Xax said. "You can stay here if you like."

"Yeah," Evie replied. "No one should be alone during this." She reached over and picked up Greene's hand, placing it in her own. It was cold and rough, like he'd already been gone a while. Xax nodded and excused herself without another word.

"I'll stay too if you like," Box said.

"I would, thank you."

The robot positioned himself on the other side of the bed and held Greene's other hand. "Just to make double sure he knows," Box said.

Evie smiled as tears gathered in the corners of her eyes. Silently she said her goodbyes as Cordell Greene took his finals breaths and fell silent.

18

If Cas thought the journey from the shuttle to Diamant's compound was long, the way back was twice as bad. They were all still feeling the effects of the *Ossak*, but it seemed to have hit Ryant the worst. Laura at least had managed to stay on her own two feet, though she swayed the whole way back. Diamant had sent the two guards to accompany them back until he could arrange allocation of the materials they needed along with one of his own ships that would be flying back with them. Cas only hoped it would give them enough time to sober up.

"What the hell was in that stuff?" Cas asked, holding Ryant up by one side while Vrij held him up by the other as they helped him stumble along through the streets. The guards remained ahead of them while Laura pulled up the rear.

"O-ossak is a rarity…or was. E-expensive. Farmed in the c-coldest temperatures of Laq. It has a c-chemical which is s-said to remove—"

"Remove distractions, yes, I heard that part," Cas snapped. Ryant was damn heavy and he was having enough trouble keeping himself from falling, much less a ninety-five-kilogram man.

"It also h-has chemicals t-that alter the neurotransmitters in the b-brain. O-other species seem to e-experience similar effects."

Fuck. The one time he'd been required to get drunk and it had put him in a precarious negotiating position. The only thing that probably saved him was his existing tolerance. He couldn't even imagine what Laska would have said if she'd seen him back there. Although she did say to keep another species' cultural norms in mind, that it was always a good idea to assimilate yourself into their standards as best you could. To show a willingness to compromise. He wasn't sure Diamant had appreciated it as much as perhaps someone else. There was something deceptive about that man, like he was running a hidden agenda but wanted you to know it. Or maybe that was just the *Ossak* talking. Whatever the reason, Cas felt like he'd done a bad job at the negotiating table. He'd given up a lot and wasn't confident it was worth the risk.

"Are we close?" Cas called to the guards ahead of him. He'd lost track of their route in his attempts to keep Ryant vertical. One guard turned back tapping his chest with his hand. *Thank Kor.* If he had to hold this buffalo much longer, they were all going to end up sprawled on the street just like the people curled up in the alleyways. Cas only hoped Diamant would lead these people to a better future. But he wasn't sure that could happen.

They rounded the corner to see the shuttle still sitting on one of the pads. Cas reached over with some difficulty and tapped the comm on his hand. "Hey, Saturn? You still in there?"

Her face appeared in the window and she threw up a hand. "You guys don't look so good."

"Get down here and help us, Ryant is...drunk." She opened the main bay doors in the back as Cas and Vrij maneuvered Ryant around the landing gear. "You okay back there?" he asked Laura.

She stumbled at the sudden attention but caught herself. "Fine."

Jann came jogging around the edge of the ship and got up under Cas's side, relieving him of Ryant's weight. "What the hell did he have?"

"Some Bulaq concoction," Cas said. "Vrij will be happy to tell you about it later." Cas turned back to Laura. "Get back on the ship. Sleep it off."

She glanced between him and the guards, who had stopped short of the ramp to the ship. "You sure?"

He felt the heft of his boomcannon under his jacket. "I'm sure."

After the four of them had departed, Cas led the guards to the crates of supplies. "Here is a sample of what we have. This is Diamant's, as a sign of goodwill."

The guards tapped their chests. "Thank you. We will deliver it to those who need it most. Keep your ship here until we return. And prepare a volunteer or two to accompany our ship."

"Got it," Cas said, his brain still foggy. That walk hadn't done him any favors. He felt like he'd been sent through a compression modulator and hadn't come out the other side. The guards unloaded the crates and when they were done Cas moved into the crew section of the shuttle. Ryant and Laura lay on two of the beds, stacked one on top of the other, each snoring softly. Vrij was nowhere to be found. A pulse ran through Cas's heart and he bolted to the front compartment to find Jann and Vrij in the only two seats, engaged in conversation.

She glanced up when he entered. "He was just explaining to me the properties of *Ossak*, is it?"

"Yes."

"Sounds like heavy stuff." She returned her attention to Cas. "What's the play?"

Cas eyed Vrij for a moment. "We're taking some of them back with us. They'll bring all our materials and when we get to *Tempest*, we'll load our end of the agreement on their shuttle and that will be that."

"Sounds simple enough."

"It always does."

"We also need a volunteer to go with them. In the spirit of *cooperation*. Since I'm the only one left standing who can't fly a shuttle, it seems obvious." Cas leaned up against the bulkhead, his head pounding. He wasn't sure he could handle spending a full day on an alien shuttle. He wasn't willing to trust Diamant as the one to accompany the rest of them.

"I-I will also go," Vrij offered. "Two t-targets."

"Two targets?" Cas asked.

"I think he means with you both there you won't have to bear the burden alone," Jann said.

Cas rubbed his head. "That makes sense. Thanks." Vrij tapped his chest. Having him there would be better because at least Cas could keep an eye on him; he trusted Vrij only marginally more than Diamant. "What is it between you two anyway?"

Vrij lowered his head. "U-used to work—were in training together. He n-never gave me a c-chance. S-said I was t-too different." He shrugged, indicating the mechanical mandibles on his back.

"You're an outcast. But I thought his thing was he wanted to save all Bulaq life. I would think with so few of you left every last individual would be important," Cas replied.

"D-diamant often says one t-thing, means another." Vrij He clicked his fingers together in a sort of rhymical tapping.

"I've gathered that much at least," Cas replied. "And yet you were the one who suggested him to us. We're here because of you."

"B-because you're desperate. B-because there are n-no o-other options."

Cas took a deep breath. "I'm going to lie down and try to get rid of this headache before we have to leave. Can you keep an eye on him?" he asked.

Jann nodded. "I'll wake you when its time." As Cas left, he heard Vrij ask what the motion Jann had made with her head meant. Perhaps on the trip back he could introduce the Bulaq to all their mannerisms, and vice versa. That should take at least a couple of hours. But the main thing was he needed to get as much sleep as he could because once he was on that ship he wasn't closing his eyes for a second. Otherwise he might never open them again.

***

Two hours later Cas was still nursing the headache while boarding the Bulaq ship. It was comparable in size to the *Hymettus* but with less frills. It was long, with increasingly-large segments toward the back, with the smallest segment at the front making up the command deck while the cargo area was composed of one large section surrounded by four diagonal "wings" which he assumed controlled the undercurrent. It was about five times as large as Vrij's ship but made of the same materials. The colors and composition made it easy to tell they were built by the same people. It also differed from the attack ships that had been strafing *Tempest* as it didn't seem to have any offensive weapons and seemed to Cas to be bulky and difficult to maneuver. Vrij led him around back to where a large ramp had extended, allowing the Bulaq to load up all their materials.

Once inside he could tell it had been more luxurious but had been chopped up and repurposed since. He had to admit, when faced with adversity the Bulaq didn't waste any time in making whatever adjustments were necessary to survive. Had an attack like that happened on Earth or any of the Coalition worlds he was damn sure they wouldn't be in this kind of position in less than three seasons. They'd still be in a disarray, but it was almost like the Bulaq had been prepared to deal with this on some level. Except for the lack of food, that was.

In the cargo section hammocks had been hung from the high walls, each accessible by ladders on the sides of the cargo bay. It was possible the Bulaq hollowed out any permanent crew quarters for parts, or this was just how they traveled on their ships. Around him a dozen—not a half-dozen as he'd been told—Bulaq loaded all the materials on the shuttle without a word to him or Vrij. They all seemed tired but didn't utter a word of complaint. Vrij directed Cas to follow him.

Deeper in the ship they passed an area full of scanning equipment that had been forced into part of the ship where it didn't belong, requiring him and Vrij to step over wires, consoles and temporary bulkheads supporting all the haphazard devices. Cas noticed not all of them looked to be of Bulaq design. He was about to ask Vrij about this when they crossed into a short corridor which could only lead to the command deck.

"H-he'll be up there." Vrij pointed two of his fingers down the hall. "D-don't take your e-eye off him. I-I don't know w-what he's planned—never the f-full picture with him."

"You're not coming?" Cas asked.

"B-better if I d-don't. I-I'll make sure all the c-cargo gets on board."

Cas nodded. "Yeah, okay." Though he didn't like the idea of facing Diamant alone, it was better than trying to keep an eye on both of them at once. He had no idea what the cultural norms were in a situation like this, but hopefully if he got tired of listening to Diamant prattle he could excuse himself for one of those hammocks.

Vrij nodded back, a move that surprised Cas, though when he did it, he accompanied it with two chest taps. With Vrij at his back, Cas continued down the rest of the corridor until he arrived on the ship's command deck. Like the rest of the ship it had been stripped of any non-essential parts to the point where there weren't even chairs. Instead, two Bulaq took up positions at the front while Diamant stood behind them, his arms folded one on top of the other. When Cas entered, he turned with a smile on his considerable lips. "Caspian, I'm so glad you decided to be the one to accompany us back to your ship. It gives us a chance to get to know each other better." He indicated the room with a sweep of his hand. "Welcome to our ship; you see what we've been reduced to. I *apologize* we have nowhere for you to sit. I'm sure after the *ossak* you're tired."

"I'm fine," Cas replied. "I got a few winks on my own ship."

Diamant cocked his head. "Winks?"

Cas fumbled. "Sorry, it's an idiom of ours. It means we slept lightly."

"Ah," the Bulaq replied. "Well I look forward to learning more about your culture. It sounds fascinating. With so many different species interacting all at once. It must make for some interesting get-togethers. Tell me, what is your Coalition's stance on religious activities?"

The question threw Cas. He hadn't expected the man to come out of the gate swinging. "Uh…well, each person is free to practice as they like. There are a few major religions within the Coalition, but there are no requirements to join, stay or refuse. It's personal preference, really."

"Is it?" Diamant lowered his head but kept his eyes on Cas. "How interesting." He returned his attention to the Bulaq in front of them. "Where are my manners? This is Jurej and Keswall. They'll be our guides back to your ship." They turned at their names and each tapped their chests twice.

Cas nodded to them. "Pleasure. How many are you bringing with you?"

"Oh, not too many I think," Diamant replied. "Enough to unload all the materials and help your people install them. If we work quick, we can have the job done in a day or two."

"But you don't even know the extent of our damage," Cas replied. "It will take us some time to modify the raw materials into components we can use."

Diamant folded his arms again. "Oh, it won't matter," he said with a smile on his lips again. "We are very good at repairs. We find speed doesn't affect the quality of our work."

"That's a valuable skill," Cas said, hoping to prompt a little less posturing on Diamant's part.

"Yes, it is," he said.

It was going to be a long ride back.

19

Evie waited in Bay One, watching the two ships approach the open end of the bay itself. She stood near the far side where the corridors connected to the rest of the ship, well out of the way of any approaching ships. And yet she felt exposed out here. Her last experience on a shuttle had caused her to avoid the bays ever since, but as captain she felt she had a duty to be here to meet their new "allies" despite being completely blindsided.

What had she told him? No unnecessary risks. And what had he done? He'd brought an entire contingent of Bulaq back with him, all of which could be nothing more than a boarding party in disguise. Cas had emphasized he'd found no weapons on any of them and their ship wasn't equipped with offensive capabilities. Regardless, Evie had made sure a contingent of Rafnkell's fighters had met the ships and she'd also had Uuma assemble a security team to greet them when they disembarked. She'd been surprised to learn he'd traveled on the Bulaq shuttle and one of the Bulaq had done the same on their shuttle. He hadn't said much about it but had relayed the information in a tone that told her he'd explain later. He damn well better because she wasn't about to have this ship overrun with Bulaq looking for an easy poach.

She'd forgone a weapon herself, the dozen armed security personnel behind her said everything she needed to. Evie *almost* stopped by her quarters for her sword but decided it might be in bad taste. She had to lead this crew now and she couldn't go off on a whim like that, not that she could have before anyway.

The *Hymettus* landed first, taking her regular spot. Through the windshield Captain Jann and Laura were visible, Laura throwing Evie a brief wink as the shuttle landed. She exhaled for what felt like the first time in three days. Everything was okay between them, good. She couldn't afford to be distracted right now, not when their survival depended on what happened in the next few minutes.

The second ship came in and executed a perfect landing in an area designated by the flight control team on the deck. Despite their unfamiliarity with Coalition procedure, they did a fair job following the team's commands. The Bulaq ship didn't seem to have a port to see on the inside, instead it was fully opaque. Evie figured they must use remote camera sensors to see what's ahead of them.

The crew of the *Hymettus* exited first, led by Laura who, upon getting a good look at Evie's face, transformed her own from one of amusement to sorrow. Had she been able to tell what had happened to Captain Greene from just the look on Evie's face? She needed to do a better job at hiding her emotional state. It wouldn't do for the crew to see her worried or angry; they needed her calm, collected, and sure of herself.

"Captain," Laura said, approaching, placing her fist to her chest in the traditional salute.

"Good trip, Lieutenant?" Evie asked.

"We'll see." Behind her, captains Ryant and Jann followed on either side of a Bulaq male. He was very similar to Vrij, except his plated skin was a shade darker and he was a bit taller. "This is Lu'mat," Laura added, introducing the man. "He's a Bulaq engineer, responsible for many of their construction projects."

"Welcome to *Tempest*." Evie nodded.

"I am honored to be here," Lu'mat clasped his hands together in front of him and gave a small bow.

"Captain, I need to head to sickbay," Ryant said, eyeing the door. Evie nodded; Cas had informed her of his adverse reaction to something while they were in the company of the Bulaq, but he hadn't elaborated. Something *else* he'd have to tell her later.

"I'll make sure he gets there," Jann said, leading him along. He did somewhat green around gills. It was never easy trying to assimilate into a foreign culture and some people just didn't take well to it.

"Captain?" She and Laura turned at the same time to see Cas approaching with one Bulaq beside him and a dozen more walking behind, including Vrij bringing up the rear. Why had he brought him *back*? The man was a criminal, despite his help. They'd come from the cargo bay of the Bulaq ship, which was now open. Inside sat crates and crates of goods. If nothing else, Cas had at least found what they needed. Now to see if it was all worth it.

Evie gave her most reassuring smile while not going overboard. She couldn't read the Bulaq beside Cas, only saw that he kept his eyes trained on her. "May I present Diamant of the Bulaq," Cas said, indicating the man beside him.

"Captain Diazal, what an honor," Diamant said in an overly saccharine tone. "I've been told you like to grasp and shake hands during an introduction."

"That's one of our customs, yes. But it isn't—"

"Then I insist you allow me to accommodate you." Diamant reached out with one hand. Evie stared at the sharp claws on the end of each finger longer than she should have before reciprocating the gesture. She clasped her hand around his and he did the same. Somehow, the claws didn't cut into her skin. "Is this correct?" Diamant asked.

"It is. Thank you. And it's a pleasure to meet you."

"Oh no, Captain. The pleasure is all mine. It isn't often we meet other species with such a *generous* nature." He let go and one of his claws caught the back of her hand. She yanked it away, inspecting the wound. "I'm very sorry. You can see why this isn't one of our customs."

She swallowed the pain. It wasn't deep, but it was like the claw had made a very shallow, but long cut that was now beading blood. "It happens, I know it wasn't on purpose."

Diamant swung his hand behind him. "These are my comrades, some of the best workers the Bulaq society has left. I have already spoken with Caspian, but we believe we can affect your repairs much faster if we help you refine and install all your repairs."

Evie had to work to keep the shock off her face. Cas hadn't said anything about this on his call. "That's…very generous of you, but we can manage."

"Oh, no, I insist. I inspected some of the damage as we approached. It will be much easier for my people to make some of the repairs. Your damage is *extensive*." She didn't mention it had been more than twenty hours since the last attack on the ship. She wasn't sure if it was Diamant directing his people not to fire on them or if they were staying away because they knew he was coming aboard. Whatever the reason, the timing was convenient.

"How about we discuss it somewhere more comfortable," Evie suggested, shooting looks at Cas. For his part he held a good poker face, not betraying anything for the moment. "While you're here we've assigned you each quarters where you can relax before you have to return. Enjoy our hospitality for a while." They really didn't have the extra room and Evie had needed to open up one of the sections they'd already closed to accommodate the Bulaq, but she didn't want them to see just how bad off *Tempest* was at the moment. If she had to fake it until they left then so be it.

Diamant clasped one hand over the other. "You are too kind, Captain. I look forward to sampling your accommodations."

"Our officers here will see that each of you reaches your individual units without delay," she added.

Diamant gave her the hint of a smile. "Of course, would you like us to help you unload the materials?"

"No, thank you, our people can take care of that. But we do appreciate your assistance." She felt like she was locked into a strange dance with him, both of them circling each other in choreographed steps. "We'll load what Caspian has promised in their place. Shouldn't take more than a few hours."

"Very well. If you'd be so kind as to show us the way." He folded his hands together like Lu'mat had when he'd first exited the *Hymettus*.

"Come with me," Ensign Folier said, leading the Tempest's security team. Diamant and the other Bulaq moved past them, following the team through the exit. Only Vrij remained.

"You too," Evie said. "I've assigned you a room as well."

"N-no more jail?" Vrij asked.

"Provided you can behave. One finger out of place and you're going right back in." Vrij clasped his hands together and bowed, following the rest of the Bulaq at a distance. Evie rubbed the back of her hand, smearing what blood had come up from the cut.

"You should get to sickbay," Laura said, taking the hand in her own. "You don't want to get an infection from something he might have had under his claw."

Evie smiled. "I'll take care of it in a minute. Can you give me and Cas a second here?"

Laura's eyes flicked between them. She glanced around then pushed up on the ends of her toes and placed a quick kiss on Evie's lips. "I missed you. I'll check in with Uuma and see where she can use me."

"I missed you too," Evie whispered. Laura smiled then turned and left the two of them there as one of the maintenance teams approached the Bulaq shuttle to unload.

"You shouldn't have brought them here," she whispered to Cas without looking at him.

"I know," he replied. "It was stupid. But it seemed like the only way to get what we needed. At first it didn't seem so bad, but after spending a whole day with him I'm not sure we can trust him. Did you notice he didn't even ask about the supplies for his people?"

She nodded. "Which means that was what he was really interested in." She cut her eyes to him. "Greene's dead."

He was still for a moment, as if he was trying to process it. "I...I don't know what to say. He was one of the best. So then..."

"*Then* I'm officially the captain and you're officially the first officer. And before you object," she said, stopping him from saying anything. "I can't do this job alone, not right now. When we get back, if all this gets ironed out, then you can go back to being...whatever it was you were before. But right now, I need to know you're a hundred percent committed. Because you just introduced a big risk to this ship, and if it goes bad—" She stopped when she saw the conviction in his eyes.

"You're right. You shouldn't have to do this alone. I know this was a bad call. I just hope it doesn't come back to haunt us." He shook his head, doubt seeping from him.

"Let's just get them loaded up and on their way as soon as we can."

"Wait a second." He smirked. "The only reason you gave them all quarters was so you could lock them inside."

"Precisely. And if they think they're getting access to sensitive areas of the ship—"

Cas folded his arms, his eyes on the exit where all the Bulaq had left. "I already made it clear to Diamant that was out of the question."

"How did he respond?" If she had to guess, he'd put on a good show. There was something about that man she couldn't reconcile. What was his true motive?

"About like you'd expect. Like he'd assumed that was the case and almost insulted that I'd assumed they thought different. You know, playing all the angles."

"Yeah," she said, her eyes narrowing. "I know all the angles."

20

"You're sure you didn't find anything?" Cas looked over the report again.

"Boss, you question my medical skills one more time and I'm twisting those nipples right off through your shirt."

Cas curled his hands into claws to keep his temper under wraps. "Look, *Doctor*, he scratched her intentionally and I want to know why. Did he deposit a disease in her skin? Something we can't detect?"

Box snatched bar displaying the holo report from Cas's hands, shutting it off and stowing it in a compartment in his leg. "Did you ever think maybe he's just an asshole?"

"I *know* he's an asshole, but he's got a hidden agenda. And until I know what it is, I can't let my guard down."

"Then why did you let them on board in the first place?" Box's eyes flashed with frustration.

"I don't know! It seemed like the only option at the time."

"Because you were drunk." Box walked to the other side of the room. Cas'd had him come meet him in his quarters rather than in sickbay. He didn't want Evie to know he was double-checking on Xax's work. It wouldn't look good to have the first officer question the chief medical officer.

He mentally sighed. *First officer*. Back when he thought Greene would recover it hadn't been real. Something he needed to get through until things went back to normal. But since when had things ever been normal on this ship? He should have known. "I know what you're going to say but it wasn't my fault. I'm almost positive Diamant never would have even talked to us if we hadn't taken part."

"If I were you, I'd be more worried about what you put in your own body while you were there. Ryant's blood was at an almost toxic level. Thankfully because you drink so much you could function at a higher level than he could. Which reminds me." Box pressed one finger to Cas's neck, and he felt a sharp prick.

He jerked away, holding the spot. "Ow! What the hell was that?"

Box held up the finger with a tiny, but sharp needle embedded in the finger. It retracted immediately. "Like it? It's my new DDS. Drug delivery system. Xax thought it was a brilliant idea."

"Did she? Let me hear the playback," Cas said, rubbing his neck.

"No. But trust me, it was gushing with praise."

"Uh-huh. What did you just shoot me with?"

"Palithasol. To get those toxic chemicals out of your system. You may not feel them, but they're still there."

Cas stood and made his way to the small window in his room. "Did you give one to Yamashita yet?"

"Don't tell me she took some as well? You humans. Just can't help yourselves." Box threw his hands in the air in an overly dramatic fashion.

"Oh, don't act so high and mighty. I remember not too long ago when you were hooked on net dramas. Those things were like lo-boz to your processor."

"Hey, I could quit anytime I wanted. I just didn't want to. It's not my fault you were so mind-numbingly boring I had to self-medicate."

Cas sighed and sat on the edge of his bed. "And you're sure there's no way he could have infected her with something."

"That's it." Box rushed him, his metal hands clamping down as they aimed for his chest. Cas rolled on the bed and off the other side, ducking the robot's hands.

"Ha! You'll have to OWWW!" Box had reached over faster than he could have anticipated, clamping down on the tender skin beneath his shirt. He smacked Box's hand until the robot released him. "Dammit, that hurt!" He glanced down his shirt. "Great, that's going to bruise. Thanks a lot."

"I tried to warn you."

"Fine. But if anything comes up on her tox screens, something hidden or dormant, you let me know before you tell her."

"I'll make a note of it. Have you spoken to Consul Zenfor since you returned?"

Cas rubbed his chest, noting Box had now caused two bruises. "No, why?"

Box shrugged. "I just thought you might have had an update on—" As he was speaking a shadow passed over Cas's window.

He turned back, studying the small porthole. "What the hell was that?"

"I don't know," Box said.

Cas pressed his face to the clear material, trying to see on the outside of the ship, but it was too dark. The running lights only illuminated certain sections of the ship. He tapped his comm. "Bridge, this is Caspian. Do we have external sensor cameras on level seven, midsection alpha?"

"No, Commander. They're down in that area," Zaal replied. Dammit, he wished people would stop using that rank.

"Zaal, I think there's something outside on the hull. Get a shuttle or something out there to check it out. It just passed above my window."

"Yes, sir."

Cas turned back to Box. "I should get to the bridge. Inform the captain. Remember what I said."

Box waved him off. "Next time I'm coming back with something for your anxiety." Cas rolled his eyes as they exited at the same time, both heading in different directions.

He reached the hypervator and got in, he glanced down to see a spot of blood on his shirt. He pulled it forward, glancing down to where Box had snagged him. "Son of a—" Great. Now he was bleeding. He was going to *kill* Box.

The doors opened on the bridge. "Anything?" Cas asked.

"Rafnkell is checking now," Zaal replied. "She didn't like the idea of anyone else out there doing it."

"I know the feeling," Cas replied. He took the first officer's chair.

"What's going on?" Evie asked, exiting from the command room.

"I'm not sure, but I think I saw something on the hull close to my quarters. Zaal sent Rafnkell out to check on it."

"You *saw* something?" Her eyes widened as she took her seat.

"It's probably nothing. Everything ready for our meeting with Diamant?"

"As ready as can be. I need to figure out what his connection is to those ships that keep attacking. I can't believe it's just a coincidence they stopped as soon as he decided to come aboard."

Cas shrugged. "He's a man of influence. And he did tell me he'd try to find the faction controlling the raids, get them to stop."

"Yeah," Evie replied, "Unless he's the one controlling them. There's just something about that guy that's—"

"Slimy?"

"Exactly." She leaned forward. "I don't want him on this ship any longer than necessary. I don't even care about the provisions anymore. I just want him gone."

Cas was taken aback. She hadn't seemed very happy about how much he'd promised the Bulaq in the way of supplies, but maybe she'd come to the same conclusion he had about how as soon as they were back in Coalition space they wouldn't need the supplies anymore.

"Ma'am, feed coming in from Chief Rafnkell," Zaal said.

"Main viewer," Evie replied. The viewer switched to show an external view of the side of the ship. "Anything Chief?"

"It's hard to tell with all the damage, but I think something is moving out here. Check out grid K-16." On the screen, it automatically enlarged to show a more detailed view of the ship. And there, among some of the damaged panels and sections that had been blown out into space, was Vrij, using his mechanical mandibles to anchor himself to the hull as he ran across the surface.

"Is that—?" Evie asked.

"Yep. Chief you better grab him." Cas couldn't believe it. He must have donned one of his suits that allowed him to stay in a vacuum. But what was he doing out on the hull? And how did he even get out there?

"I'm assuming you didn't know anything about this," Evie said. Cas shook his head. "I knew it was a mistake letting him back on board. Why didn't you just leave him with his people?"

"Diamant seemed to think it was better if he came with us due to the level of scorn he'd face from his own people. Apparently they don't like him."

"I can see why."

On the screen, Rafnkell fired a grappler from the spacewing, which Vrij didn't see until it was too late. It hooked around him like a vice and yanked him off the hull in one swift move. He flailed in the zero-gravity.

"Chief, bring him into Bay Two," Evie ordered. "Security team to Bay Two. Prepare to escort a prisoner back to the brig."

"Do you want to go find out what he was up to?" Cas asked.

"No, that's your job. I'm not wasting any more time on that criminal. I'll meet with Diamant. I don't want him knowing about this until they're ready to leave and take him with them." She turned to Zaal. "And figure out how he got out of his room and onto the hull."

"It looks like the room we assigned him to has been depressurized," Zaal replied.

"Why didn't the proximity alarms go off?"

"I'm not sure," he replied. "With all the damage to the ship they may not be working properly. Or there could be another cause. Until I investigate I won't know." Cas was growing used to Zaal not having human features anymore, with nothing but his robotic exoskeleton visible under his hood. He almost preferred him this way to the smiling, emotionally stuck face he normally had.

"Get on it," Evie ordered. "And you get down to Bay Two, I don't want him out of anyone's sight. See if you can't find a way to remove those things on his back," she said to Cas.

"Do you really think—"

"Captain, we have another problem," Uuma interrupted. "Our weapon systems have failed again."

Evie stood. "We just finished repairing those," she replied.

"It isn't from previous damage to the ship," Uuma said, studying her console. "It looks like the interruption is coming from where Vrij was on the hull. He must have gotten into the systems from the outside."

Evie glared at Cas. "Great."

"It's going to take some time to repair. And it won't be easy; we'll have to send a maintenance crew out in suits."

"Wait," Cas said. "Are you saying Vrij sabotaged the weapons? Why would he do that?"

"Because he's been a spy for Diamant this whole time," Evie replied. "He used us to get into the ship, figured out what we needed, then told us exactly what we wanted to hear to get him on board. And now I have to find a way to get the Bulaq off the ship without raising any alarms."

"Are you sure? They seem to vehemently dislike each other."

"Two people can dislike each other and still work together." Her eyes narrowed. Damn. He knew he'd screwed up. This was why they needed someone more qualified in this role. Someone who at least deserved it. Now he had to try and clean up his own mess.

"I'll go see what I can find out," he said, approaching the hypervator at the far end of the room. "And see about removing his apparatus."

"And make sure he doesn't have any more of those portable suits on him!" Evie called after him. The doors to the hypervator closed, leaving Cas with his thoughts.

What a mess.

21

He entered Bay Two just as Rafnkell was setting her spacewing down on the deck, Vrij still flailed about on the end of the extended grappler. As soon as she was down, she extended the cable and it lowered him to the ground where he was met with three security personnel, all with rifles pointed at him and led by Laura. Cas approached as one of the security officers unhooked Vrij from the tether. He cowered under their weapons.

"Cleaning up your mess again, I see," Rafnkell said, descending the ladder and pulling off her helmet. "Good thing for you I take a clean shot."

"Good work out there, Chief," Cas said. If the compliment caught her off guard she didn't show it. She only turned to Vrij.

"If I have to go out there one more time to retrieve your ass, you can better believe it won't be as pleasant." She left them there, returning to the supply lockers on the far side of the bay.

Cas stood over the cowering Vrij for a moment. "Can your mandibles be removed?" he asked. A shaky hand reached up to Vrij's forehead and held two fingers there before releasing them. *No.* Of course he'd say no. Perhaps they should take a detour by sickbay to verify. Cas turned to Laura who held one of the rifles. "I need you to bind his hands *and* those things on his back."

"Yes, sir," she replied, stowing her rifle on her back using the magnetic locks. "Don't move," she told Vrij, approaching him and he went as still as Cas assumed he could. She removed his jacket, tossing it to the side, revealing the mechanical armature attached to his back. From Cas's vantage point he didn't think it was something that could just be detached. It looked like it had been integrated into the soft tissue of his back. Crewman Tes pulled a pair of cuffs from her pocket and clapped them on Vrij's hands, which had begun to shake. She then pulled out a second pair and pressing the tab between them, elongated the magnetic chain between them. Cas had worn a similar pair of cuffs back when Evie had arrested him back on D'jttan. They weren't the most comfortable things to wear but they did their job of restricting movement.

She wrapped the long line around his chest, under his arms, pinning the mechanical appendages to his back so they couldn't move, then clicked the two cuffs together. She pressed the tab again and the slack tightened, causing Vrij to wince.

"Here, stand up," Laura said, coaxing him up by raising his arms. "Come with me. Tes, take point. Unak, cover his rear. Any sudden moves and you shoot him." She stared at Vrij as she made the orders. "Understood?"

"Yes, ma'am," they replied.

Cas was impressed. "You've been brushing up on your prisoner protocol," he said.

"What do you think I was doing that whole trip to the Hub? Reading for pleasure?" She was driven, that much was clear. He could see what Evie admired about her.

As they led Vrij through the corridors Cas brought himself into step beside the man. "First tell me how you got out there. Last time I checked you were locked in your room."

Vrij made a strange motion with his hands, which Cas recognized as someone moving through a door or portal. "W-w-window," he said.

"You opened the window? That's not possible. They're anchored deep into the hull. Plus, there would have been a proximity alarm. And a depressurization alarm. And a general alert. So, tell me another one." Vrij tapped his fingers to his forehead over and over not saying anything else. "Fine. We'll do an investigation later. But what I really want to know is why'd you do it, huh? Was it all just a ploy to get Diamant on the ship? Or was there another reason?"

Vrij tried to reach up and touch his head but with his hands and chest bound and a short line keeping them magnetically connected, he could barely move his hands. "N-n-no. I w-w-was—there w-was—o-on the h-h-hull I-I—"

"Oh my god, just spit it out," Laura said in front of them.

"I-I-I'm s-sorry. I w-w-was—"

"Is there any way to clean that up?" Laura asked.

"I don't think it's the auto-vox. I think it's just the way he speaks," Cas replied. He'd suspected as much ever since he'd met the other Bulaq. Vrij was a nervous wreck, though if he'd been caught sabotaging someone else's ship Cas supposed he'd be pretty nervous too. There was no telling what the Bulaq did to their criminals; he was probably afraid of the Coalition's punishment methods.

"I-I-it wasn't—I-I didn't d-do a-a-anything," he finally said with tremendous effort.

"Then why were you on the hull?" Cas asked. He shouldn't even bother, this man was a known thief and the sooner he was off the ship, the better. Evie had been right.

"F-f-following L-lu'm-mat."

Laura screwed up her face, turning to him. "What?"

Vrij glanced out one of the windows as they passed. "H-h-he w-w-was on t-the ssss-side of the sss-ship. M-messing w-with t-the systems."

"He's just trying to shift the blame," Laura said. "We flew back with Lu'mat. He didn't make one move out of line the entire time."

"Not to mention when Rafnkell went out there you were the only one she saw. You were alone, Vrij."

"N-no," Vrij insisted. "H-he w-was out there. J-just before s-she showed up. I s-saw—the w-weapons c-conduits, d-damaged. H-he's Diamant's m-m-most t-trusted man."

"You can't be buying this," Laura said to Cas.

"Why would Diamant want him to damage our weapons systems? I thought he came here to help," Cas asked, averting his eyes.

"I t-tried t-to tell y-you. Never the w-whole s-story w-with Diamant. H-he always h-has another a-agenda."

Cas shook his head. "So, you're saying Diamant ordered Lu'mat to disable the weapons systems because he's what? Planning more attacks? Why would he do that when he knows we have the spacewings? Not to mention he's on board which makes an attack risky. Unless they know exactly where he and the others are on the ship." Diamant wouldn't be that brash. What would be the point of bringing them all those materials if they were just going to destroy the ship again anyway? It didn't make sense. "Sorry Vrij, but it doesn't hold water."

"T-then w-what?" Vrij asked, his voice stronger.

"I don't know. Maybe you were planning on stealing more supplies and didn't want us shooting at you as you escaped in your shuttle. Or maybe the parts you needed were on the weapons control systems. Who knows? All that matters is you got caught before you could do any permanent damage."

"I-I am not s-stupid. T-taking w-weapons components a d-dumb idea. Sets off t-too many alarms. N-not good f-for borrowing." He'd pulled himself up more, walking almost fully upright again.

Cas eyed him. "Maybe you got sloppy. Like last time."

"L-last time w-was a f-fluke—a m-mistake. S-stupid t-to make a s-second one."

"Let's say you're right, and Lu'mat was out there messing with the weapons. What am I supposed to do about it? Go to Diamant and tell him you saw his associate on the hull of the ship, tearing things apart? He'll think we're conspiring against him. And for a man whose temperament seems to balance on a tightrope, I don't want to see what happens if we push him too far to the other side. For all we know he controls every Bulaq ship left. For my crew's sake, we need to get out of this in one piece and with all those materials. There's just no other way."

They rounded the edge of the corridor to the brig, which sat empty, Ensign Folier stood beside the entrance, her hands on the controls. When she saw them approach she dropped one of the force barriers to a cell.

"Take the ones on his hands off, but leave the one around his back," Cas ordered. "I don't want to unbind him until we know the full extent of how he got on the outside of the ship. And confiscate those." He pointed to the row of small canisters attached to Vrij's belt. Laura reached over and undid the clasp, handing the belt over to Folier who stored it in a drawer on the other side of the brig console.

"Y-you c-can't trust him," Vrij said. "D-do whatever n-necessary to g-get him o-off this ship. The l-longer he's here, t-he h-harder it w-will be."

"The only problem," Cas said as Laura removed his cuffs and gently moved him inside the cell. "—is I can't trust you either."

***

Cas raced on to the bridge, scanning for the captain. But she was nowhere to be found. "Where is she?" he asked Uuma. Ever since leaving Vrij in the brig he'd had a sinking pit in his stomach that had only gotten worse as the minutes had ticked forward. It was like an increasing pressure on his brain and everything was telling him he needed to get to the captain before she met with Diamant. He'd meant to go check on Zenfor and the engine situation, but this took precedence.

"She's in the command room," Uuma said.

"Alone?"

"As far as I know," she replied. Cas dashed over to the room and tapped the call button on the side repeatedly.

"*Come in,*" Evie said, her voice terse. He pushed inside faster than he thought and scanned the room. She was alone. "What the hell is so important?" she demanded.

"I was afraid to comm you in case you were already in the meeting. Have you spoken to Diamant yet?"

"No, he's waiting in the conference room. I was just…preparing."

"Vrij says he was out there chasing one of Diamant's men."

"Oh for—" Evie rolled her eyes and slumped back down into her chair.

"I know, I don't believe it either. But what if he *is* telling the truth? Vrij says Diamant has a hidden agenda."

She glared at him. "I think that much is obvious. The question is, what does he want?"

"I'm not sure. And neither is Vrij. And he could have been making it all up; there's no way to tell."

"Ugh." Evie leaned forward, elbows on the desk and placed her face in her hands, rubbing up and down. "How am I supposed to do this?"

"Do you want me to talk to him?"

She pulled her hands away, exasperation painted across her face. "I'm not looking to avoid my responsibilities."

Cas took the seat across the desk. "No, I'm not talking about that. Did you notice anything odd about all the people Diamant brought with him?"

She furrowed her brow. "Not really."

"They're all men. Not one woman among them. The entire time we were there I didn't see a woman in any kind of authority position. I don't know if it's a cultural thing or not, but it's worth considering."

"Did they even *have* women?" she asked.

"A few. But the ones I saw were destitute, beggars. I didn't see any with influence or power. I could be wrong. Maybe all their female leaders were on the planet when it was destroyed. But something about it seems weird to me."

"You might be right," she said, leaning back. "Okay. You talk to him again. But for the love of Kor, don't give away the farm here. The idea is to get him and his people off the ship as soon as possible without insulting him. We can't afford to have him turn all the Bulaq forces on us. *If* he's the one controlling them. I just checked with the cargo team. Almost all of the supplies have been loaded in their ship."

"What's the condition of the lounge?" Cas asked.

Her face dropped. "Cas, come on, are you really—?"

"No. This guy likes ceremony. He likes theater and elaborate rituals. If I can create one of my own, it might make him more amenable. At least it would put us on even footing. Last time *he* had the advantage. This time maybe I can turn the tables."

She stared at him over the bridge of her nose. "You want to get him drunk."

"Dead drunk. So much that he agrees to anything. Including leaving."

"And what happens if he turns out to have a temper when he's intoxicated?" she asked.

"I won't be alone. And I don't think he does, he stayed calm the last time, despite detailing the loss of his home planet."

She tapped her chin repeatedly. "I can't say I necessarily approve. But then again, you're the one who went through negotiation boot camp with Laska, not me. Just make sure you're not alone with him. I don't want to have to rush you to sickbay for mandible wounds."

He stood, pressing his fist to his chest. "I won't let you down."

"Uh-huh. I've heard that before. Good luck."

22

Cas entered the conference room to find Diamant standing at the window, his arms folded in front of him, staring out into the nothingness. Lieutenant Stillwater stood off to the side, keeping an eye on him but also staying out of his way. He nodded to Cas as he entered, and Cas returned the gesture. He studied the form of Diamant and saw how his exposed mandibles were set into his back almost like wings on an insect. Whatever had happened to Vrij must have been a traumatic experience to have ripped such powerful appendages off him. He couldn't help but feel sorry for him. Cas cleared his throat.

Diamant turned, his smile faltering just a tad before it was back up again. "Ah, Caspian. I was expecting the captain."

"She had something unexpected come up," he replied. "So, you're stuck with me."

"No matter. In fact, I almost prefer this. You and I have a rapport." He paused. "We already know each other's *secrets*." By Kor, Cas wished he'd been able to keep his mouth shut about Suzanna.

Cas cleared his throat, anxious to move on. "Since it is just you and me, I thought perhaps we could speak somewhere more...comfortable. This room can be stuffy. Plus, it would give you an opportunity to see more of the ship."

Diamant regarded him. "Very well. That's something I've been meaning to speak to the captain about. We've been on your ship for nearly six hours and my crew has yet to be allowed to leave their quarters. Surely you don't consider us a threat."

Cas glanced to Stillwater, indicating for him to follow them. "Of course not. But as you know we have many damaged sections. Keeping your people safe is our primary concern. We just don't want them wandering into a dangerous area."

Diamant gave him a knowing smile as he came into step beside him, both of them exiting the conference room to head to the hypervator. "I see. How very generous of you. Though I can assure you, my people can take care of themselves."

"No doubt. But we also felt some rest was in order. It was a long journey and your people have been through a lot. Did you find your quarters comfortable?"

Diamant clasped one hand around the other. "Very. My people haven't felt comfort like that in many standards. We once had ships like yours, where all our needs were provided for. But we've had to make sacrifices due to our *situation*." The hypervator doors opened and the three stepped inside.

"Level twelve," Cas said.

"So tell me. How long have you been first officer? I was surprised to learn about your position from the nice ensign who escorted me to my quarters."

"Surprised that I could have an actual job on this ship?"

Diamant smiled. "Oh no. I knew when we first met you were someone of great importance. It is a skill I have: recognizing talent. And raw energy." He made a fist with one hand. "In a position like mine you have to learn to separate those who *will* and those who only *consider*. Action is the true power in this world. And those willing to take action wield all the power."

"Like yourself," Cas suggested. The hypervator doors opened on twelve and they stepped out, Cas showing Diamant the way.

"I suppose. But I am but a humble servant to my people. You sit in the second-most powerful seat on the ship. And yet you're independent. You don't wear the uniform like your colleagues, and I don't see any markings of rank. All this tells me you have enough influence to do and say as you please. Perhaps even more than the captain."

"I wouldn't go that far," Cas said, leading him to the lounge doors, which were closed and the room behind them dark. "And I have a complicated history with the Coalition."

"I see," Diamant said, drawing out the last word. "I'd love to hear about it."

Cas used his command codes to override the door locks, and they slid open, the lights coming on automatically. "Maybe later. But first, I want to introduce you to something." He turned to Stillwater. "You can stay here." Stillwater nodded and took up position at the door as the other two men entered.

"What an opulent room," Diamant observed. Only a few of the chairs and tables had been overturned by the turbulence when the ship was damaged, and a few of the bottles along the back wall had shattered upon impact, giving the room an earthy, oaky smell that permeated everything. Cas walked over to the bar and pulled out a bottle of undamaged Firebrand.

"You were gracious enough to introduce us to *Ossak*. I feel it's only fair to repay the favor."

Diamant returned his attention to him. "How *generous*." His eyes flicked from Cas to the bottle and back again. "I look forward to the sample."

Oh, it's going to be a lot more than a sample. Cas grabbed a couple of unbroken glasses and indicated they take a seat at one of the tables close to the windows. "This is one of the better views on the ship. At least as far as the lower levels are concerned. The best are up on two and three, which is also where our Stellar Cartography unit is located."

"And do you bring all your guests here to sample your wares?" Diamant indicated the room with a wave of his arm.

"Just you. I'm not sure everyone who comes aboard *appreciates* our customs." Diamant narrowed his eyes by an infinitesimal amount, but Cas paid him no attention. Instead, he uncorked the firebrand and poured a small amount into both glasses. He pushed the glass over toward the man and picked his own up. "Cheers."

Diamant frowned but picked up his glass as well. "Cheers?"

"It means good health and good luck." Cas reached over and tapped the edge of his glass to Diamant's. The tinkle echoed through the room. "Now we drink." Cas knocked back his without even allowing the firebrand to touch his tongue.

Diamant looked at the drink for a moment then followed suit, albeit slower. He swallowed, regarding the glass, then set it down. "Interesting flavor."

"Do you like it?" Cas asked.

"I do. It has an aroma I'm not familiar with. Complex flavors. Truly a treat worthy of kings." He raised his glass to Cas again and Cas obliged him by filling it with another shot's worth. This was going better than he could have expected. But now it was time for the true test. He didn't expect Diamant would be inebriated yet, but if he wasn't receptive to Cas's next question this conversation would go nowhere whether he was drunk or not.

"Forgive me if this feels forward, but why are you really here?" Cas asked, holding his glass steady.

Diamant watched him for a minute, then set his glass down. "I'm sorry?" he said with an air of offense.

"Back on the Hub, you were right. There are way too many people for us to have a meaningful impact on your food problem. So, I'm wondering what you're really doing here? And why you decided to fulfill our request."

"We had the materials to spare." Diamant picked up the glass again and sipped the liquid. "Is it wrong to want to share what we carry in abundance?"

"No, of course not," Cas said, keeping his tone even. "It just seems like you're giving up a lot for little in return." It wasn't the case at all and they both knew it; the problem was Cas didn't know *why*.

A smile spread across Diamant's face. "I have to congratulate you, Caspian. That was a bold risk. Potentially insulting me and losing everything we've built together on a hunch. I must keep a very sharp eye on you." He drained the rest of his glass. "Refill my drink and we can have a real discussion."

Cas did as he asked, topping himself off in the process. Despite his promises to himself he'd stay clear of the bar until he was no longer first officer, he'd found himself here yet again. But this was the best way to deal with the man. And whatever the cost, he had to keep him talking. Because if he was here talking with Cas, he couldn't be doing something else to the ship.

"You're correct. I came here under false pretenses." Cas was about to interject but Diamant held up his hand. "I'm more than happy to take your supplies back with us. Though they won't make a significant impact. Thankfully our survival isn't dependent on your goodwill otherwise we would surely starve." Cas sipped his drink, allowing the insult to pass over him like a wave. "My true purpose here as the unofficial leader of my people is to find them a new home."

"And you think *Tempest* is it?"

Diamant laughed. "No, of course not. How many can your ship hold? A thousand at best?" He was right. Tempest was on the small side, built for a permanent crew of a few hundred at most. If they cleared out the cargo areas and the bays they could probably fit a thousand if they had to evacuate people say from a planet in a hurry, but it wouldn't be a long-term solution. "My desire is you take me and my men with you on your return trip home. If we find a suitable planet on the way we'll disembark and send word to the Hub to join us there. Unfortunately, the hub is not built for speed and would take probably decades to reach a new planet. But they have to know where they're going first."

Diamant leaned forward, pushing his glass back toward Cas. "You see Caspian, my people depend on me to lead them out of this...darkness. I'm the only one who can find them a new home, the only one who can fulfill our destiny and bring my people back from the brink of extinction." His face became deadly serious. "We won't let this stop us. And I won't quit until my dying breath."

Finally. The truth. Cas pondered Diamant's words as he poured them both another drink. "What if we don't find another planet on the way back?"

"You said you come from a great and welcoming Coalition." Diamant took his drink and sipped it, his eyes never leaving Cas. Was that the plan? To apply for membership and join the Coalition? Not that it was a bad idea, but there was a process. It usually took years, sometimes decades for a species to be approved. And as far as Cas knew no member had ever been admitted without their planet being within Coalition bounds. Now that the Bulaq had no planet anymore, where would they reside while they waited? "All we are asking for is a fair chance, Caspian. A chance to rebuild our lives. To regain the dignity we've lost. Can you imagine having all that stripped from you in one, swift moment?"

"I can, actually," Cas said, nursing the firebrand.

"Then you know—maybe better than anyone else—we aren't asking for much. Just the chance to live and survive."

"You make a compelling argument," Cas replied. "But I don't know how well it will go over. While the Coalition would be happy to accept your application, the approval process—"

Diamant waved his hand dismissively. "Let the politicians figure out the minutiae. We are willing to take the chance. Are you?"

Cas had to admit; he hadn't been prepared for this. He'd known Diamant had a strategy, but accompanying them back to Coalition space? Joining up? If that had been his plan from the beginning he'd done a stellar job of hiding it. Even if they made it and were accepted, how long would it take for the rest of his society to follow? Cas wasn't even sure the Hub had undercurrent capability. Which meant it would take thousands of years to make the journey. Diamant also didn't know about Zenfor's advanced drive system. No one did, except maybe some of the admirals on Starbase Eight.

"I do apologize for misleading you," Diamant said, swirling the brown liquid in the bottom of his glass. "Though you do have to admit, had I made this proposal back on the Hub we wouldn't be sitting here together right now."

"Probably not," Cas replied.

"Allow me to make it up to you. Let my men assist in your repairs. I've already managed to outline a schedule. It will take you weeks if not longer to fix all your systems. My men can have it done in *days*. And I suspect you're on a timetable. That you'll want to begin the long journey back home as soon as possible."

"It seems we're always in a hurry. No matter what." Cas drained the rest of his drink. The alcohol was producing a light fog in his brain, but not enough to affect his logic. But it was enough to loosen his tongue.

"Aren't we all?" Diamant replied with a smile.

"Are all of your men still in their rooms?" Cas asked.

A frown appeared on Diamant's face. "I believe so. You have us under guard; I don't know how they would leave. Why do you ask?"

"We caught Vrij on the hull of the ship. He said he was following one of your men."

Diamant sighed, sitting back in his chair. "That man has been a thorn in my side for far too long. Look what happens. I try to show mercy, tell you to bring him back here so he can return to his shuttle and leave and what does he do? Violates your trust. Not becoming of the Bulaq name, I'm afraid." He raised his glass to Cas once more. Cas hesitated, but filled it again.

"What is your history with him? Why does he seem so afraid of you?"

"It's not a story worth telling, trust me. Just know that we've known each other for a long time. He was in trouble a few years back, I tried to help, and it all fell apart."

"Is that when he—?" Cas motioned to his back.

"Ah. His *augmentation*. No, that occurred long ago. I assume you have him in custody." Cas nodded. "Good. Keep him there. And I'd keep a very sharp eye on him. He's slipped through my own hands more than once. Perhaps we should have left him on the Hub. But then again, he's never really fit in anywhere."

Cas couldn't help but feel sorry for Vrij. And he had been right about Diamant, just perhaps not the way he'd thought. "I'll need to speak to the captain when she's available again," Cas said. "She'll have to make the final decision on your request."

"Until then?" He examined his drink. "May we be allowed at least a tour of your fine ship? Remember, part of our original agreement was to come and assist."

"I think our original agreement is void, now that I understand your true purpose."

Diamant kept his eyes on the glass. "Fair enough."

"Give me time to speak with the captain. Until then I can authorize your people use of our mess hall on a limited basis, as long as they have escorts." Evie wasn't going to be happy about this. But the stakes had changed. Diamant was in essence seeking asylum. It changed the rules of everything.

"Is this how you treat all your guests, Caspian?" His tone had gone cold, and Cas didn't like the shiver down his back as he said it.

"You came here under false pretenses. No matter your reasons, this relationship was based on a lie. I can't overlook that. And until I feel like I can completely trust you, then it is either escorts, or nothing at all."

Diamant set the glass down, still partially full. "Then it seems like we have a lot of work to do." He turned and left the lounge in measured, but swift steps, Stillwater noticing then catching up.

Cas stared at the two glasses and half bottle of firebrand. "Well, *that* could have gone better."

23

"The regulators are fried because when he disrupted the energy flow it overloaded the system," Ensign Tileah said. Her voice was muffled from the enviro-suit and the comm link was dipping in and out. Evie made a mental note to notify Zaal as soon as their conversation was over.

"How bad?" she asked.

"I don't know yet, it's a mess out here. I'm going to need at least a full crew to come out and assist. If this had been inside the ship –ere we have gravity and air, I'd say we could fix it in a day. But out here, y—bly looking at three or four."

Evie ran her fingers across her eyebrows, massaging the skin. A headache had bloomed sometime in the past hour and had decided to stay for a visit. "And there's nothing we can do from the inside of the ship?"

"Not without removing –st of the internal hull plating. Which would expose the ship to the vacuum anyway." She could hear frustration in Tileah's voice, and she couldn't blame her. She was the weapons bay senior and knew the systems as well as anyone, including Lieutenant Uuma. But this wasn't just the defense grid overloading. Vrij had crippled the primary power conduits to the main blade and dart systems. Which meant other than the spacewings they were defenseless. Not to mention Engineering was *still* trying to get the undercurrent system back up and running. The crack in the emitter was worse than they'd originally suspected.

"Do what you can, I'll notify Engineering to have a crew meet you out there as soon as one is available. Until then, get back inside and conserve your oxygen."

"Yes, Captain," Tileah said. She cut the comm and Evie was left in silence. She tilted her head back, closing her eyes. The pressure of the headache abated as she laid her arm across her eyes, blocking out what little light filtered through her eyelids. How had Greene done this? She'd heard of his exploits back on the *USCS Sims*, which had been an exploratory vessel. It had run into some kind of spatial eddy, disabling the ship. But Greene's quick thinking and assumption of temporary command when the captain was hurt had led to zero loss of life and the ship being salvaged before the eddy could destroy it. The story was stuff of legends in the academy circles and had been one of the reasons Evie had been so excited to serve with him on *Tempest*.

In many ways this situation was similar, except they'd already lost twenty-two crew members to the ravages of these unknown aliens. It had been something of a miracle the Bulaq attacks hadn't cost them anyone. "What would you do?" she whispered into the ether. She felt like everything was balanced on the edge of a knife, and if she pushed too hard or stepped too far, it would all tumble off one side or the other.

The chime on her door rang, sending a shockwave of pain through her mind. She sighed and rubbed her eyes before resetting herself. *Get it together. You're the captain now.* "Come in."

Cas entered with a strange look on his face. She would almost have called it apologetic, but there was something else there too. Something she didn't like the look of. "Captain," he said, taking a seat.

"Tell me you have good news from the meeting," she replied.

"Sort of." She listened as he gave her a rundown of his discussion with Diamant, the pressure in her head increasing the longer he spoke. When he was done, he didn't meet her gaze.

She sat back in her chair, regarding him. "For someone who spent thirty days or more studying under one of the best negotiators in the Coalition you are terrible at getting people to do what you want."

A smile spread across his face. "I know it isn't what you wanted to hear. He threw me for a loop. Doesn't this fall under the asylum clause?"

She sighed, thinking back. Technically when a person or group of people requested asylum it was in a need for protection from a mutual enemy or because they were fleeing persecution. In this case the entire Bulaq race was the victim of an unprecedented attack which left them destitute. She could see how the law could be interpreted to cover such an event. "Did he say anything else about the aliens? About why they attacked? Or anything we might be able to use against them?"

Cas shook his head. "We didn't get into it. He told us most everything back on the Hub. But I'm sure there's more. I don't think he ever tells the whole truth about anything. He's always got something in his back pocket to negotiate with."

"*If* we can fix the engines and get back to Coalition space and he can present *everything* he has to the Coalition Council about *Andromeda* then I'm sure they'd be willing to take it under advisement. But the odds of that happening seem slim. I just got off the comm with Tileah and the weapons are in bad shape. Which means I have to pull maintenance crews who should be working on the engines off their assignments to help with our defense, in case we get raided again while we're sitting out here being completely obvious and visible." She stood and walked to the small food distributor on the far wall. "Coffee." The small slot opened to reveal a stainless-steel tumbler, steam rising from the small hole in the top. "I just don't know."

"And you think allowing them access to the mess hall is a good idea?"

"I think it's better than keeping them confined like animals which isn't doing anything to help the goodwill between us. I'm not saying let them all in there at once, but maybe one or two at a time." His posture was tense; he didn't like the idea either but what else could they do? Antagonize them further?

"And what about allowing them to help? Because Diamant is right. It *will* take weeks. If not longer. And we have no idea where the aliens are, if they're already back on course to the Coalition or if they're out here somewhere, waiting on us. Or both for all I know."

He shook his head. "I think if they were still out here we'd know about it by now. They seemed interested enough back at Omicron Terminus. I think if they still had ships in the vicinity they would have attacked when we were disabled."

"How do you know they're not biding their time?" She took a sip of the coffee. It burned the edge of her tongue, but she didn't care. She needed *something* to take this headache away.

He shrugged. "I don't. But if that ship we destroyed back there was meant to lie in wait for us, they probably figured they didn't need more than one. They probably thought we were easy prey."

She took another sip. Cas had told her all about their expedition to the ship "hiding in time" as he put it. But if the ship was meant to capture them, why had it allowed him, Zenfor and Jann to board and walk around without being captured? He'd said the ship seemed empty, but it obviously hadn't been when it started pursuing them. So, what had been the point? He could be right, it might have been the only ship they'd left behind, which meant the rest of them were already on their way. Which also meant they couldn't waste any time getting back ahead of them. The Coalition needed to know they were dealing with a temporal enemy; one that could open and hold pockets of slowed-down time. And unless they could rebuild the communications grid the only way the Coalition would find out was if *Tempest* got home.

"I don't think we can afford to play this safe. I think we're going to have to take the risk." Cas glanced up at her. "Tell Diamant we're willing to allow his people to help, but on a *limited* basis only. I'll be assigning two security personnel to each Bulaq and they are to work in non-restricted areas of the ship only. Nothing in Engineering. Nothing close to the weapons. Get them to repair the holes in the hull and working on the environmental systems on the lower decks. We'll give this a try. If everything goes well, maybe we can talk about the future of our two peoples." Was it the right call? She couldn't say for sure. But it was what they needed. They had all the parts to fix the ship, so she might as well put all the hands to use. Though it might require some creative shuffling of personnel to make sure the Bulaq were monitored.

Cas nodded. "I think that's the right call. At least for now. And hey, if the other Bulaq attack while Diamant is aboard, we'll know his influence isn't as wide as he thought."

She scoffed. "I'm going to put Rafnkell and the other pilots on continuous rotation until the ship's weapons are back up and running. And especially while we have people outside of the ship working. We can't afford to be caught off guard out here." Cas stood. "Was there anything else?"

Cas hesitated for a moment but shook his head. "Just something Vrij said. But I think it's just bad blood between him and Diamant. Not that we can trust him anyway. Did you figure out how he got outside the ship yet?"

"Oh, you'll love this," Evie said, picking up a small holo bar and handing it to Cas. "He completely disassembled his room. Somehow, he cut through the galvanium in the walls to get to the window, but before he did that he set up false readings for all the automatic sensors in there. When he finally opened the room to the outside there was a short decompression, but he'd anchored everything and himself, so it didn't blast into space. We found mandible marks on the floor where he'd held himself down."

"Damn," Cas whispered. "That's an impressive bit of work."

"Yeah," she said, taking the holo bar back. "Let's just hope they can assemble as fast as they disassemble."

24

Zenfor glanced over as the main door to Engineering rolled away, revealing Cas. He spotted her and made his way over, a determined look on his face. She wasn't scared or nervous, only disappointed in her performance. Or lack thereof. Though she probably wouldn't have been so eager to tell him had Sesster not been so supportive. He provided a level of stability she hadn't felt since Mil'less left and she found she could draw strength from it.

You are making the right decision. I'm right here if you need me.

"What's the story?" Cas asked as he approached. "And why couldn't you just tell me over the comm?"

"Because this is something you don't want getting out. Not yet," she said. "My engine enhancements are irreparable. Either I rebuild the undercurrent engine from scratch, or we use Sesster's technology. But we will not be returning to the Coalition anytime soon."

His face was unreadable, which was surprising for someone as volatile as Caspian. She'd expected him to ask for an explanation, but instead he stood there, watching her. Any shame she felt at not being able to complete the task she pushed down deep within.

He isn't angry. Only trying to figure out what to do, Sesster said.

Angry she could handle. It was this silence she found so infuriating. "There's no chance?" Caspian asked.

She shook her head. "I've been working on simulations every day since the attack. But it wasn't until we managed to return to Engineering before I could confirm my suspicions."

"Which means best-case scenario we're at least a season away from the furthest edge of Coalition space. And at least two from the inner systems." He cursed, turning away from her. "This complicates things. The Bulaq have just requested asylum. What is the status of the regular undercurrent engines?" He nodded, as if hearing something that wasn't being said.

Zenfor glanced up to Sesster. *Are you telling him the truth?*

Of course. It has always been our policy to be honest. The situation could be much worse; I'm glad this is all there is.

Zenfor was glad too. Now that her engine upgrades were no longer working she'd resigned herself to stay in Engineering and help with the repair efforts. With so many of the crew lost, everything was taking longer than it should, and the people around her were overworked and prone to making more mistakes than normal.

"Okay," Caspian said, turning back to her. "Thanks for your honesty. Now *I* get to go tell the captain." He said it in a cheerful voice but with a tone that suggested anything but. These people were a strange crop of contradictions. "If anything changes, let me know." He paused before leaving. "And thanks for getting us this far. Couldn't have done it without you."

After he'd left, Sesster returned to her mind. *The humans can be volatile, but they can also be very fair. It's something we admire about them.*

I didn't need the ego boost. But I was glad to see him take it so well. She turned back to him. *What's funny is I see many more common threads between our two people than us and the humans. Despite our physical similarities.*

She felt what she could only describe as the breath of something that wasn't there move through her. *I wonder what would have happened had your people come upon my planet instead of the humans all those years ago,* Sesster said. *Would we now be in an alliance with you, our technologies working together? Or would you have subjugated us, as you have so many other species?*

Zenfor twisted her face. She couldn't help but hear the unspoken accusation and, while accurate, it still stung. The Sil had never come upon another species with anything close to their level of technological sophistication. Except for the Claxians. The Sanctuary had first learned of the Coalition and its many world members during the initial conflict with them over a hundred years ago and at that time deemed the Coalition beneath their notice. They were to be ignored unless actively provoking the Sil and even then, only minimal resources would be used to refute any kind of contact. Zenfor remembered reading the reports when she first became consul. She needed to have a familiarity with the Coalition as her patrol area included a large swath of Sil space closest to where the Coalition drew their own boundaries. And buried deep inside those reports was the mention of a member race of the Coalition: the Claxians. Not much was known at the time other than they helped provide the technological backbone for the Coalition and were thus considered a higher priority target if war ever did come. But Zenfor saw something different. She saw the only kindred species the Sil had ever encountered. But because they were part of the Coalition, no one wanted to consider the possibility they might be equals. Zenfor would be lying to herself if part of the reason she'd decided to come aboard the *Tempest* wasn't because of Sesster.

It's a difficult question to answer. Would you have allowed yourselves to be subjugated?

Sesster was silent for a moment. *I don't believe so. From what I understand of the Sil they only require other species to remain on their planets and keep to themselves. Which is something that comes naturally to Claxians. Before the humans we were content on Claxia Prime. Most of my people remain there with few of us leaving the comfort of the planet.* She glanced up to see his arms moving across four different systems and wondered how he could focus on so many different tasks at once.

It comes naturally to us. We are born multitaskers.

Zenfor returned to her console. *I'm glad we didn't find you first. Imagine all your ingenuity and knowledge locked away on your planet. I feel as though the universe would be less whole without you as a part of the fabric.*

And what of the species inside Sil space? Do they not also possess the capability to contribute to the galactic collective?

That's different, she thought. *Those species have nothing valuable to offer. They're inferior.*

How do you know?

The question made her pause for a moment. She knew because it was what she'd been told by the Sanctuary. It wasn't as if she'd actually visited any of the dozens of inhabited planets inside Sil space. Everything was about Thislea and the supply depots. She'd never had the desire to visit anywhere else. Her purpose was to patrol her area of space for the designated time, then return back to Thislea once the assignment was over so the next Consul could take over. And then once all her work was done, she'd be able to rest with those closest to her, for that was the reward of a life of hard work. The last of life spent in leisure and family rearing.

There was no reason to travel to any of the other planets. It just wasn't done. So then why did she have a lingering doubt all of a sudden?

For the first time in her life, Zenfor questioned if the Sanctuary had told her the entire truth. *No.* She shook her head. The Sil weren't like the Coalition. They were harmonious and had been for ten thousand years. The Sanctuary wasn't keeping anything from them, it was just how things were.

I hope you're right. But I feel I must defend my own people. The Coalition is harmonious as well. We haven't been around for as long, but for an organization that has stood the test of over two millennia, I'd say we've managed well.

Oh? Zenfor asked. *Then why did you allow Admiral Rutledge to violate our borders and then work so hard to cover it up?*

She felt a strange sensation of confusion wash over her. *What are you talking about?*

For some reason she'd become angry. As if Sesster's assertion that the Coalition was as stable as the Empire was an insult to everything they'd accomplished. *I'm talking about how your Admiral took his ship into our territory and tried to capture one of our ships. And when he failed, thanks to Caspian, he hired another captain who could do the job for him. We lost ten Sil the day they finally took the ship. And all for what? A weapon you couldn't even understand or re-create?*

The air in Engineering had gone deathly still. Zenfor glanced back up to see Sesster had frozen in place. Other people in Engineering had begun to take notice as well, some of them craning their necks to see what was going on. *You're not lying,* he finally said. He hadn't known. They'd kept the information from him, and he hadn't been aware of Admiral Rutledge's betrayal. *How high does it go?* he asked.

I don't know. I suspect more of your admirals know. And of course Caspian and the captain are aware.

This can't be true, he said, desperation in his voice. *I have no doubt you believe this, but it cannot be true.*

For the briefest of moments guilt gnawed at her for revealing the secret, before that emotion was replaced with one of outrage. How dare they keep something this important from one of the key members of the crew. *No one* had told him. Not the captain, not Caspian, not anyone. And all for what? *Why keep you in the dark?* Sesster was silent and she was unable to detect any of his thoughts. *You have every right to be upset. They should have trusted you. And it shouldn't have taken me to tell you.* She finally understood why the Sanctuary had a difficult time coming to a decision regarding the information the Coalition had provided: they couldn't be sure if it wasn't an elaborate ruse. They knew more about the Coalition than they let on. And Zenfor had made the decision to come along without that information. But knowing that they kept these kinds of secrets from even their founding members put everything into perspective for her. She clenched her fists and stood, intent on making this right.

Don't do anything, Sesster said in her mind.

"No," she replied aloud. "This is wrong, and they are not going to treat you this way anymore." She noticed Lieutenant Tyler glance over at her words. He stood from his station and made his way over to them.

"Consul, is there something wrong?" he asked.

"Did you know as well?" she demanded. "Did you keep the truth from him too?"

If he'd known I would have seen it in his mind, Sesster said.

"Ugh," Zenfor said, pushing past Tyler.

"Know what? Where are you going?" he asked.

"I don't answer to you," she replied without looking back. This betrayal would not go unpunished. And she would make sure every person on this ship knew the truth before it was over.

25

Cas took a deep breath as the hypervator made its way from the Engineering level to the bridge. Zenfor's news had hit him square in the face and he was still feeling the shock. But he hadn't wanted to react in Engineering. Going off about something none of them could control would do nothing but shake what little confidence the crew had in him. He trusted Zenfor; if she said she couldn't do it, he had to take those words at face value. He was also aware at how much she hated admitting she couldn't do something. But it brought on a whole new set of problems. With no quick way back to the Coalition they couldn't afford to hand off the supplies to the Bulaq anymore. After he informed the captain, he'd have to speak with Diamant and let him know the terms of their agreement would need to be changed once again. And if Diamant didn't like it then that was *his* problem. Because the man had already lied about his true intentions. Cas was almost to the point where he could just pretend he hadn't heard Diamant's request for transport and they could just kick them all off the ship and keep the materials for themselves.

He felt under his jacket for his boomcannon, remembering he wasn't allowed to carry it around the ship; he'd had to stow it as soon as they'd returned. This place wasn't like the Sargan Commonwealth. He couldn't just steal all those materials without compensation, no matter how much he wanted too. But sometimes old habits died hard. He might have to do the job Evie couldn't, yet again.

The hypervator paused, and the doors opened to reveal a grim-looking Lieutenant Yamashita.

"Lieutenant." Cas nodded as she stepped inside. "Finally catch up on your sleep?"

"Screw you," she replied.

"Now wait a second—" Not only was she breaking protocol by disrespecting a superior officer, but she was putting her career in jeopardy. Not that Cas would report her on something so minor, but someone else might not be as forgiving.

"You brought them on board," she snapped. "It's because of your terrible skills as a negotiator we're even in this mess."

"What are you talking about?" Cas asked. Things hadn't been great since bringing the Bulaq back, but he wouldn't exactly call it a mess. They had one rogue who'd gone out and disabled the weapons systems, so what? It wasn't anything that couldn't be fixed with enough time and people.

She faced him. "I just got back from the outer hull, working on the damaged systems with Rafnkell. Guess what we found?" He shrugged. "There's indications of more than one Bulaq using their mandibles to walk around out there. We've got two sets of 'prints.'"

"Wait, so Vrij really was chasing someone out there?"

"Looks that way. Or maybe they were in it together and he's the only one who got caught. I went back and checked his quarters. The indentations he made in the floor when he decompressed the room are different than the indentations all around the weapons systems. He wasn't the one who disabled them. It was someone who didn't have mechanical mandibles."

The door of the hypervator slid open to reveal the bridge. Evie sat in the command chair and Cas noted bags under her eyes as she turned to them. Her eyes widened in surprised and without saying a word she made her way to the command room, indicating they follow. Cas really did not want to drop all this news on her at once, but what choice did they have? The Bulaq were increasingly becoming a problem and no matter what they'd requested they needed to be removed from the ship at once.

"Well," Evie said, circling her desk and taking a seat. "I'm sure whatever you've got to report can't be good so let me be the first to say that Cas, you were right. The Bulaq are good workers and seem to be holding up their end of the bargain. I've got them working on low-security systems all over the ship, still under guard, though I'm not sure it's necessary." She rubbed her eyes as she leaned back. "Okay, whichever one has the worse news go first."

Cas cursed under his breath, looking at Laura. He indicated she make her report. She pursed her lips at him then turned to the captain. "We've found evidence a Bulaq *other than* Vrij damaged the weapon systems. And before you ask the evidence is solid. It wasn't just him. He could have been assisting or he could have been pursuing, as he claims."

Evie leaned forward; her eyes wide. "That's distressing." She turned to Cas. "I'm assuming you didn't come here to tell me the same thing."

Cas shook his head. "We have another issue. Zenfor just told me her engine upgrades can't be repaired. She'd have to rebuild the undercurrent system from scratch. So unfortunately it's the long way home."

Evie stared at him. "How is that any better?" she shouted. "I said the *worse* news go first!"

"I didn't know his news," Laura replied.

"This is getting out of hand." Evie stood again. "Is there any way to find out *who* sabotaged the weapons?"

Laura shrugged. "We could perform DNA tests. It's possible some residue was left behind where they punctured the hull over and over. But the marks were made by organic mandibles, they don't match the puncture marks in Vrij's room made by his mechanical ones."

"Which means Diamant was lying. *Again*," Evie said. "Unless he's got a rogue, which I highly doubt."

Cas couldn't help but feel responsible. Each time Diamant had been a step ahead of him, making him think he had the upper hand when in reality he was nothing more than a means to an end for Diamant. Why did Cas want to trust him? Because he'd been a military leader of his people? Or because he'd survived a horrific incident where everyone else had perished? Maybe a combination of both. He'd thought Diamant was truly putting the interests of his people above his own, but now he wasn't so sure. Even Rutledge, in all his betrayals had put the good of the Coalition above all else. Cas found it telling that he no longer made the same assumption about Diamant.

"Okay. Here's what we're going to do," Evie said, her palms on her desk as she leaned over it. "First I want to get—"

The door to the room slid open, large, blue hands forcing it apart the last few centimeters. Standing in the middle of the doorway was Zenfor, her eyes like fire. Uuma lay on the ground behind her, apparently the recipient of one of Zenfor's fists to the face; something with which Cas was all too familiar. "Shit," he said. He'd seen this look in her eyes before and he instinctively put himself between the Sil and Evie and Laura.

Cas held out his hands. "I can see you're upset. Tell me what's going on." He glanced to Uuma who held her head with one hand while Zaal bent over her.

"*You,*" Zenfor seethed. "All of you are nothing but a group of dishonorable liars. You pretend to join hands in this *great* Coalition, professing cooperation and trust all the while you're doing nothing but keeping secrets from each other."

"What are you—" Evie began.

"I'm talking about *Rutledge* and the *Achlys*. The fact your chief engineer doesn't know the story tells me all I need to really know about the Coalition. I never should have come on this ship. And I certainly never should have helped you."

"No," Cas heard Evie whisper. "You told him?"

"A job you should have done," she replied, taking three steps forward. She was close enough to Cas to pick him up and toss him to the side, but he stood his ground. "He knew *nothing*. And I want to know why."

"What is she talking about?" Laura asked.

A sound like a hoarse laugh came from Zenfor's throat. "You don't even tell your lover? I should have suspected as much from a race of cowards. The Sanctuary was right, you are not worth our time and I hope this threat destroys you all."

Cas kept his eyes on Zenfor. She was fast and if she started to rampage there was probably nothing he could do about it, but it was important he stood his ground. He couldn't see Evie and so he didn't know if Zenfor's knowledge of her relationship with Laura came as a surprise or not.

"Consul. I will not be threatened on my own ship," Evie said. "Now either stand down or I will have you removed from this bridge." Cas had to give her points for bravery. He wasn't sure he would have stopped himself from calling security immediately after her outburst.

"Why should I listen to an inferior, worthless—"

"Consul, *stand down* or be removed. That is my final warning."

Cas was pressed close to Laura as Zenfor had backed them both up against the desk and he could feel her breath on the back of his neck. He pushed away any inappropriate fleeting thoughts and instead focused on Zenfor's rage, his eyes not leaving hers. "Allow her to speak," he said. "Please."

Zenfor took a step back, but her face was set in a heavy grimace. "You have two minutes."

Cas relaxed as Evie stood from her chair and walked around the Sil, to the outer bridge. She knelt over Uuma, said something in a low voice Cas didn't catch, then returned to her desk. She tapped a button on the desk. "Sickbay, please send Box to the bridge for first aid. Diazal out." Once the doors had closed she turned to Zenfor. "Have a seat."

Zenfor stood where she was. Cas moved out of the space between them while Laura remained on the other side. She looked like she wasn't sure where she was supposed to be, if she was supposed to be here at all. But Cas wasn't going to interfere.

"You are correct, we have not told Sesster or most of the crew the truth behind what really happened with Rutledge and the *Achlys*. This is partly because we are under orders not to, but also because with the *Andromeda* threat, the last thing the Coalition needs is an internal fracture. And make no mistake, there would be a fracture. As soon as the Claxians find out what the humans did, it would split the Coalition in two. One of our main tenants has always been peaceful exploration based on the Claxian policy of peace and non-aggression. This doesn't include going into another species' territory, capturing one of their ships and ejecting their crew into space. That in fact is considered a sapient crime and is punishable under imprisonment for life through the Coalition Charter."

"Then why did you allow it to happen in the first place?" Zenfor growled.

"What?" Laura whispered.

Evie glanced to her, sorrow in her eyes for a brief moment before returning her attention to Zenfor. "Most *humans* don't even know about it. It was a clandestine operation conjured up and executed by a few high-ranking individuals, including Admiral Rutledge. Even we don't know how high it goes." She indicated her and Cas.

"This is no excuse. You should have told him. You should have told *her*." She indicated Laura. "Your greatest threat is not these aliens, it is yourselves. You will tear yourselves apart from the inside and when you're gone, the Sil will rejoice as the universe will be less infected." She sneered and turned, exiting in a hurry.

Evie nodded to Cas. "Go after her. Make sure she doesn't hurt anyone."

He took one last look at the two of them and followed Zenfor out. He was glad he wasn't the one who had to explain themselves to Laura.

Cas took another look at Uuma who held her head while Zaal continued to tend to her. "Is she okay?" Cas asked.

"I'm not a doctor," he replied. "My knowledge of biology is limited." *I guess that's as good of an answer as I'm going to get.*

"Hey, watch out, robot coming through!" Cas glanced up to see Zenfor pushing past Box who'd just stepped off the hypervator.

"Hold that door!" he yelled but it closed before Box could wrap his fingers around it.

"What did you *do*?" Box asked, glancing at Uuma on the ground and then back at the hypervator door.

"Why do you always assume it's me?" Cas ran past him. "Computer, override hypervator and return it to this level.

Authorization Robeaux four-nine alpha." There was the buzzing sound of an error.

"The authorization overrides are offline," Zaal said as Box leaned over Uuma, inspecting her head. "We're working on getting them back up and running."

"*Fuck,*" Cas said under his breath and ran to the other hypervator. "Can you at least track her?"

Zaal stood and returned to his station. "She's getting off on level six, crew quarters."

Adrenaline shot through Cas's system. "Her own or someone else's?"

"Her own."

Cas took a breath. Thank goodness for small favors. Still, he couldn't let her stew. He had to try and fix this. The doors opened and he announced his destination, hoping they hadn't just lost everything they'd built.

26

"I understand."

Evie glanced up from her desk, after spending the last few moments trying to gather her thoughts. "What?"

"I understand why you didn't say anything." Laura slumped against the wall, staring at her hands. "You had your orders. You didn't have a choice."

Evie took a deep breath, standing. "No. I *should* have said something. I should have trusted you with the truth. I *do* trust you with the truth. It's just...there's been so much going on lately and we're still in this weird new place. I just—"

"Didn't want to screw anything up."

Evie nodded. "Yeah." She walked around the other side of the table, sitting on the edge. "I'm not very good at relationship stuff. I thought when you went off with Cas and the others it was because I was so late to dinner the other night."

Laura scoffed. "Do you really think I'm that shallow? You're the captain! Of course you're going to be late to dinner."

Evie pulled her lips between her teeth, ashamed. "It's just...I've never had a long-term relationship. They've never worked out before. And I guess I'm just not sure what's considered okay or not."

Laura's eyes met hers. "There's only two things that will do it: if you tell me it's over and that's your final decision. Or that I can see you don't care anymore and are just going through the motions. But other than that." She shrugged. "Fair game."

Evie chuckled. "Anyone ever tell you you're pretty great?" She walked over and wrapped Laura in a warm embrace.

"Someone has now; that's all that matters," she replied. Evie could stay here forever, holding on, just remaining in this place. But there wasn't time. There was more than one crisis on this ship, and she couldn't afford to linger. She let go, staring into Laura's dark eyes.

"I'm sorry I didn't tell you."

"Did we really attack a Sil ship unprovoked?" she whispered.

"Unfortunately. But right now, I've got to check on Sesster. I don't know how he's taking this, and I need to speak with him before he withdraws into himself permanently. Can you do something for me?"

"Anything."

"Until Uuma is back on her feet, I need you to find the location of every Bulaq on the ship, make sure we aren't missing any and they aren't out there crawling around the hull. If they've been out there before there's a good chance they'll head out again, if they're not already. We need to figure out what Diamant is doing. Once you have a location on all of them, let me know."

Laura nodded. "Got it. Anything else?"

Evie made it to the door. "Don't let anyone know what you're doing. I don't want to tip them off before we're ready. I feel like we might have accidentally invited a virus on board, and we need to kill it before it gets any worse."

"Got it."

They left the command room, one after another with Laura heading for the empty tactical station. Evie stopped over Box who was examining Karen's head. "How is she?"

"Bruised, but no permanent damage. I'm administering something for the pain," he replied. He glanced at Evie. Then at Laura. Then back at Evie. "Wait a second. What was going on in there? Nothing scandalous I hope." One of his optics winked.

"You wish," Evie replied. She made her way over to the hypervator. "Where's Zenfor? And Cas?"

"Crew quarters, deck six," Zaal replied. That was good. At least she wasn't terrorizing the ship. Or telling every person she encountered how the Coalition as nothing but a dishonest organization. But could Evie really blame her if she did? It was the truth after all. A truth she'd been complicit in obfuscating from certain individuals. She didn't like how that sat in the pit of her stomach. She only hoped it wasn't too late to speak with Sesster.

***

Before Evie even reached Engineering, the call from Tyler came through.

"I don't know what's going on, he's just frozen up. He won't talk to me and he won't move. I don't know what to do."

"Stay there, I'm on my way." She'd just stepped off the hypervator and had only a few meters to Engineering. What would she say? Would it even do any good to apologize? Not if the apology was hollow. No, she needed to be better than that. She'd intentionally kept vital information from a senior member of the crew. It didn't matter if it was under orders or not, he'd had a right to know.

The door to Engineering rolled away to reveal most of the crew standing in small groups, conversing. Tyler jogged up to her, confusion across his face. "I don't know what to tell you, Captain. He's been like that ever since the Sil left. She was agitated about something."

"I've spoken to her," Evie replied. She walked around Tyler, keeping her focus on Sesster. "Commander, can you hear me? I need you to respond." If he did hear her, he didn't move. Talking to a Claxian was difficult enough when they weren't upset. How was she supposed to speak with him if he'd withdrawn into his own mind? It wasn't as if she could make him focus on her. "Commander, I need to speak with you. I have a lot of explaining to do. Please allow me to make my case."

"Case for what?" Tyler asked.

Evie took a breath. "I'll tell you as soon as the commander is informed. He has the first right to know." She turned back to Sesster. "I'd rather not but I will make this an order if I have to."

A strange sensation came over Evie and the walls around her began to melt away, as if they were ice on a hot day. The entire room shimmered, and she was standing back on Sissk in the hot daytime sun, shielding her eyes against the blinding light. Their past few sessions she'd managed to "skip over" this part of her visions, though this time it seemed she no longer had that capability. Though this also wasn't exactly like her previous encounters. The terrain was flatter, with no mountains in the distance, and no cities either. And this time it seemed hotter. She'd already begun to sweat in the few seconds she'd been out here. She turned around to see the physical representation of Sesster standing off in the distance, staring at the blazing sun.

Shielding her eyes, she approached him. "How can you stand to stare into it like that?" she asked.

"It all looks the same to me," he replied.

"Sesster, I'm sorry. I should have told you. But I'd be lying if I thought it was a good idea. What happened? Did Zenfor let it slip?"

He turned to her. "Do not blame Zenfor. She was only being honest with me."

"I'm not," Evie replied, her hands out, supplicant. "I just mean *I* should have been the one to tell you, not her. It's my duty as your commanding officer to make sure my crew is informed about our missions."

"Why didn't you tell me?" His blank eyes bored into her.

"Greene and I considered it, even though we were under orders not to speak about it to anyone. But we thought if you knew you'd feel obligated to tell your people back on Claxia Prime. And once word got out what the humans had done, it would set off a chain reaction that could result in a rift spreading throughout the Coalition. With the Sargans pressing in on one side and this unknown threat on the other, we decided it wasn't the best time."

His nostrils flared. "*You* decided. You thought it would be more convenient to leave me in the dark," he said, his voice louder than she'd ever heard it.

"Yes," she replied. "For the time being." He made a sound of disgust and turned away from her. "I was a willing participant in this coverup, I know that now. But when we made the decision I thought I was doing it to protect the Coalition. But I get it now. The cracks of division were already there, otherwise Rutledge and the others would have informed the Council and there would have been a vote on the matter. But he knew it would never happen and he was paranoid about the very kind of threat we're facing right now. I didn't come up with the idea and I didn't initiate it, but I helped cover it up. It shouldn't have happened and I'm *sorry*."

Sesster kept his back to her, and she noticed his back rising and falling indicating deep, measured breaths. "It's illegal," he finally said.

"I know. Rutledge has already been punished. The others—they're too high up."

"How many others?"

She shook her head. It was a question she wished she could answer herself. "I don't know. But I think it goes to the top. Or at least close. Cas thinks some of the people at his hearing knew."

He turned back to her; his white eyes locked on her own. "I can feel your guilt and remorse so I know it's real, but I don't know if this is something I can forgive. I don't know that I can trust you again."

She took a few steps closer to him, the heat really beating down on her, but at the moment she didn't care. "I know I failed you. It should have been the first thing I did as captain; issue a general alert and inform the crew. Even though I was under orders, I should have spoken out. Greene seemed to think it was best we sit on it but…I'm not sure he was right about that." Greene was a great captain, one of the best, but it didn't mean he was infallible. Maybe that's where she had gone wrong: to think this man could make no mistake, that he would never take the incorrect path. Because as much as she wanted to live up to his legacy, she didn't want to hide things from her crew, even if they could be damaging to the Coalition. She needed to keep her crew's trust, and the only way to do that was to be completely honest with them. About all of it.

"You already know my deepest secrets; you have to know that I trust you otherwise I never would have continued these sessions. You know more about my past than anyone on this ship; probably anyone alive. Please believe me when I say I trust you, implicitly."

He stared at her. "Captain, I—" He took a breath, looked up, then reset himself and stared at her again. "You may not be completely at fault. I think I may have also been willfully ignorant about this issue."

"What do you mean?"

"When Caspian first came aboard I could sense he was holding something back. I could have seen it, but I chose not to, I chose to pull back so he wouldn't have to show it to me. I sensed it was something personal and dark, but also potentially damaging for innocent people. At the time I thought it would be better not to know."

"And now?" She squinted. If they didn't get out of the sun soon her skin was going to catch on fire.

"Now I'd rather know the horrible truth, than a convenient lie."

"I will be issuing a ship-wide announcement as soon as these Bulaq are off the ship. This is something the entire crew deserves to know, damn the Coalition's orders. I'm sorry it's taken me this long to see that. But before I can do that, we have to do something about our visitors. We've discovered they may be working to undermine us, and I can't allow them to disable this ship, whatever their reasons. Will you help me?"

Her surroundings melted away again, revealing Engineering around her as she stared up at the giant Claxian. The sun was gone, though the sweat on her forehead and tingle on her skin remained, as if she'd really been out in that sun. One of Sesster's appendages lifted up to "look" at her. *I will help you, captain. It is my job.*

"Thank you," she replied. "Just...thank you."

27

Cas took a deep breath and tapped the button beside the door. There was no response. He tapped it again but there was nothing. Using the override codes entered his mind until he remembered they were offline. And even if they weren't, he couldn't barge in on her. But he had to make this right. Without Zenfor's help, he seriously doubted their ability to get back to Coalition space. They were already down almost a fifth of the crew.

Instead of tapping the button again he pounded on the door. He should have brought Box down here with him; he could have made plenty of noise. On his fourth round of bangs just when he thought his hand might break from how hard he was going at it, the doors slid open, causing him to miss the last hit and topple forward. Zenfor caught his fist in her hand and pushed him back with a shove hard enough to cause him to almost lose his balance in the other direction.

"I am getting sick of finding you unannounced at my doorstep," she said.

"Let me explain this," he pleaded, not crossing the threshold of her room.

She only stared at him; her nostrils flaring. "What's there to explain? You hid the mission—against my people—from your own. It speaks volumes about your trustworthiness."

"Yes, *I* made the conscious decision not to tell Sesster. As did Evie and Greene. Imagine if he had known before we returned to Sil space to speak with you. We never would have made it. There would have been a formal inquiry and it would have been all over the media outlets. And these *things* would still be out here and on their way to the Coalition, with nothing between them and trillions of lives. It all would have been buried. We didn't tell him not because we couldn't trust him, but because we trusted him too much to do the right thing. Humans are fallible, Claxians aren't."

Her features softened. "He spoke of that to me. How you all look to the Claxians for guidance. You place them on pedestals. You should have told him; you might be surprised at the outcome."

"Maybe. And I know it was wrong. Trust me, I absolutely know. But what I find more interesting about all this is you." He braced himself. He never could be quite sure when a hit was coming, and he didn't want to be caught off-guard again.

"Me." Not quite a question and not quite a statement either. Though her features had grown dark.

"I remember a time when the internal politics of the Coalition didn't mean jack shit to you. You couldn't have cared less. And now you're up in arms over us not divulging classified information."

"It's different," she replied. "This is about trust between your crewmates. On my ship we don't keep secrets, it isn't efficient. The ship functions better as a whole if the crew is informed."

He stood his ground. "And what happens if the information is dangerous? What if you knew something that other Sil didn't want you to know? Would you still tell the crew? Would you put their lives in jeopardy for the sake of efficiency?"

She made a sound of disgust in her throat. "Our society doesn't work like that. The Sanctuary doesn't keep secrets from us. Everything is out in the open."

He scoffed. "I used to think the exact same thing about the Coalition."

Zenfor stomped into her room. "Why must everyone keep questioning me?" She slammed her hand down on the table in front of her, leaving a fist-sized dent in the metal. Cas remained at the threshold. "Well, are you coming in or are you going to stand there gawking?"

He stepped inside; the door sliding closed behind her. It was darker in here; she'd turned down the luminosity of the lights about sixty percent. He supposed it reminded her of the darkness of the Sil ships.

"I am so tired of this," she finally said. "I am tired of being here, of being away from my people. I never thought—"

"That it would be this hard?" Cas offered.

"I'm not afraid of hard." She slumped down in one of the chairs. "It's all this *breathing,* sleeping, and *eating*. It's exhausting. It's a wonder you people get anything done in your day. Most of your time is dedicated to personal maintenance; to make sure your bodies don't seize up on you."

He approached cautiously. "I still can't believe you stay in those suits all the time. Don't your people ever get tired of that?"

She made a hand gesture Cas didn't recognize. He wasn't sure if it was a rude symbol to him or something unrelated. He tried not to think about it too hard. "The suits are a requirement for military service, not the civilian population, though some still wear them outside of the ships. Usually they're veterans but there will be the odd experimenter. Children obviously don't know the ease yet. We do all the things you do; *I* haven't done them for a very long time. And when I did remove it, I would have been in comfortable settings surrounded by those I know. Becoming consul determined my life. And I am dedicated to it until the day I die or am forced to retire."

"You're homesick," Cas said, his voice softer.

"If that means what I think it means then yes. I miss my people. Here things are...lonely."

"And you found a kindred spirit in Sesster. Someone else who is cut off from his own people. *That's* why you're so upset." She only glared at him with her gray eyes. He'd had it wrong. She wasn't going rogue; she was upset because they had hurt someone she cared about. Maybe the only person she cared about on the ship.

Cas's comm beeped. "Robeaux here."

"Cas, Laura just commed me. We're missing two Bulaq. We need to get these people off this ship before they sabotage us to the point we can't function anymore. Go get Vrij out of jail, he might be the only one of them we can trust. See if he can come up with some way to help us."

"How's Sesster?" Cas asked.

"I think we've reached an understanding. We'll deal with that later. For now, meet Laura down in the brig."

"Acknowledged," Cas replied, cutting his comm. He turned to Zenfor. "Well?"

"Well, what?"

Cas huffed. "Are you going to help us get these guys off this ship or not?"

"Why should I help you? You're the one who was stupid enough to bring them aboard."

"Because we needed the materials. If you have a better idea of how I should have handled—"

"Of course I do. You should have taken what you needed and blown their shuttle to ash." She smirked.

"That's not how we do things." Though he had to admit the thought had crossed his mind.

"Even with the evidence of what they've been doing in is staring you in the face, you're not willing to see what's really going on here. Those attacks weren't random. They were designed to make you desperate. So desperate you'd do anything to get what you needed for your repairs."

Cas went cold. What if she was right? What if Diamant had been behind the strafing attacks and it had all been a ploy to get them to approach him for the materials they needed? "Shit," he said. "Why didn't you say something before?" He ran for the door.

"I can't do everything on this ship myself. If you haven't noticed I've been busy trying to repair the engines!" She stood, a scowl on her face.

"Look, if you want to hit me, it's going to have to wait. I need to get Vrij out of jail. In the meantime—"

"In the meantime, I'll go back to Engineering and figure out a way to trap all these bastards right where they are," she replied.

"That works for me." It wasn't a full reversal, but it was as good as Cas was going to get from her. He only hoped Evie had made some real progress with Sesster. He might be the only person that could keep Zenfor from tearing the ship apart in frustration. Though it would be interesting to unleash her on the Bulaq ship. See what Diamant thought about *that*.

***

Seven and a half minutes later Cas walked into the brig to find Lieutenant Yamashita and Crewman Tes staring at Vrij through the barrier. Laura glanced back as Cas entered, her arms crossed and a sour look on her face.

"Are we sure this is a good idea?" she asked.

"The captain thinks it is, so this is what we're doing," Cas replied. Vrij had been right about Diamant. And if he'd been helping Lu'mat out on the hull, he'd done a poor job of hiding his involvement.

"H-he betrayed y-ou, d-didn't he?" Vrij said as Cas approached.

"Not yet. And we're not going to give him the opportunity. We found other indications the Bulaq were out on the hull, and two are missing at the moment."

"U-undercarriage," Vrij replied.

"What does that mean?"

"I think he means underneath the ship," Laura replied.

Cas eyed him. "What would they be doing down there?"

"Y-your lower s-security systems. They'll t-take those offline f-first. If h-he's p-planning something, h-he'll want to m-make sure the b-backups—the backups are o-off." Vrij winced, as if telling Cas this information hurt him.

"Fuck," Cas said. The security overrides. They were controlled by the backup control systems. Diamant's people must have already gotten to them. But how were they getting on the outside of the ship?

He walked over to the control panel, tapping the top drawer. Inside was Vrij's belt containing his *skin curtains* as he called them. "Get him out of there," Cas said to Crewman Tes, grabbing all the remaining canisters.

She nodded and released the barrier. Vrij stepped forward. "T-thank you." Cas tossed him the belt with his equipment, which Vrij replaced around his waist.

Laura's eyes narrowed. "Now what?"

"Now we get to Engineering without running into any of Diamant's people," Cas replied. He nodded to Tes. "Get me a secure channel to Zaal."

Her face twisted as she inputted the controls. "Looks like some of the security protocols are offline," she said. "That's not right."

"Damn, he's moving fast." Cas glanced at Laura and Vrij. "Let's get going. We've only got one level to go. Even if they are under escort, running into any of the Bulaq could trigger Diamant's plan when they see Vrij out of jail. We can't show our hand yet so stay alert." He returned his attention to Tes. "Lock down this area and don't let any of the Bulaq in, understand?"

"Yes, sir," she replied, drawing a weapon from a hidden compartment beneath her station. Cas nodded, indicating the other two follow him.

The hallway connecting to the main brig was quiet and empty. If Cas remembered correctly, there was a service access junction off the main corridor about a hundred meters down which should spit them out right beside main engineering. After checking again and listening carefully, he motioned for them to follow him as they quickly made their way down the corridor.

They kept a good pace, Vrij had no trouble keeping up and Cas thought they might make a clean exit. But as they reached the last corner that would lead them to the access hatch Cas thought he heard the low murmur of voices. He peeked around the corner to see Ensign Williams escorting one of the Bulaq directly toward them. He pulled back with a grimace on his face, silently communicating the other two they were too close to turn back. His mind groped for some place to hide Vrij in the few seconds they had but there was nothing. He didn't have a choice; they'd have to knock out the Bulaq. If they even could be knocked out.

"Get ready to take him," he whispered to Laura, then turned back to the corner. As Williams and the Bulaq turned the corner Cas stiffened. Williams' eyes went wide for a second upon seeing them as if they'd startled him but the Bulaq didn't seem to react.

"Oh, Commander. Lieutenant. I didn't hear you coming."
He turned to the Bulaq. "Have you met Draz'j?"

Cas looked at the man for any sign he was up to something
or surprised to see Vrij out of jail, but he remained impassive.
That's when he felt a tapping on his shoulder. Cas glanced
back to see only Laura, but no Vrij. "Wha—" he began, then
turned back to the other two. "—uh, no. I haven't. Caspian
Robeaux." Cas then indicated Laura. "Lieutenant Laura
Yamashita."

"Draz'j," the other man said, his voice bored.

"I'm escorting Draz'j to begin work on the hull breach just
below deck eleven," Williams said, too chipper.

"Great," Cas replied. "Well, thanks for the help." Draz'j
made a motion Cas didn't understand and he didn't care to.
He had the distinct impression it was a rude gesture and that
Draz'j was probably laughing at him under the surface. They
thought they had the upper hand. "I don't want to keep you.
Carry on, Ensign."

Williams nodded and continued to escort Draz'j along,
picking up the conversation where they'd left off as Williams
told him about the history of the ship and her name. As soon
as they were out of earshot Cas glanced around rapidly.
"Where did he go?" he whispered.

As soon as he asked Vrij landed right in front of him, his
legs flexing allowing for a silent landing. Cas jumped back,
startled, but then glanced up. In the ceiling fifteen meters
above them were tiny little puncture marks where Vrij had
been holding on with his mandibles. He'd been right, the
Bulaq could *jump*. Vrij grinned.

"Did he see you?" Cas asked. Vrij touched two fingers to
his forehead. "Good work." He glanced back at Laura who
was suppressing a grin. "C'mon. Let's get there before we run
into anyone else."

28

Evie stood at the back of Engineering, going over the astrometric data from what few scans they'd made on the way to where the ship currently sat. If they managed to get the Bulaq off the ship, they'd need to engage the engines to get out of range. Tyler had assured her they would be ready and even though Zenfor's upgrades were offline, they should be able to maintain an undercurrent for a short, sustained burst.

Even though she hadn't returned to the *mind-place* she'd sensed more calm emanating from Sesster, if that was possible. It could have been her own mind telling her what she wanted to hear, but the air in the room felt more at ease and so did she. His revelation that he hadn't looked into Cas's mind put her at ease. It meant that even Sesster knew the damage such information could do to the core of the Coalition. And for the first time Evie had to admit the organization she'd grown up revering had some serious cracks inside. Cracks which she had contributed to and willfully made larger without even realizing it. Cas had been right all along; the Coalition had a sickness and it was going to take a lot of hard work to make it better. Once all this was over, once *Andromeda* was no longer a threat, the Coalition would have to take a long, hard look at itself. And Evie was going to make sure *everyone* knew what Rutledge and the others had done.

That was, if there was even a Coalition left after *Andromeda*.

The door to Engineering opened and the air in the room tightened, as if someone had frozen everything in its place. Evie glanced up to see Zenfor enter and make her way over to them, her focus on Sesster and no one else. She stared up at him for a few moments, then turned to Evie. "Is this true? You have admitted everything?"

Evie nodded. "Everything. And I'll be making a ship-wide announcement once the Bulaq are off the ship."

"He says he's forgiven you."

She exhaled. That was a relief; she wasn't sure she'd been given that much leeway yet. But it was good to know. If there was one thing constant about Sesster, he was fair. He was also a very compassionate and sensitive person. It had always been hard for her to know what was going on with Claxians, not being very receptive to their thoughts. But ever since her time with him in the *mind-place* she felt like she'd gotten to know him a lot better. For which she was grateful. "I'm not sure I deserve it, but I appreciate that." She nodded at Sesster. One of his appendages "nodded" back.

"You won't be so fortunate with me." Zenfor grimaced and turned to Sesster, staring at him for longer than a few moments. Evie prepared to excuse herself, there was obviously an intense conversation going on from the look on Zenfor's face. But just as she moved Zenfor turned back to her. "I've been *told* not to be so rash and that I should *try* to see things from your point of view." The words came out through clenched teeth and Evie could tell it was taking a great amount of restraint on her part to keep from exploding in a rage of fury. She'd seen how strong the woman was and wasn't keen to experience it firsthand.

"Sesster, it's okay," she replied. "She doesn't have to forgive me. She has a right to be angry."

Zenfor clenched her hands then relaxed her shoulders. "I would prefer to discuss events of a non-personal nature." Evie couldn't disagree there. She indicated for Zenfor to continue. "Caspian told you of the engine status?"

"He did."

"Has he informed you of Diamant's plan?"

She frowned. "I don't know of a 'plan' per se, but Lau—Lieutenant Yamashita found two of the Bulaq missing from their assigned locations. I've got Zaal looking into where they and their escorts might be. I know he's up to something."

"You are correct." Zenfor walked over to her terminal full of Sil glyphs. "I suggest once we know where each Bulaq is exactly, we use the ship's force barriers to trap them where they are. If they're contained, they should be manageable."

Evie stared at her terminal which had transformed into a cross-section of the ship. "And if we don't know where they all are?"

"I think that must be the most important aspect. They may have some way of alerting each other we're not aware of. Also, Diamant must be arrested immediately."

Evie was so focused on what she was saying she didn't hear the door to Engineering open again. Only when Laura's voice reached her ears did she finally turn to see her, Cas and Vrij standing there. "Any problems?" she asked, her eyes lingering on Laura.

"Nothing we couldn't handle," Cas replied. He glanced up at Sesster for a moment, then grimaced, dropping his head. Evie knew that feeling; the one that said you'd let down your crewmates. She turned to Vrij.

"Do your people have any way of contacting or speaking with each other that we don't know about?" she asked. "Something they can do, and we'd never know?"

Vrij tapped his chest twice. "M-my p-people have e-electromagnetic sensors—in o-our heads. T-they allow u-us t-to receive..." He screwed up his face. "N-not thoughts—impulses. D-desires. A-also m-makes us g-good e-engineers."

"Because you can read the electromagnetic spectrum it gives you an advantage when working with anything that puts out that kind of signal. No wonder you can disassemble and build things so quickly, you don't have to test as you go," Cas said.

Vrij brought his hand to his chest again but looked at it and dropped it. Instead he nodded, though the motion was jerky, like he hadn't quite gotten the hang of it yet. "Y-yes. That's r-right."

"So, then Diamant could have been sending signals to his men this entire time," Laura said. "Or to you." She stared at Vrij.

"T-the signals are g-generated and r-received through our mandibles," he said. "M-mine aren't sensitive e-enough t-to r-receive from other B-Bulaq anymore." He dropped his eyes. Cas had said he was an outcast from his people and now Evie understood why. It wasn't just the mechanical appendages on his back, it was because he'd lost his connection to his people. An innate connection they all shared; all but him. She felt like she'd seriously misjudged him.

"Okay, that's it, give me your gun," she said, holding her hand out to Laura. Laura made a face and withdrew her sidearm, handing it to Evie.

"What are you doing?" she asked.

"Arresting Diamant. This has gone on long enough. The rest of you stay here and pinpoint the location of all the Bulaq. Maybe we can use this electromagnetic signal they've got against them. Even the ones that aren't inside the ship. Once you have them all located, lock them down."

"You're not going to face him alone," Cas said.

She almost laughed. "No, of course not." She tapped her comm. "Security team to Engineering." Even though that seemed to satisfy Cas, Laura was still tense. Her shoulders were bunched up so tight Evie thought she might break from the pressure.

"I'll go get him. Give that back," she said, holding out her hand.

Evie shook her head. "My ship, my rules. No one messes with me and my crew. I'm looking him in the face when I tell him we know. And I'm escorting him all the way back to his ship. I want to see the dejection on his face when he realizes we bested him."

Laura furrowed her brow. "Are you sure that's a good idea?" she whispered.

Don't worry, she mouthed to her, then added a smile. Though she had to admit the weapon felt wrong in her hands. She'd done some basic firearms training back in the academy, but ever since had only ever armed herself with her sword. Perhaps she should go get that instead, it might be more intimidating. *No.* What was she thinking? This was going to be a simple operation, nothing more. She wasn't even going to use the weapon.

Ensign Folier entered along with crewman Unak, both of them armed. Evie turned to the rest of them. "Get to work. Once we have Diamant in custody and back in his shuttle we'll start moving the rest of the Bulaq, one by one. But I want him locked down first. I'll signal when we're right outside his door so you can make sure the rest of the Bulaq are immobilized."

"Just like they should have been from the beginning," Zenfor said under her breath. Evie pretended not to hear. She took one last look at Laura whose eyes and lips had tightened. This was going to be a problem. If either one of them was going to be compromised every time the other went into a dangerous situation it might lead to some bad decisions. She'd have to have a discussion with her about it later.

"Wish me luck," she said and made her way over to the security team.

29

Ten minutes later Evie, Folier, and Unak stood outside Diamant's quarters. She'd sent his escort, Ensign Maro—who had been stationed outside his door—back down to join the security team she'd arranged to meet them in Bay One, at Diamant's shuttle. She tapped her comm.

"Cas, how is it looking down there?" she asked.

"We think we've got them all. Vrij gave us some frequencies to work with and we think the two missing Bulaq are on the underside of the ship, doing Kor-knows-what. But Zenfor says we can decompress that section since those decks are shut down. The explosive blast should knock them off the ship and if Diamant wants them, he can go get them after they get off the ship."

"Good. Prepare to initiate the force barriers on my mark," she said.

"Ready down here."

Evie glanced to both security officers with her. They nodded in unison; their weapons ready in their hands. *Here we go.* "Mark."

"Force barriers engaged," Cas said. There was a moment of silence on the other end. "They should all be stationary, including Diamant. The deck was successfully decompressed and the two should no longer be on the side of the ship."

"Let me know when you get confirmation of that," she replied. "Until then, Diazal out." She nodded for Unak to open the door. He entered the unlock code and the door slid open to reveal Diamant, sitting in the one chair of the room, a blue glow around him.

"Ah, Captain! How nice of you to come and visit. You could have knocked." He raised his hand, indicating the door. "I would have let you in."

"I don't know what you think you're doing here, but it's over," she replied.

His visage didn't break. "Of course it is. I see now I never should have tried to best you." He glanced to the two security officers. "So, what happens now, hmm? Am I to be shot?" His eyes returned to the gun in her hand.

"No, you're leaving this ship. All of you. And you're not coming back."

"I see," he replied, too comfortable for Evie's liking. "Then I suppose we best get on with it. May I stand or will this field cut off my head if I try?"

Evie tapped her comm. "Drop the field in quarters Io-76." The blue field disappeared, but Folier and Unak kept their weapons trained on Diamant. He stood slowly. "If those things pop out from your back you can trust we will kill you."

"I have no further quarrel with you, Captain." He held up his hands in front of him. Evie smirked. It was possibly the one hand gesture their two species had in common. "And I certainly don't wish you harm. You'll have no trouble from me."

Somehow his words didn't make her feel better. She'd prefer it if he was fighting them, or if he at least looked surprised. But he was neither. To Diamant, this was just another day with nothing out of the ordinary. It unnerved her.

"Let's go," she said, indicating he go first.

"Whatever you say, Captain." He inched his way forward and made sure not to touch any of them as he walked past. He didn't turn his back on them, but stopped at the door anyway, his hands still up.

"Turn around and start walking." Evie lowered her weapon. There was no need for all three of them to keep guns on him; that was just overkill. But she wasn't about to put it away. They exited into the corridor with Diamant in front and the three of them behind.

"I'm curious, captain, what gave me away? Surely it couldn't have been my performance," he asked.

She considered not answering him. Everything he said was some stretched version of the truth. "First you tell me what you're really doing here. Why did you want to get on this ship so badly?"

"When the Cho'ju'itsa came for my planet, it wasn't on a mission of benevolence. Or mercy. They came to kill. No opportunity was given to my people; we were helpless against their attack." He sighed. "I'm not sure an offworlder could understand. You didn't watch your planet disintegrate before your eyes. You haven't been shunned and turned away by every other species in the quadrant. You live on this...palace of a ship and you dare question my motives?" His face turned in fury. Folier and Unak raised their weapons again, keeping them locked on Diamant. "I know the Cho'ju'itsa aren't done with us, Captain. I know it in my heart. And because of that we need to leave this place. We need to get away where they can never find us again. Your ship with your advanced engines is the only ship in existence which can outrun them. Surely you must see how valuable that is to us." He'd calmed from his anger, but Evie didn't tell the others to lower their weapons.

"Turn back around," she said through her teeth.

"Very well, but you're the one who asked," he replied, resuming his original posture. He straightened, and walked forward, as if he were leading them instead of being escorted.

"How are you so sure they'll return?" Evie asked after a few quiet minutes.

"Because, they didn't stop with our planet," he replied. "The Cho'ju'itsa didn't attack our stars until we had tried to fight back. Until after we'd tried to stop them. We were doing nothing but *defending ourselves*."

Evie screwed up her face. "Wait, you're saying they destroyed your stars because you fought back?"

"I witnessed it myself," Diamant replied keeping his gaze ahead of them and walking at a consistent pace. "I saw what few ships remained in the system attempt to fire on them. When they did, the Cho'ju'itsa became *vindictive*. They destroyed our stars, and as a result, all our settlements in the system, along with most of our stations and ships. Within hours everything had been annihilated."

"I thought you had been knocked out before any of that happened."

He turned, showing only the side of his face and a smirk. "Caspian does make a thorough report; I will give him that. And here I'd thought he'd been so high on Ossak he wouldn't remember." He paused. "I don't tell the true tale to many as they might get the wrong idea. But no, I witnessed it all. I witnessed the destruction of my world, my stars, and most of my society. Those who were out of the system at the time—they were the lucky ones."

Evie felt a growing discomfort in her stomach. She couldn't help but feel bad for them and she knew they were desperate, but to try and steal their ship was unacceptable. "If you'd been honest with us from the beginning we might have been able to come to an agreement."

"Oh, come now, captain. Don't tell me you'd have taken the time to ferry a bunch of nomads back and forth to a new home. It would have taken years. And from what I understand, you're on a schedule."

"We could have at least helped with the preparations. Even helped you find a new planet as you originally suggested. What was your eventual plan? Control of the ship?" She caught Folier and Unak exchange glances.

"Temporary control," he replied. "And your resources. But we wouldn't have left you destitute. My people know all too well what that is like. It isn't something we could impose on another culture. We would have taken your ship back to the Hub, filled it to the brim with my people and begun our search for our new home. And then once we were there and settled, we would have allowed you to leave. Simple. Though time-consuming."

She dropped her gaze. "I wish we could have come to an understanding. I feel for your people, I really do. But deception and subterfuge are not the ways to get what you want."

"I regret we had to resort to such *barbaric* practices, but my people are desperate. And now, because of you we will only become more desperate. By removing me, you are diminishing our chances for survival."

She shook her head. "My original offer still stands. You can have the supplies and we will give you information to help you increase your food output on the Hub, but nothing more. We just can't afford it."

He clasped his hands in front of him. "It's a very generous offer, Captain. But I'm afraid it is too late. The trust between our people was broken the minute you pointed those weapons at me. If I gave in now, I would be accused of playing into your hands and people would revolt. I must keep the peace. No matter the size of the sacrifice." He stopped and turned around again. The security officers held their weapons to him. "You should feel honored; it isn't often someone manages to get the drop on me. Will you tell me now what gave me away?"

"We found more than one set of mandible tracks on the outside of the hull," she replied.

His head flinched back. "But how—?" Realization dawned on him. "Of course. Vrij's tracks are different than everyone else's. I should have anticipated that." He smiled and turned around again. "You've caught me in a rare moment of weakness, Captain. I applaud you."

"No applause necessary." They were almost to the bay. She'd feel so much better once he was back on his own ship. Perhaps it would be a good idea to sedate all the Bulaq before sending them back off. She should call Xax and get a medical team down here to administer it to each Bulaq they collected. It would make the job much easier. "Go ahead and take him inside," Evie told the two security officers. "I'll be in there in a minute."

"Yes, ma'am," Ensign Folier replied, pushing Diamant forward. He still had a grin on his face Evie couldn't help but dislike. Despite everything, he was still toying with her. She glanced down to tap the comm on the back of her hand when something hard rammed into her, knocking her to the ground and the weapon from her hands.

Chaos erupted.

30

"I don't like it." Laura paced the width of Engineering. Cas watched her as Zenfor continued to work on the engine systems behind him, as did the rest of the engineering crew. "That bastard is still hiding something, I know it."

"Like what?" Cas asked. "He has Evie plus two other guards escorting him. What else is he going to do? Besides, Diamant doesn't come across to me like the kind of person who gets his hands dirty. If he were going to do something rash, he'd get someone else to do it. And we have everyone else locked down."

"H-he's d-deceptive," Vrij said from the corner of the room. He'd backed into it and stood there, as if being smashed up against the walls was the only thing keeping his sanity.

"See, even he agrees with me." Laura motioned to Vrij. "I'm calling her, I gotta know everything's okay."

"And what are you going to say?" Cas asked.

"I'll make something up about the weapons systems." She tapped the back of her hand. "Captain, come in." There was nothing on the other end. Laura screwed up her face. "Captain?"

Cas noticed an unease forming in his stomach. The kind that always came along when one of his courier missions was about to go south. He turned to Zenfor. "Anything out of the ordinary on the sensor logs?"

"I was just going over those." She glanced up to Sesster, whose arm moved over to the primary sensor control units adjacent to him. "He's worried too. There are anomalies in the system."

"Evie, come in," Laura said into her comm. Maybe her concerns weren't misplaced after all. But how could Diamant have gotten the upper hand? She wasn't stupid and she wouldn't have turned her back on him.

"Are the force barriers still holding?" Cas asked.

Zenfor moved over to another monitor to check. "Yes. They're all still in place and most, if not all the Bulaq are under guard by one or more security officers."

Which meant the frequencies Vrij had given them were accurate and Diamant's people weren't still roaming the ship. So why did something feel wrong all of a sudden? Laura gave up and stared at him, her eyes accusing as if to say *I told you so.*

"Okay, fine, let's go check," Cas said. "Vrij, you come with us. I'm willing to bet you're better at hand-to-hand combat with your people than we are."

He nodded again. "T-they w-would slice y-you to r-ribbons."

Laura's eyes went wide. "We need to *go*. Now!" She ran over to one of the supply lockers in Engineering and pulled out a pulse rifle. Cas instinctively reached for his sidearm, but it wasn't there. It was in the security lockup on level twelve, near the Bays. He should swing by and grab it, just in case.

"Try and figure out what's going on," he told Zenfor. "Comm us as soon as you have some information."

She'd pulled up an image of Bay One where they were supposedly escorting Diamant. Everything looked normal as far as Cas could see, though Diamant and the escort hadn't arrived yet. What could be taking them so long? It wasn't *that* far of a trip.

"Are you coming or am I doing this alone?" Laura asked, already at the door to Engineering. Cas and Vrij jogged to catch up with her.

He wasn't sure if it was Laura's insistence or the fact that his mind had been somewhere else while they all waited in Engineering but the hairs on the back of his neck now stood straight up. He turned to Vrij. "Can I count on you to help us?"

Vrij tapped his chest twice, though he was clearly nervous. For a moment he thought about calling Box as well; the extra muscle wouldn't hurt. As they followed Laura down the long corridors Cas tapped his comm.

"Yeah, boss," his friend said on the other end.

"Get down to Bay One, I think we've got a problem here," he replied.

"Caspian problem or actual medical problem?"

"A Bulaq problem," he said, breathing hard as they picked up the pace. Laura was *fast*.

"Caspian problem then. Shall I bring the bazooka or the grenade launcher?"

"Just get down there! We're on our way." He ended the transmission. *Grenade launcher*. What had he been watching now? Wasn't Xax supposed to be keeping him too busy for net dramas?

As they ran Vrij's mandibles extended out and in front of him, almost like protective blades. Cas really didn't want this to get bloody, but as he studied the gleaming metal blades he could see how they might easily slice a person in half. This could go bad fast.

They took the nearest hypervator down two levels to twelve but in their haste Cas didn't even bother veering off toward the weapons lockup. It was too far away and between Laura and Vrij he was confident they had enough weapons.

When they arrived in Bay One it became clear to Cas that they had severely underestimated Diamant's cunning. Instead of a contingent of security officers waiting to escort Diamant to his shuttle, the Bay was a wreck. A second Bulaq ship had seemingly appeared out of nowhere and was perched in the middle of the deck while at least forty men under Diamant's command subdued and restrained the Bay crew and security officers. Cas noticed the adjacent Bay where the spacewings and pilots were stationed was blocked off by a force barrier, though it hadn't been one of the ones Zenfor had set up. And in the middle of the crew the Bulaq had rounded up so far was Evie, on her knees with her hands behind her head while one of the Bulaq bound her wrists together.

"Let her go, motherfucker," Laura said with perfect calm in her voice. The pulse rifle was outstretched in front of her and she took slow, calculating steps toward the group. Diamant turned with a smile on his face. He surveyed the three of them, though Vrij held back with Cas right behind him.

Cas tapped his comm. "Box, abort, we have boarders," he whispered.

"Ah, Caspian, how good of you to join us," Diamant announced. "You've saved me an awful lot of trouble by delivering yourself to us. And there is no use calling for help." He turned to Laura. "Because if you value the life of your captain…" In his hand was Evie's gun, pointed right at her head. "Such crude weapons. Perhaps we should demonstrate how we deal with unruly prisoners. Ju'lid, if you don't mind."

The Bulaq standing behind Crewman Abernathy smiled. Abernathy never saw it coming. One moment he was staring at Cas, his face drawn in confusion and the next his head had been severed clean from his body and was rolling across the floor, leaving a trail of slick blood in its wake. His body, which took a moment to register it was in the process of dying and remained upright for an almost comical amount of time, flopped over, blood pouring from the severed neck.

"You son of a bitch," Laura growled behind the rifle.

"Now you wouldn't want a similar fate to befall your captain, would you?" Already one of the Bulaq stood behind Evie, despite Diamant pointing the weapon at her. Evie's face was one of fury.

"Just shoot the bastard already!" she yelled. Cas was sure she was pissed at herself for letting him get the drop on her.

Laura winced then unshouldered the rifle, throwing it to the ground. "Get away from her," she said, too much emotion in her voice. Cas was sure Diamant would take notice.

"Of course. Now that we all have an understanding." He passed the pistol off to one of his men. Cas couldn't stop staring at Abernathy's severed head, his surprised eyes bulging from their sockets. "Now, Captain, we were in the middle of a negotiation if I'm not mistaken."

Three of the Bulaq came over and restrained Laura, Cas, and Vrij, taking them to join the others.

"This isn't a negotiation, this is a hostage situation," Evie spat.

"You say comette, I say cometé. In the end, does it really matter how we label our respective positions?" Diamant smiled.

"What does he want?" Cas asked as he was pushed to his knees and his hands bound behind him.

"Control of the ship," she replied.

"You will make a ship-wide announcement telling your people to surrender themselves willingly, otherwise one member of the crew will die every fifteen minutes until either they comply, or we run out of people to execute," Diamant announced. "If I were you, I would encourage them to cooperate. We will deposit you on the next planet we pass."

"You never had any interest in trading, did you? Your only goal was to get on this ship. Zenfor was right, you were behind the attacks."

Diamant placed his right hand on his left cheek. "You flatter me. It's true, my influence does have a far reach. Who knows what others will do in my name? I control what a rogue faction of radicals does when they *happen* to see a vulnerable ship passing by? But there is one thing for sure; it's for the good of the Bulaq people. We will be strong yet again." He turned to Evie. "Now, would you like to make the announcement, or witness the severing of your first officer here?" He blinked, still smiling. "Or perhaps your tactical officer."

"Take me to a comm panel," Evie said through her teeth. Cas glanced back at Laura who had dropped her head.

"Hey," he whispered. "It's not your fault. It doesn't matter what we would have done, they always had the upper hand."

"Yeah." She lifted her head enough so her eyes were barely visible under her drawn brows. "And who let them on the ship in the first place?"

Cas turned back around and sat back on his legs. She was right. All of this was his fault, Evie never should have put him in charge. *Dammit.* And he knew better too. It was too much to hope that the second time would be any different. Why? Why had he assumed he could do things any better this time around? Because it wasn't official? Because he didn't technically have a rank? Those things didn't matter in the slightest. Leadership came from character, and it was clear to Cas he'd never had the character to begin with. Otherwise he never would have put his crew in this position. And now, unless Zenfor and Sesster could figure out what was going on before it was too late, they would be removed from the ship and left for dead on some barren planet. *Andromeda* would find their way to the Coalition and destroy it just as they had the Bulaq and there was nothing he could do about it.

And it was all because of him.

31

Zenfor stared at the feed coming in from Engineering. The captain had just made a ship-wide announcement informing the crew they were not to resist the Bulaq and to do as they said. But Zenfor wasn't having it. Diazal wasn't in command of her. She was her own consul and she would be until the day she died. And in the little time they still had before Bulaq invaders flooded every corner of this ship, she had been trying to figure out how they had gotten past ship's security.

It doesn't matter. We need to prepare. Don't do anything rash.

"They're not taking me into custody," she muttered, going over the information on the screen. It looked like the Bulaq had managed to break into the internal sensor data and put everything on loop. But they had done it with such skill it was difficult to tell any changes had been made at all.

If you fight them, you're putting the crew at risk.

"So what? They do nothing but lie and deceive each other. It's what they deserve," she replied.

You don't believe that. I know you too well.

"You don't know me as well as you think. Weak elements must be purged. Everyone on this ship is a liability; what matters is getting the information back to Mil'less and the others." Her mind searched for any option. If she could reconfigure the same kind of probe they were going to use back at the Excel Nebula and load it into a shuttle with an undercurrent, it would reach the Coalition. It might not be soon enough to make a difference, but it would at least get there. That was more than she could say for this ship. But did she have time to configure and launch one?

Does that mean I'm a liability as well?

She'd been so intent on working she hadn't even realized what she'd said. She stopped and glanced up. Most of the crew in Engineering had stopped working, instead they stood huddled in small groups, watching the doors precariously. All except for Tyler, who continued to work regardless. His face was centimeters from his screen. Whatever he was doing, it looked intense. "No," she replied, looking up at Sesster. "It doesn't include you. And you're right. It doesn't include the others. But you have to admit, things would be so much simpler if you all stopped lying to each other."

The humans have had a hard time with it in the past. It was one of the failings of their old societies. We're working on it, but not hard enough it seems.

"Consul!" Tyler yelled, running over to them. "I need your help. I'm trying to lock out the main computers so the Bulaq can't use them. But I need a foreign encryption key." He glanced up to Sesster. "And I need your security clearance. Mine only goes so high."

"Will that work?" Zenfor asked, glancing at the door. They couldn't be far now.

"I don't know. We have protocols for when ships are boarded but with the amount of damage we've sustained a lot of the backups are offline. Including the security protocols."

"That's not from the damage," Zenfor said. "The Bulaq did that on purpose."

"We need to lock out what we can before it's too late."

She had to admire Tyler. Despite everything he wasn't giving up. While the rest of the crew had already stopped, anticipating what was on the horizon, he charged on. She felt as if she'd misjudged him before.

The door to Engineering rolled away, revealing a dozen Bulaq, half with pulse rifles and the other half brandishing nothing other than their back mandibles. Zenfor had the immediate urge to rush them and begin tearing them limb from limb.

No, we can't put the others in jeopardy.

"I know, I know," she muttered. She'd been too late; there hadn't been enough time to even load a probe with their data, much less launch it. She watched the Bulaq spread out, taking each person individually. One with its mandibles out approached her and Tyler.

"You, come with me. You," he pointed to Tyler, "stay here."

Zenfor flexed her fist. Just how hard were their skulls? Could they take the full impact from a Sil fist? Especially one that had been trained using the ancient fighting technique Kailocution? She really wanted to find out. "Hands out," the Bulaq said. She slowly extended her hands, fighting the urge to grab him by his tiny head and crush it, but instead she allowed them to be bound together. She tested the magnetic lock between them and found it was stronger than she'd anticipated. Though she might still be able to break them in a pinch. "Follow the rest," the Bulaq said, indicating the rest of the Engineering crew who had been rounded up. Only Tyler and Sesster remained. The Bulaq weren't stupid; they knew they needed both of them to use the undercurrent. Diamant had been busy since coming aboard.

Zenfor followed the rest of the crew out into the corridor. Similar scenes were playing out across the deck as Coalition crews were led out of their respective rooms and down corridors until reaching the hypervators where they were escorted to places unknown. For all Zenfor knew they were taking them all to the Bays and kicking them out into open space. If that turned out to be the case, she'd take as many with them as she could.

It turned out to be a short trip up one level to nine where she and three of the other Engineering crew were led out. Zenfor noticed one was Ensign Jackson, the same idiot who'd interrupted her goodbye ceremony with Mil'less. He was tense, cowering as they led him away.

The two Bulaq guarding them escorted them down the corridors until they reached the brig, which already had a few occupants, including the robot and the doctor. Another Bulaq had already taken over the brig's control station and he looked up when Zenfor and the Engineers entered. "Over here, he wants them all in one place," he said, indicating Zenfor and the others file into the left-most brig. It was a space built for one or two at the most, not four and though they weren't cramped, it wouldn't be comfortable.

Once they were inside the Bulaq raised the barriers. Zenfor noticed the cell beside her empty, but in the next cell over stood some of the bridge crew. Lieutenant Zaal, Uuma and River, the navigator. She didn't see the helmsman.

Just as the two Bulaq who'd escorted them here left, the door opened again to reveal the captain, Caspian, Lieutenant Yamashita and Vrij all being escorted in where they were stored in the middle unit. Behind them was Diamant, a big smile on his face.

"There," he said. "Isn't that more comfortable?" The force barrier went up sealing the four of them inside. They looked unharmed as far as Zenfor could tell.

"I expect you to keep your word," the captain said, her eyes never leaving her captor.

"Captain, I'm insulted. Are you insinuating I might not be telling the truth?" he asked, his mock sarcasm dripping. It made Zenfor want to rip his head from his body.

"No more of my crew has to die, Diamant. Promise me that."

"If they behave, everything will be fine," he replied. "Despite what you might believe I have no quarrel with you. You just happened to be in the wrong place at the wrong time. But I am going to get what I need for my people, one way or the other." He surveyed all of them. "If we have any problems, I know where I need to come and ask. Rest assured the remainder of your crew will be waiting in your cargo areas, under heavy guard. And your elite space fighters are safely contained in your other shuttle bay. As long as we have an understanding there will be no problems." He clasped one hand over the other fist and bowed, then turned and left with the other Bulaq. Only the one manning the control station remained.

"Yeah and stay out!" the robot yelled.

"Are you okay?" Cas asked, staring at Zenfor.

"Fine. Were all your materials worth it?"

"Stop. We're not going to bicker in here," Captain Diazal said. "We're all in the same situation. We needed parts and Cas found them. It just happened that he brought back some unwanted guests at the same time." She stared at the Bulaq who only smiled back with nothing but smarminess.

"Great, so now what do we do?" Lieutenant Yamashita asked, slumping down on the small bench in her cell.

"We don't do anything," the captain replied. "We can't risk harming the rest of the crew. We don't have much of a choice."

Zenfor turned in frustration, staring daggers at Jackson who'd sat on the small bench in their cell. He saw her and jumped up, moving aside. She slumped down on the seat in his place, crossing her arms. Nothing like this would have ever happened on a Sil ship. If it detected a person they didn't want aboard that person was ejected into space. However, if the person required a trial they would be kept, as Caspian was. But here there were no trials. Only actions. It was so uncivilized.

And it only made her miss home more.

***

As Cas watched Zenfor sit in the other cell he couldn't help but think about how he was the world's worst repeat customer. All of this could have been avoided if he hadn't been so adamant about finding the Bulaq and helping them. He still found it hard to believe Diamant was just doing this for his people. Was this really the best way to go about trying to find more resources? Had they not come upon the Bulaq would *Tempest's* crew have resulted to similar tactics to get what they needed to survive? He supposed it made sense, looking out for a new planet would give them a lot of opportunity, but how many planets could there be that didn't already have some kind of dominant species? In Cas's experience, if a planet was habitable, it had at least one occupant. Some planets had many, many more.

He glanced over at Evie who had the most dejected look on her face. He couldn't even imagine what was going on inside her head. But without asking he knew it was because she blamed herself for this, for not being able to get out of it like Greene might have. He hated he'd caused her to question her ability to lead this ship. All this was his fault, not hers.

"Hey," he said, standing beside her. He could feel Laura's eyes on the back of his neck, but he didn't care. Evie didn't say anything; only acknowledged him with a glance. "So, what's this awesome plan you have to get us out of this?"

Her eyes narrowed. "What?"

"I figured you had some mastermind plan you'd come up with in the past five minutes that would save the ship. You know, something easy." She dismissed it with a shake of her head, but there was a tiny smirk at the end of her lips. "I don't know what to say. It was nice of you to defend me, but this really is *my* fault. I never should have brought them aboard without your authorization. I guess the first officer title doesn't exactly fit anymore."

She eyed him. "Why, because you made a bad call? Didn't you ever make any bad calls working on the *Hartford* or the *Achlys*? Was every decision you made the perfect one? Because that's remarkable."

He shook his head. "You know that's not the case."

She considered it. "Maybe. But if you hadn't done what you did on the *Achlys*, you'd be dead along with the rest of the crew right now, right? And Rutledge would still be out there, experimenting. Or trying to at least."

"What are you saying? This is a blessing in disguise?"

She scoffed. "No. Absolutely not. I'm just saying we need to make the best of a bad situation. Whatever that means." It was clear she was struggling to keep it together for the crew. There had to be something they could do.

Cas glanced around the cells, then at the guard by the door. His eyes hadn't left them, and Cas wasn't sure how good his hearing was, but he didn't want to take any chances.

Dejected, he took a seat beside Laura. But his eyes landed on Vrij's belt. And it all became clear.

32

Cas stood and turned his gaze to Box, who looked like he was scrawling something on the far side of his cell's wall. Cas cleared his throat and Dr. Xax glanced up, but Box remained oblivious. Cas slid his eyes to the guard who had taken an interest in something on the station's console. He nodded to Xax to get Box's attention, which she did by tapping him with two of her four hands.

"I'm drawing here." Box scrawled with the tips of his fingers. She hit him harder. "What?" he yelled, turning around. "Can't you see I'm trying to design a more efficient sperm delivery system? See, this here is the flagella, and this is the porstamen, and this goes into this like so—" The guard perked up at the noise, his eyes now on Box. It wasn't what Cas had planned but it would work. He tapped his comm.

"Ryant? Jann? Do you copy?" he whispered.

"This is Ryant," the reply came through. Evie perked up.

"Remember you told me about that training run you guys did on Takar? I think it'd be a good idea to do that again."

There was a pause on the other end. "Are you serious? What about—"

"Don't worry about the details. Just be precise. *Very* precise."

Ryant coughed. "Yeah. Okay. Maybe twenty minutes. There's something we have to do first."

"My freedom of speech is being suppressed!" Box yelled. "I can draw whatever I like!" Cas glanced up to see the guard had walked over to Box's cell and was yelling something at him to which Box was yelling right back. Xax stood off to the side, her eyes sliding to Cas and a smirk on her face. He nodded in appreciation. "Call when you're ready. Robeaux out." He cut the comm.

"What was that about?" Evie asked.

"We might not be sunk quite yet," Cas replied. "But the margins will be razor thin." He turned to Vrij. "Hand over your skin curtains."

"Do I even want to know what that is?" Laura asked, leaning away.

"They're like our repel fields, only better," Cas said. Vrij unhooked three from his belt and passed them to Cas, Evie and Laura. "How many more of those do you have?"

Vrij counted. "S-seven." Cas glanced around the brig. It wasn't enough for everyone, even if Box and Zenfor could go without one for a short time. He only hoped Ryant was as good a shot as he thought he was.

"Shut up or I'll come in there and disassemble you myself," the guard grunted at Box.

"I'd like to see you try! I'll break your hands in five places before you get one on me. I know the seven most deadly ways to kill a man and half of them I can do without even looking. Come on in here big boy, come on!" Box yelled. "What's the matter, can't back up your threats with any action? Don't want to try your pincher thingies against some real steel?"

"Mandibles," Xax said.

"Try some *mandibles* against real steel?" Box repeated. He'd come right up to the force barrier and his eyes were blinking in wild patterns. Cas couldn't tell if it was all for show or if really did want to take on the guard. For all his bluster, the guard wasn't taking the bait. He merely bared his teeth then returned to the control station.

"Jerk," Box said. "You put me in a confined space, I'm gonna draw in it." He returned to his erotic drawing.

Cas turned his attention to Xax. "How did they grab you so quickly?"

She shook her head. "I'm not sure. A couple of them came in, threatening us just after the Captain's announcement. This one had been prepared to needle them all in the necks." She indicated Box. "I persuaded him it probably wasn't the best thing for the crew."

Cas couldn't disagree. If Diamant had found out he probably would have executed Evie. He turned to her, but she was watching him carefully, as was Laura and Vrij. Even Zenfor had perked up. They still had some time; so he might as well gather as much information as possible. He focused his attention on the Bulaq.

"Hey, guard." The man glanced up. "Aren't you one of the ones that accompanied our shuttle back from the Hub?" The guard remained impassive. Cas took that as a yes. "So, you should have been restrained by a force barrier. How did you get free?"

A smile appeared on the man's face. "You think we're so primitive," he replied. "When actually we probably know this ship better than you do. Diamant planned for your contingency. We already had an easy way out."

"You disabled my program?" Zenfor asked. She'd stood and pushed through the others in her cell to come to the front.

"Leaving you any recourse would have been sloppy," the man replied. "And just as predicted, you tried to restrain us. I guess it didn't work out too well for you."

From the look on her face Zenfor was furious. Cas wasn't sure Sil skin turned red when they were angry, but it had gone from a light blue to a much deeper shade. He was glad she was behind the force barrier otherwise he was sure she would rip the man apart.

"So they've been sneaking control this entire time," Evie said more to herself than anyone else. "And we didn't see it."

"We saw it, we just thought it was something else," Laura said. But Evie only shook her head.

Cas placed his hand on her shoulder. "Don't worry," he whispered. "I think we have a plan. But I need you to do something first."

***

"The next person who speaks will be shot," the guard said, surveying the spacewing pilots seated in a loose cluster on the floor of Bay Two. He'd heard Ryant speaking into his comm and threatened him with the pulse rifle he'd confiscated from one of the security officers. Dorsey Ryant sat back with his hands up and mouth shut. All of his friends, his fellow pilots, his *family* was in this one small, confined space being held by a group of aliens who'd nearly killed him with their fucking ossak drink. Xax had ended up needing to pump his stomach. He'd had a bad reaction to the substance and could have ended up critical had he continued to drink it. But he'd known the risks when he first took the bottle and now he was ready to get some justice.

Only...what Cas suggested was suicide. How the hell was he supposed to get to his ship and launch from the bay without the Bulaq killing everyone in sight first? Sure, there were twelve of them and only four Bulaq, but they each had those razor-sharp knives on their backs and Ryant was pretty sure those could cut through almost anything he could throw at them. He needed another way.

He glanced over to Saturina and catching her eye made a few hand signals in their shorthand. It was a backup system they used when they were out in the field if they lost comms, which was more common than one would think. *Cas just called. He wants us to re-create the run on Takar.*

She glanced at the guards, who had gone back to watching the bay instead of the individual prisoners. Her forehead creased. *Is he serious?* she signed back.

He shrugged. Assuming Cas and the others were in the brig, it would mean a delicate operation at best. Ryant flipped down his goggles, bringing up an interior map of *Tempest*. The brig was located deep in the ship, at least three horizontal decks in from the outer hull. They'd have to be amazingly precise. *Any ideas?*

Jann shook her head. He wasn't going to give up though. He'd told Cas twenty minutes and he'd meant it, even if he hadn't quite known how they were going to accomplish it at the time. Ryant stared at the end of the bay where the force barrier kept out the vacuum of space and an idea dawned on him. It might be their only hope, but it would mean perfect coordination between *all* of the spacewing pilots. Everyone needed to be aware and ready, otherwise they couldn't take the chance.

He caught Saturina's eyes and nodded toward the opening. Her eyes went wide, and she shook her head.

No other choice, he signed.

She had a pained look on her face. *Raffy's not going to like it.*

Does she ever? Start informing everyone. Saturina shook her head again but tapped on Iavarone's shoulder, informing him of the plan. Silently he passed it along to Coley and Blackfield, and then on to See, Squires, Utley and the rest, all of them glancing back at Ryant like he was crazy. But no one had outright opposed yet.

Finally Wilmouth made the signs, passing the word along to Linkovich and Rafnkell. Their leader turned to him and immediately shook her head *no*. There seemed to be a collective breath of relief from the other pilots who had been willing but not confident about their chances with such a stunt. But Dorsey Ryant wasn't swayed. He was doing this, one way or another. And they'd had fair warning.

From where they sat on the ground he began to inch backward, keeping an eye on all four guards who were positioned around the main doors to the Bay and the adjacent doors to Bay One, which was still cut off by the force barrier. Ryant was pretty sure he'd have to make a break for it, and he had no clue how fast the Bulaq were. From what he'd seen in their city most of them were on the edge of starving, but for whatever reason these that had boarded the ship from the second shuttle seemed well-fed and healthy. Which meant he couldn't take any unnecessary chances. With those powerful hind legs they might be able to make huge leaps; he wouldn't know until it was probably too late.

Rafnkell's eyes flared as he continued to scoot back. All the pilots were watching him now, with the exception of Jann who had begun her own movement toward her spacewing. Ryant glanced behind him, the end of the bay was a good hundred meters away. He flexed his legs. He could probably do it in fifteen to twenty seconds if he pushed it. All that time in the gym hadn't been for nothing. He nodded to the pilots, holding up his hands and extending all ten fingers twice. That's all the time they'd have. Rafnkell mouthed *no* but he turned around anyway and got into a crouching position.

"Hey, what are you—" Before the guard could finish his sentence Ryant took off like a shot, bolting down the bay toward the open end. "Hey! He's running!" the guard yelled. There was chaos behind him—people were yelling, there were scuffles, the sounds of metal clanking against metal—but

Ryant paid no attention. His entire focus was on the small panel at the end of the bay. Out of his left ear he heard one of the spacewings start up. Then another. Then a scream. He couldn't bear to think about who it had been or the *thump thump* of heavy footsteps behind him, gaining. He was so close.

He skidded to a stop right at the panel before something heavy and solid ran into him, knocking them both over as they hit the force barrier at the end of the bay. Beyond there was nothing but empty space, but Ryant's focus was on the Bulaq who'd chased him down. His sword-like mandibles were out and already coming around to slice into him when Ryant sucker punched the Bulaq, sending his head back and a spray of maroon blood flying from the alien's nose. He winced and the mandibles stopped, his focus on his face. Ryant punched him again before he had the chance to recover and the man fell off to the side, in serious pain.

"A lot tougher than you thought, huh?" He stood and entered the code that would drop the force barrier, exposing the entire bay to open space.

"You can't!" The Bulaq said and one of his mandibles freed itself from under him, coming up and impaling Ryant through the back. He glanced down to see the mandible hadn't gone all the way through, but he felt the warm rush of blood spill from his back. Surprisingly, there wasn't a lot of pain. Either it was the adrenaline or getting stabbed didn't feel much worse than being punched. It wasn't enough to stop him, that was for sure. He hit the final sequence and a moment later everything in the bay was sucked into space.

33

"He's close," Evie whispered, her eyes closed, and her mind focused on what was happening on the ship. Cas had told her to reach out to Sesster as he was the only one who could keep the ship out of the undercurrent now. Because once the ship jumped to faster-than-light speed, his plan wouldn't work anymore. They needed to do everything they could to keep the ship in one place, at least for a little while.

"How close?" Cas asked.

She shook her head. She couldn't "see" exactly as she could feel. She'd never been further than a few meters from Sesster when they'd gone to the *mind-place*. But now she was a full deck and several hundred meters away. She wasn't even sure she was connecting with him, but she could almost feel what he was feeling.

Evie felt a reassuring hand on her back. "You can do it, sweetheart, I know you can." Laura. Sweet, sweet Laura. Evie had put her through so much already and yet she had stayed strong beside her. How could she have ever thought she'd get mad over something as simple as coming home late for dinner? "Just focus." Evie nodded. She could do this.

"Shit," Cas whispered. "The guard is looking over here. Keep working on it." She sensed he'd left her side while Laura continued to rub her back supportively.

"Hey!" Cas yelled. "I have a medical condition. I need to see my doctor. He's over there in that cell."

"That's right!" Box yelled back, turning from his drawing. "I'm his *doctor*. I've got everything that ails him. I need to administer medicine."

"I'm not stupid," the guard replied. "You're just going to have to suffer."

"Boss, it looks like he doesn't believe you," Box said, goading the guard. It was difficult for Evie to concentrate.

"Don't worry about what they're doing," Laura said. "Just focus on Sesster. Nothing else matters." Her hand slipped from Evie's back and took hold of her hand instead. Evie smiled, but kept her eyes closed. Laura was wrong, *this* mattered. She took a deep breath, filtering out the obscenities Box was now hurling at the guard. All her thoughts were focused on Sesster, and his physical position on the ship. She could do this, she just had to *concentrate*.

Slowly the world around her seemed to melt away, and Evie opened her eyes to find herself back on Sissk, standing in the middle of the desert. A lone figure stood a few meters away, turning to reveal himself to be Sesster in his "human" form. "Captain?" he asked, frowning. "How—did you bring us here?"

She surveyed the area. "I guess I did? I focused really hard. But that's not important now. We need you to keep Diamant from initiating the engines."

"That won't be easy, he's had all his people down here working on repairing our issues. The Bulaq are fast and efficient. I would daresay our engines have never worked so well. Zenfor might even be able to get her drive back up and running."

"Sesster, do everything you can to keep this ship in one place. If we move everything is lost. Is Diamant there now?"

He shook his head. "No, he's on the bridge. But there are others here in his place. I can sabotage the engines, but they'll know it was me. They might take it out on Lieutenant Tyler."

"I think that's a risk we'll have to take," she replied. "Hopefully they realize they need Tyler as much as they need you. We'll be as fast as we can. I promise we won't leave you there alone with them."

He considered it a moment. "Very well. I trust you, captain."

She smiled. "Thank—"

The scene dissolved around her and she was back in the cell, Laura still gripping her hand while a cacophony of consonants and vowels flew through the air with fury.

"—my pet Rulag had a face like yours I'd shave its ass and teach it to walk backward!" Box yelled. "You're nothing but a niffle-eating cumberbunch."

"Box, I think he's got it," Cas said. Evie turned to see Box back at the edge of his cell, his yellow eyes blinking like wild as the insults flew from his mouth. The guard wasn't having it, though it was distracting him from Evie's cell. Cas turned back around. "Good?" She nodded. "Then I'd say we're about ready." He turned to Vrij. "How do we use these things?"

Vrij pointed to the top of the small canister. "H-hold down on the top and i-it takes care of the r-rest. F-fifteen-minute supply of o-oxygen."

"Hopefully we won't need that much." Cas said, palming the device back into his pocket. He checked his comm for the signal then shook his head.

Evie really hoped everything was okay in the bay. She hadn't been happy about this plan, but they were out of options and Cas said Ryant was confident he could make it work. She'd gotten in contact with Sesster so now all that was left to do was wait. She glanced at Laura and gave her hand a squeeze, grateful they were in this together.

"Here," Cas said. The comm on the back of his hand blinked. "That's the signal. Activate them now." Evie let go of Laura's hand and fished the small canister from her pocket. She held the top and at once felt a strange shudder up her back. She didn't feel much different, though when she reached out to touch Laura her finger stopped just millimeters from her shoulder.

"B-better hold on to s-something," Vrij said. Evie nodded, grabbing one end of the bench in the brig. She glanced over to Zenfor who stood at the edge of her own cell with her arms crossed and her attention focused on them. This was either going to work great or they'd all be dead in the next minute. There way really no way to tell.

Just as Evie saw the guard notice they had all taken strange positions in the cell, the back wall exploded in what should have been a blast that would have killed them all, but instead of blowing into the cell, the wall itself and the concussive energy was sucked backward, along with all the air in the cell itself. An alarm blared in the brig as Evie and the others were jerked toward the hole. Vrij lost his grip but his mandibles extended, holding him on the plating as the air was completely emptied from the room. She checked the rest of them, everyone seemed unharmed.

She turned to see Box yelling something but couldn't hear a thing anymore. She tapped her personal comm. "Okay, let's go," she said. The other three nodded and they all floated through the hole into the next section of the ship. Behind them lights continued to flash but Evie knew the guard wouldn't drop the field. That small amount of magnetic separation was the only thing keeping him alive. Though he'd surely be making a call to Diamant.

The three corridors separating the brig and the outer hull of the ship had been expertly blown away, creating a tunnel they could travel through. Evie hadn't been worried about anyone in those sections because all the crew were in the cargo holds, and thus anyone unlucky enough to be in those sections when the spacewings blew into them would have been Bulaq. As she grabbed a charred piece of bulkhead to pull herself forward, she didn't feel an ounce of pity for them. Not anymore.

They reached the outer hull to find at least eight, if not more of the spacewings attacking *Tempest* herself.

"Ryant, Ryant, come in," Cas yelled into his comm. One of the spacewings flew alongside the opening. It was Captain Jann's ship.

"He's been injured," she replied. "I got him back into Bay Two and repressurized it, but he's going to need medical attention. Fast."

Shit. Xax and the rest of the medical personnel were still locked up in the brig. They'd have to move fast to regain control of the ship. "Just keep them occupied, captain," Evie said. "We'll take care of the rest. And good work." She turned to them of them as the spacewing peeled off to re-engage the fight. If *Tempest's* weapons weren't at full capacity yet, they soon would be and if the Bulaq fixed the auto-targeting they wouldn't last long out there. "How do we get back inside the ship?"

"Easiest way will be to go into that breach on seven," Cas said, pointing up. "Then we're only one level above the bridge."

She nodded. "And how do we keep from floating off into nothingness?" As if to drive home her point the ship shook with the blast from a spacewing.

"H-hang on to me," Vrij said. "I c-can get you t-there." His mandibles extended from his back, punching small holes into the bulkheads around him. Cas reached out and took his hand, Laura took Cas's and Evie took Laura's, forming a chain. Vrij's mandibles "walked" around the edge of the bulkhead to where they were outside of the ship. He moved quick, each puncture a measured step designed to cover the most ground with the smallest amount of effort. The ship shook again but Vrij held on without a problem, headed for the open section on seven. It had been a long time since she'd been on a spacewalk, and then it had been in a full enviro-suit. Nothing like this. She'd never felt like she could reach out and touch the stars before.

The mine had blown out a series of eleven separate crew quarters on this level, and even now it was easy to see the remnants of what hadn't been sucked into space when the mine hit. A few tables and other personal items which had been magnetized or bolted down still remained, but otherwise everything else was gone, including some of the walls separating quarters from each other. Evie could barely stand to look at it.

Vrij brought them into the relative safety of what little overhang remained as they approached one of the doors that would open to the outer corridor. But it wouldn't open without a security override and they could still be offline. Evie could only pray the Bulaq were thorough; that if their real goal was to take this ship, they wanted it operating in perfect condition, which meant fixing every broken system. If they hadn't, she wasn't sure what they would do.

"Armor's up," Cas said, glancing back. Evie followed his gaze to see he was right, the spacewings weren't having as much success anymore, many of them had pulled away to get out of the line of fire. Evie could see Jann's ship was still heavily engaged in battle.

"Just get us inside. The best thing we can do to help them is get to the bridge and retake control," Evie replied. Cas hovered over the control unit to the door, tapping in his override code. The doors slid open, but a blast of air knocked them all back. Had they not been holding onto Vrij they would have been blown out into space.

Vrij, grimacing, pulled them with both hands and using the mechanical mandibles, shot forward through the blast of air until they were on the other side. Once inside he clamped down on the wall and floor bulkheads as they tumbled back toward the opening. Cas reached over and shut the doors, closing off the suction. As soon as they were closed the four of them collapsed against the walls.

"Y-you can d-deactivate your c-curtains now," Vrij said, sitting up. His mandibles had folded back behind him.

"I think I'm gonna throw up," Laura said. "Let's not do that again."

"C'mon," Evie said. "We need to put an end to this."

34

The entire time they ran through the corridors all Cas could think about was Ryant down in Bay Two. How bad had he been injured? And was it too late? He needed to find a way to get a medical team down there, though there were probably a dozen Bulaq between them and the Bays.

"Here," Evie said, after they'd run a long length of corridor, coming to the door to her quarters. It opened upon sensing her personal pattern and she brought them inside. Cas was surprised they hadn't run into any Bulaq yet, though they were probably trying to figure out what had happened to them after leaving the brig. As soon as they got eyes on the outside of the ship they'd see Vrij's marks leading them right to level seven. They didn't have a lot of time.

"There are two guns in the locker under my bed," she said, heading for the closet. Laura ran over and pulled the case out, unlocking it and withdrawing two standard Coalition pistols.

"I didn't think weapons were allowed in personal quarters," she said, smirking.

"Being the captain has privileges," Evie replied, removing her sword from its mount on the wall. She ran a cloth across its blade, then sheathed it and slung the strap securely over her shoulder.

Laura handed one weapon to Cas, keeping the other for herself. "I assume you don't need one," she said to Vrij. He touched his forehead with two fingers. Then shook his head. He was getting better at Coalition hand signals. "So what's the plan?"

"We make our way to the bridge, remove Diamant from power, retake the ship," Evie said.

"And we need to get someone down to Bay Two to check on Ryant," Cas said.

Laura checked her weapon. "I'll take care of Ryant. You three get to the bridge."

"Wait," Evie said, "why you?"

"Because it's going to take all of you to take on Diamant. He won't be expecting both of you at once and you can get the drop on him. And plus, if things go bad, you'll compromise your decisions if I get in trouble."

"She's got you there," Cas replied.

Evie sighed. "You're right. You *are* a distraction." She winked at Laura. "Just be careful getting down to Bay Two. Don't take any unnecessary chances. And keep an eye out for the Bulaq. You saw what they did to poor Abernathy."

Laura stuck the pistol into her waistband. "Got it. Don't worry about me." She pushed up on her tiptoes and kissed Evie's cheek, then disappeared through Evie's door.

Evie took a moment to reset herself. "Okay. Let's get moving toward the bridge. We should avoid the hypervators."

"And the large corridors." Cas turned to Vrij. "You okay to go? We'll need you as backup."

"I am h-happy to h-help," Vrij replied.

"Quite the change from someone who wanted to *borrow* all our parts on a few days ago," Cas said, regarding him.

His eyes fell to the floor as if in shame. "Not all of u-us think as Diamant. T-there are other ways to g-get what you need. You've b-been more than f-fair."

"We'll talk about that later," Evie said. "Right now we have a job to do. Everyone be on guard. We have no idea where all the Bulaq are or when we'll run into them."

"Yeah and apparently they can climb on the ceiling so don't forget to look up every now and again," Cas said.

A crease formed in Evie's brow. "Really?" Vrij nodded, the motion smoother than Cas had ever seen it. "Okay then. Let's move."

***

The journey to the bridge was unsettlingly quiet and Cas couldn't figure out why. He suspected by now the Bulaq knew they had survived the explosion and were on the ship somewhere, but they hadn't seen or heard any of Diamant's crew since leaving Evie's room. She'd kept her sword sheathed but remained alert, managing to find one of the access corridors close to the stern of the deck. That had led them down one floor to eight and then back over into an adjacent access corridor next to standard hallways that would eventually take them to the bridge. Evie thought it was better to stay out of sight as long as possible, despite the halls being empty. Though he couldn't disagree, Cas wasn't sure if the lack of people was a good thing or not. On one hand it could indicate Diamant was short-handed and didn't have enough soldiers to keep every area under surveillance. But on the other it might signal he was expecting them and prepared to spring a trap. It was impossible to know until they got there.

"Here," Evie said, crouching low as not to hit her head. "This junction connects to one more that will take us right beside the conference room off the bridge. Vrij, when we arrive can you use your mandibles to cut through the bulkhead to give us access?"

He nodded, a smile on his face. He was happy to help, and Cas couldn't blame him. After everything Diamant and his people had put the man through, Cas would want to see revenge at almost any cost as well. And he'd want to take part in that revenge as much as possible.

"Okay, moving on. Stay low, stay quiet. And cut through that bulkhead as quickly and with as little noise as you can." She picked up the pace through the cramped access tunnel before turning a corner and then turning one more. She stopped, pointing at the wall. She then crawled further along while Vrij squeezed past Cas. He hadn't been close enough to tell before but the man had a clinical smell to him, like antiseptic. Cas wasn't sure if it was his natural pheromones or it was something artificial he'd added himself. Regardless, Cas held his breath.

The scissor-like mandibles extended out from Vrij's back, cutting into the bulkhead beside him, creating an opening just large enough for them to crawl through. Once he was done, he backed out of the way to allow Evie to step through first. She checked both sides before disappearing through the hole. Cas followed with Vrij right behind him.

The conference room was in the same condition as always, there was little, if anything out of place. "Okay," Evie whispered. "We'll have to make this quick. Cas you go in and get the jump on as many as you can. Hopefully he doesn't have a lot of crew up here. Whoever you can't cover, Vrij, I need you to detain. I'll come in behind you and take Diamant."

Cas glanced at her sword. "You mean you're going to stab him?"

"Whatever it takes," she said, her eyebrows drawn so low he could barely see her eyes. "He took my ship and killed Abernathy. He's not getting away with it. He had his chance to leave."

"That...doesn't square with the Coalition Charter."

She withdrew her sword. "A lot of things don't."

Cas hadn't realized just how upset she'd been at this whole situation. He couldn't exactly fault her for feeling betrayed and used though; Diamant had played all of them. And while Cas was fed up, he wasn't to the point of killing the man. But maybe she was right, maybe this was what it took. Maybe they all had to adapt.

"Ready?" she asked. He and Vrij nodded. "Go."

Pistol in hand, Cas charged through the door connecting the conference room to the bridge.

His first impression was he'd done exactly what he'd meant to, catching everyone on the other side off-guard. But then he saw Diamant with his own pulse pistol in his hand, aiming it right at Cas's chest. Almost as if his brain predicted something else, Cas saw the pulse shoot from Diamant's pistol in slow motion, his brain telling him this wasn't how it was supposed to go; that he was *supposed* to be the one shooting *them* and his eyes were deceiving him. The blast from Diamant's pulse pistol hit him square in the sternum, the pain causing him to collapse behind the specialist's console as the world sped back up. Cas hit the ground, holding the wound with one hand while still gripping the pistol with his other. The pain was intense, debilitating. He wasn't even sure how much longer he'd survive; he'd never been shot in the chest before.

"I'm afraid your efforts are in vain, Caspian, though I applaud you for escaping from your own brig. I've been doing some reading and understand you've had some history with prisons. Having your people blow a hole through three corridors just to get you out was inspired." There was laughter in his voice.

Cas could see the edge of Vrij's silhouette on the other side of the still-open door and he shook his head. Before he'd fallen, he'd seen only two other Bulaq on the bridge: one at the helm position and the other at tactical, probably coordinating the fight against the spacewings. Evie had been right, Diamant was short-handed. It was an even match-up, or at least it had been before Cas had stupidly gotten himself shot. He adjusted himself and with a great deal of pain peered around the side of the console itself. He might still be able to take down one of the other two even if he couldn't get Diamant himself. "How'd you know?" Cas said, breathless. The person at tactical had his own pulse pistol as well and though he was holding it, his attention was focused on keeping the ship safe.

"I'll tell you what. A tale for a tale. I tell you how I knew, and you tell me how to get the engines back online," Diamant replied.

"I guess it's good to know you don't know everything," Cas replied, honestly relieved his plan had worked.

"I don't need to know everything. Only the things that matter. Like I know you're not alone, but your friends are smart enough to stay out of my line of fire," he replied. If he knew Evie and Vrij were with him, he must be using a modified internal sensor. Could they have had time to repair all those systems already? Vrij said they were good, but it was hard to imagine they were *that* good. Then again, Diamant had told him the ship would be ready in a matter of days. Perhaps it was possible.

Cas exhaled a deep, ragged breath. The pain was only getting worse. If Diamant had set the pistol on its highest setting he'd already be dead, but that didn't mean the end result wouldn't be the same. He needed medical attention immediately. "So, what's the plan? I stay here and we sling insults at each other until one of us runs out of breath? Because it seems like I don't have much time left."

"Caspian, you *are* entertaining. No, if you decide not to tell me I'll wait until you are a corpse and then I will just torture one of your compatriots on the other side of that door for the information. Unless you decide to tell me now and I'll allow them to live. I'll never forget how guilty you felt over what happened to Suzanna. Surely you wouldn't allow that to happen *again*."

His heart thrummed in his ears and he couldn't think straight. The pain from the blast and the pain of his past conjoined, forming one giant ball of living, writhing fury rising up from him. He needed to kill Diamant and the sooner the better. He pointed his pistol around the edge of the station and fired wildly, not caring if he hit anything or not. He didn't have a good line to any of the occupied stations and to his surprise, Diamant had disappeared. When he pulled back from the corner Diamant was suddenly *there* and grabbed his head with both hands while his outstretched mandible knocked Cas's weapon from his hand. Cas was so focused on the intense pressure against his skull he suddenly didn't care about anything else except getting free.

"Hurts doesn't it? I'm slowly applying an increasing amount of force to whatever is inside that soft skull of yours." The claws at the ends of his hands dug into Cas's skin. "But only enough to cause you a massive amount of discomfort." He leaned in close. "The real discomfort will come as you watch your friends suffer and die by my hands. And don't think I won't do it.

"After all," he whispered, "If I'm willing to kill my own people, there's no telling *what* I'm capable of."

35

Evie stared at Vrij, all her focus on him. Because he'd been ahead of her, she hadn't seen what had happened on the bridge as soon as Cas went in. And now the doors had closed again, cutting them off from whatever was happening over there. "What happened?" she whispered.

"Diamant—h-he s-shot—"

"He shot Cas?" Vrij nodded. *No.* He'd been ready for them. Which meant he knew she and Vrij were here as well. "Was he still alive?"

"Y-yes but hurt." Vrij dropped his gaze. That sealed it. She was going in; she couldn't allow Diamant to harm Cas any further. She gripped the hilt of her sword with both hands, focusing on it intently. She hadn't used it since D'jattan. There had been a part of her that thought she'd never use it again. But she'd come to realize the sword was a part of her, and she wasn't going to discard part of her history because it was uncomfortable. She was going to embrace it.

She drew a deep breath and calmed her senses, standing close to the door. "Follow me if you can, I'll need all the help I can get." She took one last breath and stepped forward, the doors sliding open as she approached. In front of her Diamant held Cas by the head and they both turned to look at her as soon as she came through. Evie raised the sword above her head and brought it down at an angle, meaning to slice right through Diamant. Instead, he pushed Cas away, the force allowing him to dodge the sword as he twirled in place and produced a pistol from somewhere she didn't see.

Evie ducked to the side, keeping the sword low as she dodged back and forth in a zig-zag pattern. Diamant fired twice, both shots missing her as she moved around him in an unpredictable pattern, only hoping to get back within striking range.

"Look out!" Cas yelled as another Bulaq at tactical aimed his own weapon at her. She crouched low and rolled away behind the bridge engineering station, coming to a stop.

"Most impressive, Captain. Had I known you were an accomplished swordswoman I would have been better prepared," Diamant said from somewhere near the front of the room. "As it is, I suggest you give yourself up. Your first officer has severe wounds and may not survive much longer. I promise to give him medical attention if you tell me what is wrong with the ship's engines."

Adrenaline surged through her system. How badly had Cas been shot? And could she afford to wait around to find out? But what if it was another lie?

Evie peered around the side of her cover to see Vrij come barreling through the door and running into the Bulaq at tactical, his mandibles fully extended. They disappeared behind the station and the only sounds were metal hitting something hard, and the tearing and ripping of flesh. She couldn't imagine what they were doing to each other.

"I must say, I never would have expected it. Meek Vrij, attacking a Bulaq soldier head-on. Very brave. Stupid, but brave," Diamant said. "Time is wasting, Captain; I need your answer."

"Tell him to go to hell," Cas coughed from somewhere off to her left. He must have crawled behind the specialist's station for cover. Did he still have his weapon? A weapon blast permeated the air and Evie glanced around again to see Diamant at the far end of the room with a smile on his face and the weapon outstretched. She could just make out Cas across from her behind the other station. She gripped the sword tighter.

"I suggest you make your decision quickly, Captain. You and I may have all the time in the world, but poor Caspian does not."

"S-she doesn't need to make a d-decision," Vrij said, standing from behind the tactical station. He was covered in cuts and wounds, as well as a generous amount of maroon blood, but his face was set. Diamant's visage cracked for just an instant as he realized Vrij had been the victor against the other Bulaq. He turned his weapon on Vrij but didn't fire. "You are n-not our s-savior, you are nothing m-more than a weak m-man who m-makes others do the hard work."

Diamant's face twisted into a smiling sneer. "Now, Vrij, why would you say such a thing about your old friend?"

"W-we are n-not friends." Vrij stood his ground with his mechanical mandibles extended, though one had been shorn off halfway along its length. The other Bulaq hadn't gone down without a fight. "Y-you won't kill anyone w-with that. D-don't forget I k-knew you before all this. A-and under all your d-deceptions you're j-just a s-scared little boy."

Without flinching Diamant placed the end of the pistol to the head of the Bulaq who was in control of the helm and fired. The man didn't even have a chance to register what had happened before he slumped over in his seat, dead. Evie was too shocked to move.

"What did you say about not doing the hard work?" Diamant asked. "The problem, Vrij, is you don't know your old 'friend' as well as you thought." Evie kept her eyes on Diamant; he had the gun trained on Vrij again. "You weren't there. You didn't see those *monsters* destroy everything we held dear. And when it was over and I realized I had survived, I made sure I would never find myself in a compromised position again."

Vrij took two steps forward and Evie thought she saw Diamant's hand shake slightly. His mandibles were still folded behind his back. "I'm n-not afraid of you," Vrij said. "N-not anymore."

"You should be. As I told the late Caspian over there, I am willing to do anything to ensure the survival of our people. Even if it meant killing a few in my way. Starting with the crew of my ship."

"Y-you didn't."

"I couldn't very well put myself in a position of influence if someone of higher rank than me survived, could I?" he asked, the question being the first genuine thing Evie thought she'd ever heard from him. "History is written by the survivors. And that's what I am. It's what you are. We can make it like old times again. Help me and we'll both be hailed as heroes of our people."

"You're not a hero, and neither am I," Vrij said, Evie noted, stutter-free.

Diamant's eyes went wide and Evie saw her chance. She rounded the station out of cover and kept the sword low, only swinging it as she rushed into Diamant's personal space. He leaned back, the blade only catching the pistol, slicing it clean in half and taking two of Diamant's fingers with it.

He screeched in pain as his mandibles unfolded from his back and began to parry Evie's attacks as she tried to cut into him. Vrij joined on the other side but with only one mandible its effectiveness was halved. Even at two-against-one they were evenly matched as Diamant fought with both his bloody fists and his natural blades.

The moves were hard and hurried. Evie would strike as hard as she could, but Diamant's mandible would block the hit, knocking the sword away as the mandible moved to strike her. It was like sword fighting with two different people. Because as his mandibles blocked the main hits, his hands, with their sharp claws, scratched and reached for her and Vrij, sometimes clipping them as they fought.

In her periphery Evie tried to see Cas, to make sure he was still alive but she couldn't see him behind the station. She only hoped he could hold on a few more minutes. But her distraction caused her to miss a strike from Diamant which sliced into her abdomen, producing a rush of warm blood over her uniform. She winced, but didn't withdraw, instead fighting harder to get a good blow in. She only needed one.

***

Cas could feel his body shutting down. It was a strange sensation, feeling the life drain from his limbs. But he wasn't down for the count yet. He could still make this work. His pistol lay just a few meters away. He gathered all the strength he could, hoisting himself up on his knees. His chest burned like fire and everything tingled. There was no telling how much longer he had. He was barely conscious enough to see Evie and Vrij fighting off Diamant at the front of the bridge in a flurry of blows. He wasn't sure they could beat him. Which meant there was only one other recourse.

With great difficulty he tapped the comm on the back of his hand. "Jann," he said, breathless. "You still out there?"

"Everything's good out here, the ship has stopped firing," she yelled.

"I need you to do it one more time," Cas said.

"Do what?"

"The Takar maneuver. On the bridge."

"You can't be serious," she replied. But he was. It was clear Vrij and Evie wouldn't last much longer. And they both still had their canisters Vrij had handed out. They could survive in space for a few minutes. Diamant couldn't.

"I'm dropping the armor now. Target the front of the bridge, right at the viewscreen," he replied, his words weak.

"Are you okay?" she asked.

"Fine, just...just do it," he replied. Cas crawled to the tactical station, every part of him hurting as he moved. He just managed to pull himself up and disarm the ship's armor. "Clear," he said.

Diamant grunted as he was hit with an onslaught of blows, but Cas was too tired to care. He was too tired for everything. All he wanted was to sleep, he couldn't believe this was how it was going to end. After everything.

With what little strength he had left he pushed himself fully upright, feeling as though he would pass out any second though he didn't. "Use...use your canisters," he yelled with as much force as he could. He noticed Evie catch his eye. She ducked and rolled away from Diamant's mandibles and Cas noticed she left a sizable trail of blood in her wake. Once she was out of range, she shoved her sword into the floor, holding its hilt as she reached into her pocket.

There was a massive explosion at the front of the room and for a second Cas thought Jann had miscalculated and destroyed the bridge and all of them with it. But then the main viewer disappeared into the darkness of space and the dead Bulaq at the helm followed it, along with anything that wasn't secured down on the bridge. Vrij managed to dig his one mandible in the floor and hold on, as did Evie, her head down and grip on the end of the sword. Diamant had also shoved his mandibles into the ground and had managed to resist being pulled away, though the force of air ripping through the space was intense. Cas, having expected it, had lowered himself down behind tactical so that he wouldn't be pulled away, but he'd activated the skin curtain in his pocket just in case.

Surveying the scene, it was clear Diamant wasn't going anywhere unless he did something. Wrenching himself around the console was harder than he anticipated, especially since all the strength had left him. Somehow, he managed to pull himself around, and felt the harsh pull of decompression yanking him toward oblivion. All he had to do was line himself up…and…release.

As he flew toward the opening, his body barely on the ground, he pivoted just enough to miss Vrij and slam into Diamant's surprised face, grabbing him as the force knocked them both through the opening into open space. Once all sound had left him Cas pushed Diamant away, watching the man tumble along with the same inertia, *Tempest* growing small in the background. This was okay with Cas. He'd gotten Diamant off the ship and he'd disabled it so the Bulaq couldn't use it. Without their leader and no ship to capture, the crew should be able to retake *Tempest* for themselves.

Cas could barely keep his eyes open. Things were a lot colder than they'd been the first time he used the skin curtain, and he found it difficult to breathe. He glanced over to Diamant who wore a triumphant smile on his face. In his hand he held a canister that looked exactly like the one Vrij had given him. Cas's heart fell as he felt the hole in his pocket. Diamant had stolen it off him. Diamant said something but Cas couldn't hear anything. The silence permeated everything around him and he could feel the actual crystals forming on his skin. It seemed the cold would kill him before Diamant could stab him with those mandibles. He cursed himself for not being able to do more.

Diamant exploded in a mess of blood and guts right in front of him, some of the matter splashing up against him as it flew out in all directions. Cas turned to see one of *Tempest's* shuttles approaching, flanked by two spacewings. Exhausted, Cas finally closed his eyes as the shuttle grew closer and closer.

The danger was over.

36

"—won't hurt him, I just want to take some samples while I can. How often is he in here?"

Cas cracked his eyes open, allowing the light of sickbay to come in a little at a time. He wasn't sure where he'd just been, but Box's voice had pulled him out of it.

"Unless he's signed a formal release for his genetic material, you can't just harvest it from him," Xax replied. Cas glanced over to see her and Box standing near the foot of his bed, arguing.

"But I'm his emergency contact. And when he's incapacitated under Coalition medical guidelines, I have the authority—"

"That's not how it works. You only have the authority when a life or death decision needs to be made, not when you want material for your experiments," she shot back.

Cas let out a breath, causing Box to turn to him.

"Great. Now he's awake." He came to the side of the bed and leaned over Cas. "Do I have your permission to remove ten percent of your sperm? I'm working on a project."

Cas flinched. "What? No. What happened?"

Box threw his hands up in the air, walking away. "I'm *never* going to get this thing off the ground."

"Captain to sickbay," Xax said, then smiled at Cas. "How do you feel?"

"I'm not sure. What's going on?" He remembered everything, but his body felt strange, like either it wasn't all there, or it wasn't all his. He felt like a stranger in his own body.

"You suffered severe trauma, but we managed to bring you back for a while longer. Hope you don't mind," she said, humor in her voice.

"My body feels weird," he said, flexing his fingers and toes to make sure they were all still there.

"That's because about twenty percent of it is new," she replied. "We had to regrow and replace one of your lungs and your spleen and remove the parts of your skin that were either burned beyond recognition or frostbitten from exposure. You're lucky to be alive."

Cas sat up, alert and the room spun. "Whoa there," Xax said.

He put his head down until the spinning stopped. "What about Evie? Are the Bulaq—?"

The doors to sickbay slid open to reveal Evie, walking toward him with a smile on her face. "Thank goodness," she said. "It was close there for a while."

"What?" Cas asked, his voice rising.

Xax gave him a reassuring smile. "No, everything was fine. You're fine." She turned to the captain. "We don't need to increase his anxiety. He's fine."

"Right," Evie said, stumbling for a moment. "You're…looking good."

"Are you okay?" he asked.

She lifted her left arm, massaging her abdomen. "Just a puncture. Nothing Xax couldn't fix for me."

"*I* did that one," Box called from across the room.

Evie smirked. "Right, Box did that one."

"And Ryant? Is he—"

"Lost a lot of blood, but Lieutenant Yamashita and the others reached him in time. He's fine; he's already back to work in Bay Two," Xax replied.

Evie either saw Cas's confused look or decided to explain anyway. "Instead of heading straight for Bay Two, Laura returned to the brig first, taking out the guard and releasing the prisoners there. She and Zenfor fought their way down to the Bays where Xax took care of Ryant and Box commandeered a shuttle to come find you."

"I figured you'd try something stupid," he yelled from across the room.

"He pulled me out?" Cas asked.

Evie nodded. "And Jann was the one who took care of our Diamant problem. He snatched the skin curtain right off you."

Queasiness bubbled up in Cas's stomach. "Can we please not call it that?" He swallowed, making sure it wasn't coming back up. "How could he do that?"

"Oh," Evie said, her face turning pink. "Vrij told us the membranes of the curtains can be penetrated with something sharp enough. I think you can figure out the rest."

Cas might have figured that out if he'd had his wits about him, but he'd been on the verge of unconsciousness, so a lot of things may have escaped his notice. Still, none of it would have changed his decision. "What about the rest of the Bulaq?"

"Restrained, loaded back on their ship, and hauled to the middle of space by one of the shuttles. We weren't taking any chances. But with Diamant gone, the fight seemed to go out of them."

"Is everyone else okay?"

She nodded. "For the most part." Her demeanor darkened. "But we need to talk as soon as you're well enough. There's a lot to fill you in on." She turned to Xax. "When?"

"Another few hours. I want to make sure all the new organs have integrated without rejection and everything is functioning as normal. Human bodies react differently to unconscious and conscious states."

Evie turned back to him. "As soon as you're cleared, meet me in my quarters. The bridge is…under repair."

Cas nodded, noting he didn't hear any blame in her voice for what happened to the bridge, despite he'd been the one who made the order. Her eyes lingered on him a moment and then she was gone again.

"So," Box said, approaching. "Now that you know I've saved your life; I think you owe me a little favor." He held a syringe with a small bottle attached to the other end. "Spread 'em."

* * *

Zenfor stood at the doors to Engineering, debating whether to enter or not. She was strangely nervous to face him again after everything that had happened; she hadn't been back since when the Bulaq had come and escorted them to the brig. She had been so full of emotions then, going off about how terrible the Coalition was and how everyone on the ship deserved what they got when in reality she was frustrated with her own performance. Or her inability to execute. She hadn't seen the Bulaq modify the sensors so they couldn't be seen taking the captain hostage. She hadn't been able to set up a backup system to take them down when they took over the ship. She was a failure and she didn't want to face the one person on the ship whose opinion actually mattered to her.

She'd never been one to back down from her failures before, but those had been different. This was something more. She felt like she'd let *him* down. And that was a difficult position for her to stand in.

Taking a deep breath, Zenfor walked back into Engineering, ignoring the rest of the crew. She didn't care what they thought, and they could watch and gawk at her or not; all her attention was focused on Sesster. She reached his massive cradle and stared up at him, trying to decide how to begin.

But before she could begin the world melted away around her, and she found herself back on the plains of Thislea, even though it wasn't quite the same. Night stretched above her in an endless sky and the purple-tinged horizon betrayed no city lights or civilization. Sesster stood in front of her, smiling. "I was wondering when you would show up," he said.

"It's been...difficult," she replied. "I don't handle failure well."

"What failure? That you didn't see a coup coming?"

"I saw it coming, I just thought I'd be able to stop it before it could get anywhere. But I've been distracted lately. I think it's affected my performance." He didn't ask the obvious question because he already knew. It wasn't like it was a secret between them or anyone else. Their minds had already connected on an intimate level. But it hadn't been like the other couplings she'd experienced before.

"I wanted to thank you," Sesster said, pulling her from her thoughts. "For telling me about the Coalition's dealings regarding the *Achlys*. Had you never told me I might not ever have known what the humans did. And while I don't agree with why they kept the information from me, I understand why the captain and Caspian didn't tell me."

"I only did what was right," she said, still angry over the situation. "The humans don't deserve your pity. Not after what they've done."

"But they do. Their species is still young, and they need our guidance and our help. We must be patient with them, as parents are patient with children. They'll learn one day and then, our futures will truly flourish."

She scoffed. "You give them too much credit."

"Maybe. But not all humans are alike. And I feel we must evaluate each on their own merit. Because of your actions, my relationships with many of the humans on this ship have already improved. I have you to thank for that."

Zenfor smiled. "For what it's worth, you're welcome. I can't tell you how…grateful I am to have a kindred spirit on this ship with me."

"I agree," he replied. There was a moment of silence where they just stared into each other's eyes. Even though Zenfor knew she wasn't really looking at his physical form, she felt as if this was his true self. His astral self as it were. And that was good enough for her. "Did the captain speak to you about her plan yet?"

Anticipation and dread arose in her, both in equal amounts. "She did."

"I'd be interested to hear your thoughts."

She couldn't say she was disappointed necessarily, but it seemed like an extreme measure. At least for the time being. But things on the ship were dire and if they didn't do something drastic, none of them might survive. "I'm on board," Zenfor replied. "As long as we do it together."

37

Cas tapped the small button beside Evie's door. Xax had discharged him not more than twenty minutes prior and he'd taken a short detour to grab fresh clothes from his quarters. When he made his way over to this side of the ship he couldn't help but think about Vrij leading them across the hull of the ship. He'd never experienced anything quite like it.

"Come in." The doors slid open to reveal Evie at her desk, her sword back on the wall behind her. It looked pristine as ever. "Feeling okay?" she asked, looking up.

He still felt weird. Even walking around knowing he had new organs inside him was enough to make his new skin tingle. It was almost as if all his body wasn't his anymore, but he clamped down the feelings. "Fine. What's the emergency?" He took the seat across from her.

"The ship is in bad shape. And even though we have all the materials we need to repair her; the repairs are going to take some time. A long time. And we've only got about a week of life support left."

"What?" Cas asked, almost shooting up out of his seat.

She shook her head. "When Diamant and his men were repairing the ship, they also built in a couple of fail-safes. One blew the entire life support system to hell. Zenfor and Sesster are working on it, but it's going to take longer to repair than we have."

"What about the shuttles? Isolating part of the ship off? Something—"

She held up her hands. "We've already been over all that. We can keep minimal life support running for a while, but not for the entire crew. We're going to have to set down somewhere until we can make repairs."

"You mean land the ship? I don't think—"

"No. I mean we need to find a planet where we can take refuge as we send repair crews back and forth to fix the ship."

He slumped back in his chair. "Great, so we've become Diamant after all."

"I don't see another way around it," she replied. "And even though we've gotten rid of them for now, there's nothing saying they won't regroup and come at us again. If there is one thing I know it's that behind every maniacal leader there is someone ready to take his place. So our first priority is moving the ship."

"I just don't understand how they were so many steps ahead of us the entire time," Cas replied.

"Vrij told me it has something to do with the way his people can determine intention. It extends beyond their own species, but someone has to be trained to recognize it for what it is and not just one's own mind talking to itself. I'm willing to bet Diamant was an expert, and he read us as easily as someone could read a book, knowing what we wanted and how we wanted to get it." She stood, walking over to the small table underneath her sword. "I think he found out about our ship and orchestrated the whole thing."

Cas frowned. "Is Vrij—"

"He's requested to stay, but I wanted your opinion. He's an excellent builder, he could help with the repair efforts. As long as he doesn't share his old friend's desires. Apparently, they'd been friends since childhood."

"Is that why he refused to shoot him?"

She shook her head. "I don't know. Maybe there was a decent person in there once. But circumstances changed him and pushed him too far. I don't want that to happen to us."

"It won't. Diamant was alone. Our crew is united in this endeavor. No more lies and no more secrets." Cas watched her carefully. She had been under a lot of pressure lately and it was his job as first officer to determine if the captain was still fit to command. He smirked. It had been the first time he'd thought of himself as the first officer in an official capacity.

"I just don't know. In the meantime, the engines should be up and running for a short undercurrent jump. I've had the shuttles out searching the area for something we can use, and we found a planet a few light years away, one we hadn't charted before."

"Inhabited?" Cas asked.

"I'm not sure yet. Probably. But maybe we can barter for some space temporarily. Vrij told me this area is full of a variety of species."

Cas leaned forward, placing his forearms on her desk. "Evie. What are we going to do about *Andromeda*? They're still out there and they're headed for Earth. And we have no way to get back to the Coalition."

She sighed. "I know. I think our only hope is to fix the long-range communicator and send them what we have, not that it's much. Depending on what Zenfor can do with the engines we might still be stuck out here for a while and if they're still on the same course they were on when we left Cypaxia they're due to reach the edge of Coalition space in just under eighty days. We can't beat them back without Zenfor's enhancements, to say nothing of developing an effective counter-measure against their time shifting."

"What do you think they want? Really?"

She turned back to him, taking her seat again. "I honestly don't know. But if it's anything like what they wanted from the Bulaq; the Coalition is in big trouble. They could destroy all the inner systems in a matter of seasons if that's their goal. If not, I don't have a clue what they could be thinking." She paused. "But that isn't our primary concern at the moment. It's my responsibility to protect this crew so that's what I'm going to do. We need to get to the planet, set up a base camp of some kind and then begin repairs on the ship. *Then* we'll worry about *Andromeda*."

She was right. Any earlier reservations he had about helping Evie lead this crew had vanished. It didn't matter that he didn't have an official rank anymore and that he was acting in the capacity without the authority of the Coalition. Diamant'd had the full support of his people and he had been crazed, almost to the point where it was dangerous to his own kind. It hadn't mattered that he was once a great military leader. It was his actions that defined him. And it had taken Cas seeing the man for who he truly was before realizing he'd already gained the crew's respect and admiration. And he wasn't going to do anything to jeopardize that now.

Cas nodded. "Sounds like a plan to me."

***

Evie walked into engineering to find Cas, Zenfor and Box all there, while Vrij stood off to the side near the corner. Sesster was in his cradle operating the various systems that had propelled them into the undercurrent. He'd warned Evie it might damage the ship further, but if they stayed out in open space things would only get worse. At least inside a system they could harvest energy from the star using the energy collector and would have a place for refuge while *Tempest* was repaired.

She didn't think it was an order Greene would have made, and while once that might have frightened her, today it only gave her more resolve. This was the right decision. And just because it wasn't one he wouldn't have made didn't make it wrong or dangerous. She was going to get this ship out of this situation, no matter what it took.

"Where are we?" she asked, tightening the loop on the sheath strapped to her back. She'd begun taking her sword with her everywhere over the past few days. Not because she felt paranoid or like she needed it for protection, but because this was a new era and that was what she'd decided to do. And if when they got back to the Coalition and someone wanted to report her for carrying a deadly weapon around the ship, then that's just what *they'd* have to do. To her, this was more important.

"Just dropping out of the undercurrent," Cas said, staring at one of the screens near the master systems display in Engineering. With the bridge out of commission it had become the ship's temporary command center.

"Hey," Laura whispered, indicating Evie over to the side of Engineering. She smirked and went over to her. "Have I told you how much I'm liking this?" Laura ran her hand down the strap across Evie's front. "Makes you look badass."

"I am badass," Evie replied, not hiding the smile on her own face.

"I know. Now everyone else knows it too. If we meet anyone down there, they'll think twice before tangling with you." Laura reached up placing a lingering kiss on Evie's lips that promised more in the future. "I am so proud of you."

"Thanks," Evie whispered back, her heart suddenly fluttering.

"Hey, *females*," Box yelled, breaking the moment. "Do you want to see this planet or not?" Evie smirked and rolled her eyes, as they both walked over to the primary monitor. "I can't wait to get back on solid ground for a while. It's been *years*."

"You were just on that asteroid a few seasons ago," Laura said.

"That doesn't count. Asteroids are like planet larvae. They *wanna* be planets someday, and maybe they will. Or maybe they'll just be swallowed up by the next gas giant they run into."

"Ignore him," Cas said. "He's expanded his studies to include the entire biological spectrum now."

"Did you know," Box began, "that a larva is often adapted to completely different environments than their fully-grown adult forms?"

"Yes, Box. Everyone already knew that," Cas said, exasperated.

"Well, excuse the hell out of me. I'm just trying to raise the collective—"

"Shut up," Zenfor replied. "We're here." She indicated the screen before them.

At first Evie thought she was hallucinating. But as she moved closer to the image and it didn't change, all of a sudden her heart started beating rapidly.

"Evie, sweetie, what's wrong? What is it?" Laura asked, taking her arm. The room had become deathly still. She glanced up at Sesster, had he recognized it as well?

"What's going on?" Cas asked.

"The planet," Evie said once she'd found her breath. "It's the same one I've seen in my visions. It's the same one with the creatures."

"What creatures?"

She stared him right in the eye. "*Andromeda.*"

Thank you for reading **SECRETS PAST**! I hope you enjoyed it! The easiest way to keep up with future releases is to sign up on www.ericwarrenauthor.com and you'll get access to all the ancillary INFINITY'S END short stories, absolutely free!

The adventure continues in **PLANETFALL**. Turn the page for a sneak preview!

PLANETFALL: INFINITY'S END BOOK 6

PREVIEW

As Caspian Robeaux stared at the emerald planet in the distance, he realized he was looking through something other than the view screen. He was looking through *himself.* The smoky image reflected a person he didn't recognize, and someone who would have been foreign to him just a few short seasons ago. His face betrayed none of the discomfort or pain which he'd become accustomed to long ago. Cas had to give himself credit; he'd made big strides. There had been a time when stepping back on a shuttle had seemed like an impossibility, but he'd managed this mission without any trouble. Though, when twenty-five percent of your body wasn't your own, it tended to change one's perspective on things.

Cas had always prided himself on his resilience, and this often included his physical characteristics. He'd managed to survive childhood without breaking any bones or needing the removal of errant or malfunctioning organs. He'd had perfect eyesight and straight teeth for as long as he could remember, and he'd never needed any artificial augmentation. So maybe he didn't hit the gym much, but that hardly mattered. The point was, his body had always been reliable. He'd never worried about it shutting down on him.

But all that had changed because of Diamant. Four days ago, he'd woken up in sickbay having been informed three major organs had been regrown and new skin had been grafted onto dead tissue. Doctor Xax had done an excellent job; he couldn't see a difference at all. But he could *feel* the difference. And for the first time in his life, he didn't quite feel like himself. Maybe that was where he found the willpower to continue to go on shuttle missions again and again. Maybe it came from the other him. The *new* him. Or maybe he no longer had anything to protect.

Then again the fact their ship was only days away from losing all life support might have had something to do with it.

"Bring her around for another go?" Box asked from the pilot's seat.

Cas shook his head. "We're not getting anything else out of this trip, the atmosphere is too thick. If the captain wants to know what's on the surface, she's going to have to send a team."

They'd found this planet two days ago, after a harrowing series of events with the Bulaq, and their leader, Diamant, had attempted to steal their ship for his own purposes. He had also been the man responsible for all of Cas's injuries, and Cas had almost died trying to stop him. But in Cas's haste to retake the ship, he'd damaged the *USCS Tempest* more than she already had been. They couldn't even access the bridge as it was open to space.

The only recourse had been to use this planet as a temporary haven, except they had no idea what was on the surface. Three survey missions covering different parts had all come up with little to nothing. They could *see* the surface itself; it was about sixty percent water and forty percent land, with ice caps on the poles and a deep green atmosphere which made everything appear a different shade of olive. Parts of the planet had dense forests and deserts that stretched for kilometers, all tinged a shade of green. But the scanners couldn't read through the atmosphere. And as far as they could see, there didn't seem to be any cities or settlements anywhere on the surface. Though the captain insisted the planet had to be inhabited.

"Are you sure?" Box asked, his mechanical hands moving over the controls. "We could always...*penetrate*."

Cas turned up his nose. "Why do you have to say it like that? Nobody is penetrating anything. The captain was clear, we stay out of the atmosphere and gather whatever information we can. Nothing else. As much as I know you'd like it."

"But the situation seems to require…*thrusting* through the atmosphere in a strong, deliberate movement, like one might see in—"

"Stop. Stop it right now. You're not even supposed to be here. Aren't you supposed to be 'doctoring' down in sickbay?" Cas used finger quotes to emphasize his point.

"A person can be more than one thing," Box replied. "I can be a doctor and a pilot. And don't forget, it was my piloting skills that saved your ass out in space and my doctoring skills that did it again in sickbay." Box made a sound like a sigh. "But I guess I shouldn't expect too much from someone who has never been anything more than an engineer."

Cas wasn't about to let him win. "We both know the only reason we're even here was because you wouldn't stop pestering Evie about your superior piloting skills and how you could come up with more than the other survey teams had. Wasn't that what you said?"

"I never said that."

"Funny, because whenever you hear something pleasant you always seem to conveniently have it recorded. But when it's something not to your liking—"

"Captain Diazal could have saved herself a lot of time if she'd assigned me on the first survey mission. I would have informed her without…*certain actions*…we'll never figure out what's down there." He glanced over at the series of rings circling the planet. "At least *I* figured out there are some useful materials in those. None of the other survey teams checked the rings."

Cas scoffed. "Not that we have time to gather them. We've got maybe another two or three days before we have to evacuate anyway. That's barely enough time to load all the shuttles. *If* that's what she decides to do."

Box turned to him, his yellow eyes blinking in a pattern Cas recognized as annoyance. He'd been with Box so long he'd learned to read the patterns in his eyes, which—since Box had no other facial features except for a faceplate and a visor covering those eyes—was the only way he could tell what was going on in that mechanical mind of his. "I'm sorry, why are *you* here again? Other than to take up space?"

Cas laughed and stretched his arms out in front of him. They'd been in the shuttle for a few hours; he was ready to get back to *Tempest*. "I'm here to make sure you don't abscond with a shuttle."

Box made a sound like the sharp inhalation of breath, despite not having lungs. Or a mouth for that matter. "I am *appalled*. Shocked and appalled. If anyone should be monitored for stealing shuttles it is you, my good sir," he replied in one of his annoying accents.

He grinned. Box wasn't wrong. There had been a time when he would have taken full advantage of this situation: him and Box in a shuttle with undercurrent capability, and *Tempest* out there, unable to move or give chase if they took off somewhere.

"What's so funny?" Box asked in his regular voice.

"All of this. If we'd been in this position a few seasons ago I would have told you to fly to the far side of the planet and engage the undercurrent as soon as we were out of scanner range from *Tempest*. We would have been *gone*."

"Ahem. *You* might have been gone, but I'm quite happy in my position *thankyouverymuch*. You would have been flying off by yourself. And since everyone knows you can't fly worth a damn, you would have ended up crash-landing on the planet, destined to spend your days on a remote world. And I would have covered all of it up, altered the ship's scanners to make it look like the shuttle disintegrated on re-entry. I would regale them the tale of your tragic, yet foolish venture to escape to parts unknown. Simple, really."

"It bothers me you've planned that far ahead."

"You didn't think I was going to stay with you forever, did you? I always needed a contingency plan," Box replied. "One can only fly a ship for so long before they grow...restless." He tried to say it with a sinister tone, but it ended up coming out comical. Box had never been sinister in his entire life.

"Well, it seemed like you were pretty happy watching net dramas all day."

"You have no clue, boss. I was three days from dropping you on the next planet when Captain Diazal showed up."

Cas rolled his eyes. "Can we head back yet? Or do you want to keep stalling?" The planet peeled away from view as Box altered the shuttle's course, only the rings circling at a forty-five-degree angle visible through the viewscreen. "Speaking of which, I can't wait for you to tell Evie about our *success.*"

"It's your fault we didn't make more progress. You didn't let me p—"

"*Don't*...say it," Cas interjected. "If I hear that word one more time, I'm going to reach in there and wipe it from your processor."

Box made an errant sound, but Cas paid him no mind. He thought about everything that happened since he'd been that person who Evie had found back on Devil's Gate. It hadn't been that long ago, but now he couldn't even imagine leaving *Tempest* to her fate. There was too much at stake; yet despite all their efforts they were even further from their goal than ever. The Coalition was at least two seasons away and the mysterious threat known only as *Andromeda* was on its way to Earth. After Diamant had told them about their encounter with the powerful and destructive aliens, Cas was more convinced than ever the alien's only goal—once they reached the inner planets of the Coalition—was to destroy them. And despite the fact the Coalition was thousands of years old, the loss of the inner systems would completely destabilize the region; Cas didn't think they could survive. And while he had no love for the organization that had once exiled him, he couldn't stand by while trillions of innocent lives were at risk.

He ran his hands down his face as *Tempest* came into view, her gray hull standing out against the field of black. Even from this distance the damage was visible, whole sections of the ship blown out by either mines from their brief encounter with *Andromeda* or their attempts to retake the ship from the Bulaq. Whatever the reason, *Tempest* was in dire shape and needed serious help. He only hoped this planet might provide a temporary solution until they could get her up and running again. Cas realized Box said something but chose to ignore it, instead hoping nothing else would go wrong. If they could just get the ship repaired—that's all it would take.

At least, that's what he kept telling himself.

To be continued in PLANETFALL, available soon!

GLOSSARY

Planets/Stars/Outposts

Cassiopeia Optima – Sargan homeworld (settled by humans millennia ago)

Claxia Prime – Claxian Homeworld

Cypaxia – planet often used for relaxation. The planet is lush with flora, the dominant fauna having been killed off thousands of years ago when the Coalition first settled

Dren – secret Coalition penal colony

Earth – homeworld of the human species. Inside the Horus system

Excel Nebula – stellar nursery deep within Coalition space

Hommel – Class G yellow star, primary star to Sissk

Laq – homeworld to the Bulaq

Omicron Terminus – Trinary Star System including two gas supergiants far outside Coalition space

Opaous – Class H yellow star in uncharted space

Quaval – one of the few charted systems inside Sil space

Rrethal – Class F white star, primary to Cypaxia

Set – outer rim planet in the Horus system

Sissk – border world just inside Coalition space. Unique as it has twelve sentient species who evolved at the same time

Starbase Eight – Coalition stronghold and first line of defense against Sargan incursions

Thislea – Sil homeworld, much is unknown about this planet

Species

Ashkas – One of the twelve distinct intelligent races inhabiting the planet Sissk. Prefer to be known as Simmilists rather than *reptiles*, as many off-worlders refer to them

Bulaq – A race of scavengers after their world was destroyed. Resemble one of the species on Sissk known as Ashkasians. No hair, hard plates make up skin. Born with two razor-like mandibles attached to their backs

Claxian – Founding members of the Coalition and pacifists with advanced technology. Lived as isolationists until first contact by the humans over two thousand years ago. Helped form the Coalition to spread peace through the galaxy

Human – one of the founding members of the Coalition and central to its operation. Humans can be found on any of a hundred different worlds in the Coalition and often hold high positions of power within the organization. Worked with the Claxians to be the founding members

Sargans – Generally human but can also pertain to other species who have joined the Sargan Commonwealth. Sargans are humans who want to be lawless, or at least out from under the thumb of the Coalition

Sil – Unknown species of great power. The Coalition has reached a tentative treaty with the Sil not to violate their borders under any circumstances. Their empire is large. Sil seem to share symbiotic relationships with their ships but not much is known about this phenomenon at this time

Untuburu – Early members of the Coalition. Highly religious to their god Kor. Untuburu are the only Coalition members not required to wear uniforms as their religion requires the sacred blue robes be the only garments worn off world. Wear metal exoskeletons to help them integrate with Coalition society

Yax-Inax – Early members of the Coalition. Studious, have perfect memory and can retain huge amounts of information. Often integrate themselves into other cultures to learn as much as possible. Easily identified by their six eyes and four arms

Miscellaneous

Alchuriam ore – an obsolete type of metal

Calorcium – a medical material filled with nanobots, injectable into wounds in order to repair/rebuild

Cyclax – a type of metal used in ship reinforcement, mined by the Coalition

Firebrand – liquor much like whiskey

Galvanium – a type of metal used in ship construction

Grande-Grande – a spaceborne creature

Guursel – four-legged animal native to Thislea. In ancient times was used to pull carts. Very docile

Palithasol – drug used to reduce blood toxicity

Rulag – a type of canine on Procyon Four. Often found in people's homes

Scorb – a heavy-type of brewed drink

Yaarn – a mammalian by-product grown for consumption

Author's Note

Well, this is it. We've officially reached the halfway point in the INFINITY'S END saga. I hope you've been enjoying the ride so far and I have to assume if you've made it this far, you are. Nothing could give me more pleasure than knowing you're out there, reading and enjoying the books I write. A little behind the scenes: if you'll recall way back in book 1 I said to watch out for callbacks to some of your favorite Space Opera shows and this book had a big one. I specifically wrote the character of Diamant based on Gul Dukat from Deep Space Nine. If you go back and re-read, you can almost hear Dukat's voice coming from him. If you heard it before reading this, congratulations! You're officially inside my head, lol.

As always, I have plenty of people to thank for making this book happen. To all my ARC readers, but particularly Meenaz, Mandy, Kay, Barrie and my sister Katie, thank you for all the time and feedback you've continued to give me in this series. Your input makes these better books.

To Dan Van Oss, your covers are always stunning and this one is no exception.

To Tiffany Shand, thanks for always fixing my mistakes and steering me in the right direction when you know I've gone wrong.

To all the authors out there who have helped me along the way, whether you knew it or not, you crafted me into the writer I am today. Especially all the friends and acquaintances I made during conferences. I'll always cherish those moments.

To my friends and family who put up with never seeing me because I'm strapped to my desk during all hours of the day, thanks for your indulgence. This is the first thing I've ever done in my life where I feel like I'm actually making a difference. And you help make that possible.

And finally, to my loving wife who has always supported me, thank you for being you. I couldn't do this without you.

Sincerely,

Eric Warren

About the Author

I've always been an author, but I haven't always known I've been an author. It took a few tragic events in my life and a lot of time for me to figure it out.

But I've never had a problem creating stories. Or creating in general. I wasn't *the* creative person in any of my classes in school, I was always the kid who never spoke but always listened. I was the one who would take an assignment and pour my heart into it, as long as it meant I could do something original.

I didn't start writing professionally until 2014 when I tackled the idea of finishing a novel-length book. Before then I had always written in some capacity, even as far back as elementary school where I wrote pages of stories about creatures under the earth.

It took a few tries and a few novels under my belt before I figured out what I was doing, and I've now finished my first series and am hard at work on my second (which you hold in your hands now!). I am thrilled to be doing this and couldn't imagine doing anything else with my life.

I hope you enjoy the fruits of my labor. May they bring you as much joy as they bring me.

Having lived in both Virginia and California in the past, I currently reside in Charlotte, NC with my very supportive wife and two small pugs.

Visit me at my website

SECRETS PAST

Printed in Great Britain
by Amazon